WHITE POPPY

WHITE POPPY

Margaret Gaan

DODD, MEAD & COMPANY
NEW YORK

c. 1

Copyright © 1985 by Margaret Gaan
All rights reserved
No part of this book may be reproduced in any form
without permission in writing from the publisher.
Published by Dodd, Mead & Company, Inc.
79 Madison Avenue, New York, N.Y. 10016
Distributed in Canada by
McClelland and Stewart Limited, Toronto
Manufactured in the United States of America

Designed by Claire Counihan

First Edition

Library of Congress Cataloging in Publication Data

Gaan, Margaret.

  White poppy.

    1. China—History—War of 1840–1842—Fiction.
I. Title.
PS3557.A2W5   1985   813'.54   85-6984
ISBN 0-396-08668-3

WHITE
POPPY

John Carradine
1753 - 1820

William
1775 - 1842

Andrew
1805-1875

Martha m. Mathes

How-kwa
1745-1839

Yin-kwa
1802-1872

Donald m. Edith
1836-

Olan _ _ _ _ _ m. _ _
1835-1900

Julie
1856-1906

Great
1862

Noelle
1901-

* The Red Barbarian

rge Tyson
53 - 1845

Wei
? - 1842

rlie *   m.   Ling-ling
-1842   1813 - 1842

Jin-see   Concubine
1832-1900

gon m. Ching-mei   Alfred Pratt m. Mei-mei
                                1847-

Didi   Great Fish   Belle
36 -   1886 -   1889-

DONALD

John Carradine = His Wife
1753 – 1820
Scotland

Other children · · · William = His Wife
b. 1775
Scotland
d. 1842
Chapoo

Andrew   Martha m. Mathes
1805-1875
Scotland &
China

many illegitimate   Donald m. Edith
offspring in China   b. 1836
                            London

                                Noelle
                                b. 1901
                                London

Chapter I

July 1860

THE Poison Trade . . .
　　Donald stared down at the night-shimmered harbor, at the bobbing lights clustered around the dark bulk of *Hormunjee*, depot ship for the continuous stream of opium that Andrew's clippers brought from India, that his fast cutters, serviced from the ship or from his great stone warehouse on the beach, busily ran to the smuggling points along the South China coast. Other depot ships dotted the harbor, other warehouses lined the waterfront, other cutters threshed the smuggling routes. The Poison Trade, they called it, joking in the lofty halls of the Hong Kong Club and the long bar of Madam Ellie's.

　　The faraway lights, winking, blinking, twinkling on the dark waters, mocked Donald. Angrily, he pushed aside the mosquito netting that screened the french windows of the large, airy bedroom and stepped out onto the broad verandah. The mosquitoes attacked at once and he slapped at them, his face twisting wryly as he remembered his astonished resentment of his first mosquito bite. What a bright-eyed innocent he'd been when he stepped ashore in Hong Kong a month ago! What silly pride he'd felt as he passed from hand to hand around the Club, Andrew's friends slapping his back, patting his shoulders. Donald Mathes, y'know. Andrew's nephew, who Andrew's chosen to be heir to Carradine & Co. Lucky young devil!

Stupid young devil.

Naïve simpleton.

That day five years ago, his nineteenth birthday, when Andrew had told him that he'd been chosen, he hadn't asked a single question, only gaped with speechless joy into Andrew's handsome face. Andrew had taken his arm confidentially, spoken in his deep, impressive voice.

"Make no mistake about it, Donald. London's a far way from Hong Kong and not much is known here about matters there. But Carradine & Co. is a great house. A *princely* house. Main office in Hong Kong and branches in all the Treaty Ports—the ports, y'know, that the Chinese were forced to open up to us under the 1842 treaties. My father was a prime mover in shaping those treaties. Great man, my father. Founder of Carradine & Co. and sole owner before me. There's no 'company' about it, really. Should be called Carradine & Son. And now . . . nephew."

He'd thanked Andrew then, stuttering with pleasure, with never a thought about what princely business the princely house might do. But even if he'd asked, Andrew wouldn't have told him. What could he have said? "I'm prince of the opium trade, the Poison Trade, that Hong Kong's the center of"?

Hong Kong was center, too, of the Pig Trade: thirty thousand coolies a year shipped to San Francisco under fictitious indentured labor contracts in conditions every bit as bad as those of the old slave-trading days. And of the Pirate Trade. Since Parliament had misguidedly offered twenty pounds per head for "piratical persons" captured alive or dead, thousands of pounds had been paid out to British naval units stationed in Hong Kong—and none of the Chinese heads they'd accounted for had been alive to tell whether it had belonged to pirate or fisherman.

Hong Kong, the Fragrant Harbor, a sink of iniquity, full of these damned voracious mosquitoes whose bite could give one chills and fever, forever hot and humid with a poisonous kind of miasma that induced boils and carbuncles and upset the workings of the stomach in a humiliating disease called dysentery. Damn and blast Hong Kong!

He didn't *have* to stay, did he? He hadn't actually given Andrew his word. But if he left, the last five years would be wasted—five years of slogging at the Chinese language. He was fluent in it now, although the coolies' chatter escaped him. But that wasn't the issue. The issue was his loathing of the Poison Trade; of the fat, smug, loud-voiced arrogance of the Poison Traders, his compatriots; of this pestilential island.

He turned and strode along the verandah to the drawing room and pushed open its french window. Andrew was sprawled in an overstuffed armchair under the soft illumination of a crystal chandelier. He seemed both native and alien to the opulent room: his attitude of careless ease claimed possession, but his head was lolling drunkenly, his shirt collar was askew, and his hand held a crystal goblet so loosely that it threatened to fall to the silken carpet.

Even thus, by God, he was handsome! At fifty-five, he still outshone most younger men. Donald, knowing himself to have a strong family resemblance, still felt himself a shadow of Andrew, not as tall, eyes less blue, hair less golden.

Handsome, spoiled-bachelor Andrew! That was another thing Donald had asked no questions about. Five years ago he'd had a romantic vision of Andrew remaining forever faithful to some great lost love. Now he knew that Andrew had never even been tempted to marry. Women were only too glad to shower him with favors, and there were ever more women to do so—English society in the Treaty Ports was growing fast, to say nothing of the continuous succession of Andrew's Chinese mistresses.

Andrew jerked up his head and growled blurrily:

"Pour yourself a drink."

Donald poured brandy and seated himself in a matching armchair opposite Andrew. He must speak now before Andrew had him running circles again.

"Uncle Andrew, I want to withdraw from our agreement."

His voice was louder than he'd intended, and it fell into silence. For a long moment Andrew said nothing. He poured more brandy for himself and slowly raised the goblet, his startlingly blue eyes staring at Donald over its rim. Then:

"D'you realize how stupid you're being? And how damned ungrateful?"

Dismay began to prickle in Donald's breast. He ignored it and tried again.

"I don't mean to be ungrateful, Uncle, but—"

"There're no buts!" Andrew cut him brutally short, then with a visible effort softened his tone. "I know you're disappointed in Hong Kong, but you'll find the Treaty Ports more to your taste. Canton's still the center of the tea trade. In Shanghai it's silk and porcelains. Rice in Amoy, Foochow, and Ningpo." His lip lifted a little. "Nice, respectable trades. I'll let you travel a bit later."

From somewhere outside a great shout shattered the silence of the slopes of Victoria Peak. For a moment the silence

4

seemed to return, deeper than ever. Then there was a fusil-
lade of shots. Andrew jumped up.

"Come on!"

Donald ran out after him. At the bottom of the garden the
darkness was fractured by the jerking lights of hand-held
lanterns. The shouting was continuous now, and there was
much thrashing about and the sharp crack of snapping
branches. Andrew rushed down a sandy path, cursing.

"They're breaking my shrubbery, God damn them!"

The garden had been cultivated every inch by hand. Hong
Kong had been a barren island when the British took it over
in 1841, and all the trees and bushes now covering the slopes
had been brought from England. Azalea had taken well, and
Andrew's garden was often brilliant with the lovely colored
blossoms of the hedge that was now being demolished.

But the noise was subsiding. By the time Donald arrived
to stand beside Andrew, there was silence except for the
panting of many men. Someone briefly shone a light on them,
then turned it on himself, on the starched white, gold-braided
uniform of a sergeant of police.

"Beg pardon, sir." The man spoke deferentially to Andrew. "Afraid we've made a bit of a mess of your hedge. Orders of the Governor, sir. Roundup of Chinee criminals who've
taken refuge in Hong Kong. They're to be sent back to Canton to be dealt with by the Chinee authorities. These men escaped, and we cornered them here."

He turned his light on five Chinese who stood in the grip
of British policemen. As though the light loosened their
tongues, the Chinese broke into loud chatter. Donald lis-
tened a moment and then sighed. It was hopeless! He'd never
understand the coolie language . . . though, by God, some
of the sounds they were making were nudging at his ear. "Ssss
. . . tao . . ." A long, sibilant syllable followed by a short,

5

rounded one, repeated over and over in tones full of fear. The meaning of the sounds hovered and then jumped into Donald's mind. *"Chop head!"* That's what they were saying! They were afraid of getting their heads chopped off! By God, were they members of the Triad? The Viceroy of Canton boasted that he'd chopped off the heads of a hundred thousand Triad rebels. . . . Donald stepped forward.

"Sergeant, are you sure these men are criminals? They could be fugitives. If they're members of the Triad—"

Andrew broke in smoothly. He had resumed his public personality. All signs of drunkenness had vanished. His collar was buttoned, his clothes were neat.

"Donald, don't you think the sergeant knows his business? And he's under orders from the Governor!" He smiled paternally at Donald and turned to the policeman. "Better cut along, Sergeant. Never mind about my hedge."

The sergeant shook his head.

"Oh no, sir! I'll get some prisoners sent up to replant it."

Andrew laughed lightly.

"Good idea, Sergeant. You'll go far, I'll warrant!"

The sergeant grinned, saluted smartly, and waved to his men. They marched off, the Chinese looking very small and frail in the hands of the burly Englishmen. Donald shivered as they passed out of the lantern light into the darkness.

"Donald!" Andrew took his elbow and walked him back toward the house, talking fast, the rough little edge back in his voice. "I'd have thought that by now you'd have absorbed more of the talk at the Club! God knows I've exposed you to enough of it! *We do not care* whether the Chinese sent back to Canton are criminals or fugitive rebels. In fact, we *prefer* it if they're rebels—"

"I'm sure those men *were* rebels!" Donald broke in bitterly.

Andrew ignored him. They had reached the house and Andrew pushed into the drawing room, shoving Donald to-

6

ward a chair. He poured brandy for himself. All of a sudden he was drunk again, his voice loud and insistent.

"So don't go trying to save rebels! The more of them executed, the better. We have our differences with the French and the Americans and the Russians, but on that point we're all firmly agreed. It's easier to deal with a central Chinese government, no matter how weak, than with a China fragmented among the rebels."

He stood over Donald, his eyes hard and shining like turquoise gemstones.

"You understand that, I hope! There're too many of them. The Triad in south China, the Tai-ping in the Yangtsze Valley, the Small Swords around Shanghai, a dozen others, all hating the Manchu, all trying to overthrow him. If they do, China'll be split up among them, and who the devil would we deal with then? Like it or not, we've got to support the Manchu."

He gulped brandy and began to pace the room restlessly.

"Not that it's easy! The new Emperor's only nineteen years old and already far gone in debauchery, so my sources tell me. Spends half the day in bed with his favorite concubine."

He paused, his glass half raised, staring into space.

"She has a strange name. Yehonala. There's a prophecy about her—that she'll usurp the dragon's throne and sit upon it for fifty years. It may be coming true already. She's borne the Emperor a son, and he's proclaimed her Empress over all those who have far more right."

There was a little pulsing silence. Then Andrew became brisk again.

"However that may be, that debauched young pup is the Emperor who's got to ratify the new treaty"—he sat down beside Donald, his eyes translucent—"the treaty Lord Elgin negotiated two years ago, the one that's going to make opium legal. Listen, Donald. We *need* China. We *need* this enormous market. In 1842 our navy whipped hell out of the Chinese, and we made them sign a treaty that opened up the Treaty Ports and gave us all sorts of concessions. But now, eighteen years later, the balance of trade is still in their favor, damn them! Last year we bought tea and silk to the tune of fifteen million pounds sterling, and all they bought from us was three million pounds worth of raw cotton from India. A difference of twelve million pounds in their favor, which we'd have had to pay in silver, if not for opium."

His eyes glittered.

"Whether you like it or not, Donald—whether those puling anti-opium societies at home like it or not—*opium is the biggest moneymaking commodity in the world today*. In 1842 we tried to get the import of opium legalized, but that was the only thing the Chinese absolutely balked at. The Emperor said nothing would persuade him to earn a revenue from the vice and misery of his people, and the Chinese negotiators refused even to discuss it. But what we couldn't get out of that tough old Emperor, we're going to get out of this new young debauchee. As soon as the new treaty's ratified, opium will be nice and legal."

He grinned, eyes shining. Donald's heart sank so heavily that for an instant he fancied it would thud into his boots. He wasn't going to be able to withstand Andrew! Andrew was winning. Andrew would always win.

He summoned his forces.

"Legal opium's worse than smuggled opium, in my opinion."

In high good humor, Andrew laughed.

"I'm surprised at you, Donald! Legal's legal, after all. It would have been legal last year already if we hadn't messed up the ratification. The Chinese don't *want* to ratify, you know. We've got to *make* them."

Once again, there was a startling interruption. From out-

8

side, a great burst of light bounced on the glass of the window, winked off for an instant, then repeated itself over and over in regular flashes. Grabbing Donald's arm, Andrew rushed him out onto the verandah to peer over the balcony. The light was beaming up from the beach below, the flashes made by a deliberate covering and uncovering of the source of light. Andrew spoke excitedly:

"By God, that works well! It's a signal I arranged with the warehouse manager in case I should suddenly be needed down there." He grinned at Donald, all anger gone, face and amazing eyes once more sparklingly attractive. "Never can tell in the Poison Trade when one might be needed in a hurry!" He turned to shout over his shoulder, "Chong! Tell the bearers to bring the chairs around at once!" and to Donald, laughing, rushing for the door, "Come on! It's time for you to jump out of your ivory tower!"

Helplessly, Donald followed him.

They went quickly downhill from Andrew's aerie perched halfway up Victoria Peak. The chair coolies thudded along with their fast, rhythmic stride; the chairs bounced gently on their flexible carrying poles. It was past midnight, late enough for the day's humidity to have been absorbed by the breeze, for the stars to twinkle clearly, no heat-haze between them and the earth. If only Hong Kong could always be like this! But all too soon they were on Queen's Road, dust kicked up by the coolies' feet clogging Donald's nostrils, the lovely luminescence of the sea blocked from his sight by the long row of warehouses that loomed darkly between the road and the beach. This was the true Hong Kong, the name of whose god was Money—a greedy god who demanded sacrifice, the peace of the mountain slopes, the beauty of the sea, the lives of coolies seeking refuge.

The bearers set the chairs down before the largest of the waterfront buildings, Andrew's great stone fortress-ware-

9

house, stuffed full of opium, guarded by a private army of bully-boys. Andrew jumped out of his chair and moved ahead into the building with the swirl that always seemed to surround him. Donald heard his surprised exclamation.

"Sir John! Didn't expect *you*, sir, at this time of night!"

Sir John Bowring, the Governor of Hong Kong? What the devil was brewing?

Donald stepped into Andrew's private office. Sir John—high-browed, spectacled, his frizzy hair upstanding—turned from shaking hands with Andrew to give Donald a beaming look.

"Well, young man! You're making your mark very quickly! Why d'you think I've bestirred myself to come here in the middle of the night? I've a message for you from no less a personage than Lord Elgin!"

"Elgin?" Andrew's voice rose excitedly. "He's here?"

"On his way." Sir John was almost as excited. "He's been put in charge of getting the new treaty ratified. After that fiasco last year they're not taking any chances. This time there's an armada of more than two hundred ships, British and French, behind Lord Elgin and the French plenipotentiary. And that's why I've got you down here in the middle of the night. . . ."

He smiled at Donald.

"I've just been called upon by Captain Hughes of H.M.S. *Kestrel*, one of our new steam frigates. Lord Elgin sent him ahead to fetch Donald. He heard in London of Donald's proficiency in the Chinese language and he wants Donald on his interpreting staff, in addition to Harry Parkes, who, of course, will be the official interpreter. Hughes has gone back to his ship, but his launch is waiting to take Donald aboard."

"*Now?*"

For the life of him, Donald couldn't keep the hostility out of his tone, and Sir John's smile faded.

10

"As soon as you can get your duds packed. Hughes's instructions are to take you to Canton, where you'll meet Parkes, who's our consul there. You're to get to know each other, discuss methods and so forth. As soon as Parkes is able to settle his affairs, Hughes is to bring you both back here to rendezvous with the fleet, go north to the Gulf of Pei-chi-li, and thence to Peking up the Pei-ho River."

Donald stood silent. He knew that he was glowering, that any words he said would be angry. By this time Sir John was cold and frowning. Andrew stepped into the breach, smiling charmingly; Donald imagined he could see the bulge of Andrew's tongue in his cheek. How delicious! Donald, who thought legal opium worse than smuggled opium, obliged to go and help ratify the treaty that would make opium legal!

"I'm *proud* of you, Donald!" Andrew's tone was unctuous. "It's a wonderful honor that Lord Elgin is doing you. Come at once. I'll help you pack."

His amused eyes glinted in the lamplight. For a moment longer Donald stood still, trying to control the bursting feeling that filled his chest. Then he bowed to Sir John and swung on his heel to precede Andrew from the room.

Donald stood beside Captain Hughes on the bridge of H.M.S. *Kestrel*, watching moodily as the sun peeped over a clear horizon and the charcoal sea acquired tints of silver and then of blue.

"Why the devil does Elgin want me if he's already got Parkes?" he growled.

Hughes chuckled.

"Seeing as how his lordship's the plenipotentiary, I reckon it's what he wants that makes what's official. And I reckon he doesn't like Parkes. I was with his lordship in Tientsin two years ago when he negotiated the treaty, and I reckoned he couldn't abide Parkes's rude manner to the Chinee. Real

11

gentleman, his lordship is. Moreover, with all the hurry-scurry, orders pouring out of the Ministry, get that damn treaty ratified double damn quick, I reckon his lordship wants his staff as strong as can be. I heard as how that treaty'll be a dead letter if it be not ratified within the year."

"That's true," Donald admitted sulkily.

"Tried to get it ratified last year, didn't they?"

"They did. My uncle says it was stupid. Lord Elgin's brother was in charge. Tried to sail up the Pei-ho in a kind of victory parade of ships, and lost four ships and five hundred Royal Marines to fire from the Taku Forts. The Chinese had got a new general from Mongolia, Prince Seng. First time ever British ships were lost in a fight with the Chinese."

"Everyone at home's bloody fed up with the whole business." Hughes grinned at Donald's gloomy look, his weatherbeaten face crinkling pleasantly. "Cheer up! It'll be quick this time!"

Donald stood at a window on the top floor of the old Carradine building, staring down at the ancient cobbled court that bordered the Pearl River for perhaps five hundred yards outside the high walls of Canton. For the past two hundred years foreigners wishing to trade with the Chinese had been restricted to this court and the tall stone buildings that lined it, in which they had lived and worked during the tea trade season.

"It's called Jackass Point," Parkes had said. "We shouldn't still be forced to live here. According to the 1842 treaty we have every right to enter the city. But that damned Viceroy says the people hate us so much he couldn't guarantee to protect our lives. Damned incompetence! Still, old Jackass Point has its attractions. It reeks of history!"

To Donald it reeked of dirt and decay, and Harry Parkes

reeked of the same kind of arrogance that infected the Poison Traders in Hong Kong. The prospect of spending God alone knew how long in the company of the sharp-faced young man with his prominent and mobile Adam's apple was not enticing.

Donald sighed and turned away from the window. It was time to pack his bag. Parkes was downstairs putting the last of his affairs in order, and *Kestrel*'s launch was waiting at the dock.

Donald began to gather his possessions. When a light tap sounded on the door, he thought it was the coolie come to take his bag and called for him to enter. When nothing happened, he went to open the door.

The Chinese who stood on the landing was no coolie. He was tall and thin, with ageless black eyes, unwrinkled ivory skin stretched over high cheekbones, black hair falling thickly in an old-fashioned queue. He wore a magnificent dark brocade gown with embroidered neckpiece.

Expecting a coolie, Donald stared at the man in confusion. The man smiled slightly and said in perfect English:

"My name is Yin-kwa."

Donald almost gasped. The fabulous Yin-kwa! Andrew's Chinese partner—his compradore—who lived in seclusion in Canton in, so they said, a palatial complex of moon-gate houses and marble courtyards, from which he directed the activities of his sons who represented him in the Carradine offices. . . .

"May I come in?" Yin-kwa said.

Donald started. "Of course. Please—" He set wooden chairs at the old, worn table. "I'm sorry I've nothing more comfortable to offer."

Yin-kwa seated himself, smiling. "How often do you think I've sat upon these chairs? This is a familiar place to me."

13

"Of course, I hadn't thought of that." Donald seated himself, then jumped up again to fetch bottle and glasses. "You will have a glass of sherry wine, sir?"

Yin-kwa inclined his head. Donald poured, and they lifted their glasses to each other.

Sipping, Donald suddenly felt resentment begin to take the place of his first astonishment. Why the devil should he feel so honored that Yin-kwa had come to visit him? Yin-kwa was Andrew's partner in the opium trade! He was worse than Andrew, really, for he was helping to enslave his own people to the drug! With the beginnings of anger, Donald glanced across at Yin-kwa.

The flat, black eyes were regarding him mildly.

"I have just come back from Hong Kong," Yin-kwa said. "Your uncle and I spoke of you. I suggested to him that he shouldn't insist on keeping you in the Hong Kong office. You can learn the business as well in Shanghai."

He leaned forward, the fading light glinting from his eyes.

"I think you will like Shanghai better. It is a very ancient town. In the year 200 before Christ, according to the foreign calendar, it was a fishing station in the Kingdom of Wu, called Hu-tu. It is not mentioned again in our histories until a thousand five hundred years later, when it was a town important enough to have a wall around it with six gates and twenty arrow towers. At that time it was called Shanghai, which, as you know, means 'Above the Sea.' Now it is one of the Treaty Ports, and will become the most important of them, the premier trading city of China, because of its position at the mouth of the Yangtsze River. Yes, I think you will like Shanghai."

Donald swallowed hard to control the anger that had been rising steadily. What right had this millionaire Chinese opium smuggler to discuss him with Andrew, plan his future, attempt to push him about?

14

"It's kind of you to be interested in what I might and might not like," he said coldly. "May I ask *why*?"

"Because you don't like opium," Yin-kwa said softly.

Donald almost snorted. "But you do? You and my uncle. It would be more comfortable for you if an opium-hater like myself were far away from Hong Kong?"

The flat eyes, which had been veiled in politeness, were suddenly sharp and clever and very arrogant. Donald felt his heart pumping. Andrew's arrogance was boastful and threw its weight about. Yin-kwa's was disdainful and drew into itself. It was formidable. How had he dared to speak thus to Yin-kwa?

Yin-kwa said icily, "Should the English be allowed to debauch our people, and no Chinese try to control them?"

Donald was silent. What did he mean? What *could* he mean? He was Andrew's partner!

Yin-kwa went on more mildly, his eyes once again veiling themselves.

"You are going from here to join Lord Elgin for the ratification of the new treaty, which will make it legal to trade opium in China. The English think they're very clever, but what will prevent the Chinese farmer, then, from growing poppies? What will prevent the Chinese from creating a system to handle the opium trade, as the English have created a system? The opium market will no longer be at the mercy of British smugglers."

Donald stared at him, thoughts and feelings tumbling in his head and his heart. What did he mean?

Yin-kwa spoke again, his voice now very soft:

"In England the treaties have names. The one of 1842, the Treaty of Nanking. This new one, the Treaty of Tientsin. In China we call them simply the Unequal Treaties."

He rose, his gown rustling richly, and turned to the door.

15

Donald followed him, searching for something to say, something that would detain him. But there was nothing. Yin-kwa was the one in authority. Yin-kwa was the one who planned and executed secretly, not telling the tyros what he meant.

Yin-kwa turned in the doorway, smiling gravely.

"The compradore of Carradine & Co. in Shanghai is my adopted son, who is married to my only and beloved daughter. His name is Wei Jin-see."

An instant later the door had closed behind him.

Donald went again to stand at the window. It was dark now, the river below him inky black, a lonely light or two marking a homing sampan. He stared into the darkness, breathing fast and lightly in time with the beating of his heart.

What was the name Yin-kwa had mentioned?

Wei Jin-see?

Chapter II

August–October

1860

"Y OU'D BETTER GO BELOW," Captain Hughes shouted. "You're doing no good here."

Donald hardly heard him over the drumming of the swirling, sheeting, dark gray rain that had been pouring from the metal skies for the last ten days. *Kestrel* hardly budged at her anchors, weighed down by the tons of water that sluiced over her every minute. All around her, vessels of the British/French armada were anchored, but they could be glimpsed only vaguely when the curtains of rain shifted. *Kestrel* seemed isolated in the vast, gray, wet, thrumming wilderness that was the Gulf of Pei-chi-li.

Not more than a mile away, if only it could be seen, was the mouth of the Pei-tang River, with the one little fort that guarded it. The plan was to land troops here, who would take the fort, then march back overland eight miles to the mouth of the Pei-ho River, where the five Taku Forts stood, two on

17

the north bank and three on the south. The rest of the British/French armada was anchored there. When the overland troops arrived at Taku, a coordinated attack would be made on the forts, from the front and back, from the sea and from the land.

Kestrel, carrying Donald, was here at Pei-tang in case interpretation should be needed. Harry Parkes was on Lord Elgin's flagship at Taku. When the forts had fallen, they would join each other in Tientsin for the negotiations.

The incredible strength and length of the rainstorm had delayed the landing of the troops from day to day. Donald stared dully into the murk. When Hughes had said, "It'll be quick this time," he'd somehow imagined a span of two or three weeks. He'd be lucky if it took two or three *months*.

Was the rain slackening? He picked up Hughes's spy-glass, wiped it on his shirt-tails, and peered. Indeed, it seemed that the other ships were clearer, even that launches were leaving them, making shoreward toward the mouth of the river. Hughes banged him on the shoulder, and he handed the glass to Hughes, who peered too and grunted.

"Rain's clearing."

During the next half-hour, as though some giant hand were turning off a million faucets one by one, the rain slackened and at last stopped. The huge black clouds allowed a fresh breeze to blow them into tatters and whisk them off to the east toward Korea. Now, from all the surrounding ships, cutters and launches could clearly be seen setting out for shore, filled with troops and horses and armaments.

"Odd!" Hughes, frowning, was again peering through his spy-glass. "There's a boom across the river mouth, but it looks like nothing more than a chain and some buoys. And the fort is silent. Fort should be booming by now. Damned odd—"

He cut himself short to turn his glass toward a forest of

18

little flags that had sprung up on the shoreline and on each ship, wig-wagging messages. In a moment, he swore in astonishment.

"By God, the fort's empty! The cannon be wooden dummies! And it's all marshland there. It's a *bog*! After all this rain, our troops be hip-deep in mud! And the horses! How're *they* going to get through that? And the *guns*! By God, how're they going to move the howitzers and Armstrongs?"

Donald began to laugh. All those men and horses and huge, heavy guns, laboriously transported by those swarms of little boats, into a bog, for the sake of capturing dummy cannon in an abandoned fort! He roared with laughter. Hughes regarded him, frowning, and he laughed the more. It was very funny, wasn't it? *Wasn't it? Why wasn't Hughes laughing?*

Hughes muttered: "They'll take the town."

Donald's laughter bubbled into blankness. "There's a town there?"

"Small one, maybe twenty thousand people. Our men will take it. Waiting ten bloody days, nerves screwed up, then squelching through a bog, and no fort to take? Nobody'll be able to stop them taking the town."

Donald picked up the spy-glass and peered through it. The coast was clearly visible now, the cutters and launches clustered at the entrance of the river, looking tiny at this distance.

A town? What had taking a town to do with ratifying the treaty? A fort, yes. But a *town*, people living in it, mothers, fathers, children, old people?

Slowly, Donald lowered the glass. There was a trembling in his breast. Hughes cocked an eyebrow at him.

"Didn't realize, did you? There's going to be many a heart broke and buckets of blood spilled afore that treaty gets ratified."

At dinner, when Donald sat with Hughes and his officers in the stuffy saloon, a delegation came from the men to ask permission to go ashore.

Hughes said briefly: "Nay."

His first mate cleared his throat and muttered:

"Maybe better let some go. We be the only ship that ain't got men ashore."

Hughes said: "So be it. Let 'em sulk if they don't like it. There'll be at least one ship with a clean sheet, willy nilly. Who's the Provost Marshal?"

"Captain Con of the Third Buffs."

Hughes grunted. "Lots of work for him and his sergeants tonight. Hope they're up to it."

Donald chewed on his dried beef and felt glad that no *Kestrel* men had gone ashore.

In the night, tossing in his narrow bunk, the porthole and the cabin door propped open to create a draft in the sullen heat that had swooped down when the rain stopped, he heard the low voices of the first and second mates down the passage.

". . . flogging tomorrow. Thirty men, Jack said. Thirty lashes each. It'll take all day."

"British and French?"

"No, just our chaps."

"What about the Froggies?"

"Don't know. Jack hadn't heard."

"But they must have started it! They always do!"

"Come on! How d'you bloody know that?"

"Because they bloody did in the Crimea!"

"Come on! *We* say *they* start it, and *they* say *we* do. Anyway, this time Jack says definite our Punjabis started it. Real apt at rape they are, as well you know!"

"So are the Froggies! And at loot too! I know! I seen 'em!"

Donald slipped from his bunk and closed the door and went back to his sweltering bunk, shivering.

When, a week later, *Kestrel* steamed back to Taku, she was greeted with wig-wagging that Hughes translated as meaning that Lord Elgin was anxious to see Donald. Hughes gave him a sympathetic clap on the back.

"Cheer up! You'll like his lordship!"

His lordship was tall and broad—broad-faced, broad-nosed, broad-browed. His eyes were penetrating and sensitive, and his manner very gracious. Shaking hands, Donald felt his tension ease.

"Sit down, Mr. Mathes," his lordship said. "First, I must apologize for dragging you away from whatever you were doing in Hong Kong. Was it very important?"

"No, no!" said Donald hastily. "It was just that . . ."

When he hesitated, Lord Elgin smiled sadly.

"I understand. The more one sees of war, Mr. Mathes, the more one detests it!"

He poured brandy for the two of them and sat back.

"But we have this treaty that must be ratified. Extremely important for English commerce. I think that once we're past the Taku Forts there'll be no more need of fighting. The treaty, after all, was fully agreed upon when I was last here two years ago. The generals tell me that the assault on the forts will take place tomorrow. Two of the Armstrongs have been dragged into position six hundred yards behind the Great North Fort. I understand it took teams of six horses to drag each gun, its carriage up to the axles in mud, but it has been done."

He paused. They raised their glasses to each other, and sipped. The brandy tasted fine in Donald's mouth, all the finer perhaps because it was being drunk with this man, who detested war the more, the more he saw of it. Donald said suddenly:

21

"Thank you, sir."

Lord Elgin smiled and nodded.

"Well—about the ratification. As soon as we are by the forts, we will sail for Tientsin, where I expect Imperial Commissioners will hurry from Peking to meet us. Parkes is fluent in Chinese and quite competent. You will sit with him. You may not need to do any talking, but I wish you to assert yourself, if need be, should civility be lost at any time during the talking. Do you understand?"

"I do, sir."

"Good. I feel I have entrusted my wishes in this matter to good hands."

The sensitive eyes were warm and friendly. Donald felt his heart move.

"It is an honor, sir."

His lordship laid a hand upon his arm.

"Well, let us hope the fighting will be over by nightfall tomorrow, and we on our way to Tientsin and ratification."

Two weeks later, Donald stood in the flapping entryway of a tent, looking over peaceful millet fields to the low black roofs of the little town of Chang-chia-wan. Beyond, hazy in the blue mists of evening, lay the walled city of Tungchow, and beyond that, ten miles distant, Peking itself.

Thank God it would soon be over! His lordship had had his wish. The Taku Forts had fallen in a few hours. At first glimmer of light on the twenty-first of August, eight allied warships had steamed over the first of the river booms, their guns roaring at the southern forts, and the Armstrongs behind the Great North Fort had begun to speak. The forts had answered, and for half an hour thunderous fire and billowing smoke had made havoc of the dawn. Then a lucky British shell had fallen directly into the powder magazine of one of the forts and it had blown with a series of ear-cracking bangs.

22

By noon, allied marines were swarming up ladders into the forts, and by evening Union Jacks and Tricolors were flapping lazily over two thousand Chinese dead. That same evening, *Kestrel*, one of a long line of British and French ships, had steamed into the river on her way to Tientsin. As she puffed past the desolate forts, Donald had gazed with awe and a peculiar sorrow at the high, dun-colored walls. The scaling ladders were still in place. In an embrasure, a Chinese crossbow sat neatly.

The talks in Tientsin had started as soon as they arrived and had gone civilly enough until the sixth day, when it came out that the Chinese envoys were not qualified to make decisions: they had to report back to Peking.

Parkes had lost his temper then, cursed violently, shouted at the envoys, and walked from the room, redfaced and explosive. Donald had stayed to decide what should be done next. The older envoy, head trembling with an old man's ague, lips trembling with distress, had whispered that there had been much confusion in Peking. The proximity of the foreign armies had made the Emperor—*nervous*. No one had known what to do until Tzu Hsi had decided that he and she must go to the hunting lodge in Jehol, with Prince Seng to convey them there safely.

"Tzu Hsi?" Donald asked.

Yehonala. Tzu Hsi were the first two syllables of her long title as Empress.

"She is acknowledged as Empress?"

"Oh, yes!"

"And Prince Seng has gone with them to Jehol?"

"Yes."

"With his cavalry?"

"With some."

The old envoy and his companion had returned to Peking, and two days later the Emperor's brother, Prince Kung, and

23

the President of the Board of War had come, fully authorized to negotiate, they assured a foot-tapping Harry Parkes. Agreement had soon been reached. What the Chinese really didn't want was the full array of the British and French armies at the gates of Peking. They were prepared to exchange ratifications if the armies would approach Peking no nearer than three miles west of Tungchow and if, from there, Lord Elgin and his French counterpart Baron Gros would ride to Peking with escorts of only a thousand men each. And so it had been agreed, and so it would take place two days from now, thank God!

Donald shivered and buttoned his jacket against the growing chill of evening. It was mid-September. Although the daytime sunshine was still warm, as soon as the sun set winter hastened to hint of its coming. He turned to enter his tent, taking a last look around at the busy scene.

Over to his right, nearest to Chang-chia-wan, was the French encampment. Behind him were the bulk of the English. To his left were the Sikhs and the Punjabis; the breeze wafted the smells from their cook-tents to his nostrils, and he grimaced, his stomach shifting. What the devil did those fierce-grinning, turbaned men *eat*?

"Mathes!"

The call came sharply over the noises of the camp. Donald sighed and turned back. Harry Parkes was striding toward him, bouncing with his usual nervous energy.

"Mathes, d'you think the Chinese fully understand the protocol? Do they understand that Lord Elgin must deliver the Queen's letter into the hands of the Emperor *himself*? Not any of the princes. The *Emperor*. Which means they'll have to get him back from Jehol in time to receive it."

"Oh God, Parkes!" For many long days Donald had sat listening to Parkes quibble, and now exasperation suddenly exploded in him. "Let it be! What damned difference does it

24

make? It's Prince Kung who's going to sign the ratification, not the Emperor!"

"Nevertheless, a sovereign's letter can be delivered only into the hands of another sovereign."

"The Emperor may be a sovereign, but didn't you notice that the princes consider him a liability? Scared witless, he was, at the proximity of our armies. I told you, the envoys said it was the Empress who made all the decisions. Maybe you should insist that the *Empress* be present to receive the Queen's letter!"

Parkes gave him a withering look.

"That concubine! Whatever your views may be, Mathes, I'm going to make sure that the Chinese understand the protocol. I'm going to ride over to Tungchow."

"D'you think that's wise? Prince Seng's cavalry is intact. It wasn't involved at all in the action at Taku."

"You said he's off to Jehol. And anyway, we've reached agreement. Why should he attack us now?"

Parkes swiveled on his heel and marched away.

Shrugging, Donald entered his tent.

The night was loud with the sounds of thousands of men and horses in close quarters, and Donald slept fitfully, half waking toward morning to hear what sounded like thunder in the distance, a low growl that quickly grew and became the hoofbeats of galloping horses. Voices made themselves heard, unintelligible at first, then separating into words: "Prince Seng." "Caught them." Then, loud and clear just outside his tent:

"Mr. Mathes, sir, Lord Elgin wants you at once. They've all been trapped, Parkes and his whole party. They decided to spend the night in Tungchow, and Prince Seng arrived with his cavalry. Mr. Mathes, sir!"

The tent bellied as the messenger tugged at the entry flap. Donald was already pulling on his pants.

"I'll come immediately."

That idiot Parkes!

When Donald pushed his way into Lord Elgin's crowded tent, his lordship, hastily dressed, was sitting on a wooden chair behind the table, head bowed. He looked up as Donald came up to him, and Donald felt a thrill of shock. The sensitive eyes, full of pain, were sunk so deep that the cheekbones shelved out from under them. When he spoke, his voice was toneless.

"Mathes, at first light I want you to take this message to Prince Seng. If he does not release Parkes and his party at once, the English and French armies will occupy Peking."

Murmurs rose all around, and he held up a hand.

"I know, gentlemen. The position is very delicate. Ratification of the Treaty of Tientsin must remain our primary objective. England is counting on us to secure this enormous and lucrative market for our manufacturers and merchants. We cannot therefore push the Manchu government so hard that it will crumble and China fall piecemeal into the hands of rebels. Also, God forbid, we cannot push so hard that they will harm the prisoners. I have talked with Baron Gros, and we have agreed that the best way is to show no weakness. Whether or not we will actually attempt to occupy Peking is questionable, but for the moment we will threaten it. Gentlemen—you have your orders."

As Donald reined in his horse, the first rays of the sun beamed over the horizon and touched the whitewashed walls of Chang-chia-wan with dainty pink. But Donald had no eyes for pretty sights. Ranged before the town were rows and rows of ragged-looking horsemen astride small, shaggy ponies: Prince Seng's Mongol cavalry. Their prowess was supposed to rest on their magnificent horsemanship, the tireless strength of their sturdy little mounts, and their deadly marksmanship with bow and arrow from the saddle.

Donald eyed them, his heart beating heavily. Fifty yards behind him were ranged two hundred Sikh cavalry, all big men on big chargers, with weapons far superior to the Mongols' bows and arrows and short swords. And behind them, in turn, were three howitzers, their crews at tense attention. Yet the sight of those wild horsemen was disquieting.

Now, from their midst, a man rode out, trotting his hairy pony to within ten yards of Donald. A short, burly, thickset man with a round, shaven head and a thickly pockmarked complexion. The level of his eyes was a good foot below Donald's, but he stared up at him arrogantly.

Donald bowed.

"Prince Seng?"

The man gave a brief nod.

"I am instructed, sir, to salute Your Highness and to say that unless the English prisoners are released at once, the British and French armies will proceed to occupy your capital city."

Prince Seng hawked and spat a glob of phlegm so close to Donald's horse that it shifted uneasily. In an accent that Donald had to strain to understand, he said contemptuously:

"I am a soldier. I take prisoners. Prince Kung is in Peking. He can make peace if he likes—if you get as far as Peking."

He whirled his pony and rode back among his horsemen and in a moment was indistinguishable from them.

Lord Elgin, his face stiff as a deathmask, waved a hand at his general.

"Then there's nothing for it but to attack Seng and his cavalry."

The general saluted and strode from the tent. Elgin lifted

27

his head in a weary gesture and closed his eyes.

"He says that Seng has twenty thousand Mongols. We and the French together have seventeen thousand men, including the Sikh and Spahi cavalry. But he says our men are a well-balanced force of foot, horse, and guns, well trained to respond to generals who know how to fight battles. He says the Chinese tactics are from the Middle Ages—as, of course, are their bows and arrows. We shall see." He opened his eyes for a moment and smiled tiredly at Donald. "You did your best. I wish Seng had agreed to release the prisoners, but since he is determined to oppose us, on his head be it."

Was it a prayer? Was it a malediction? Was it a judgment? Donald watched the drawn face. Whatever it was, Lord Elgin was a man in mortal suffering.

Donald sat on a horse on a knoll that overlooked the wide plain of tidy millet fields and, far to the right, the white walls and black roofs of Chang-chia-wan. The millet was still young, but lush and verdant. The fields were neatly squared off by narrow pathways on which men and animals could pass without disturbing the plants. The sun was hot, the air drowsy. It could be any day of ordinary peace and prosperity, the farmers gone indoors in the noontime to rest and eat their meal.

But it was not. Beside Donald was an ordnance officer with a timepiece, checking the accuracy of his howitzers, which were dropping shells on the Chinese rear position. At this distance, the booms were dull and the clouds of dust they raised slow and lazy, a fantasy background for the long, long line of Prince Seng's cavalry, which was no longer shabby and shaggy and wild-looking but magnificent, the chorus of some great ballet swirling onstage to an unheard drumbeat, each man one with his animal, clear and shining in the bright sunshine.

The ordnance officer's laughter grated on Donald's ears. "By God!" the boor cried. "I thought that tactic had gone out with the Dark Ages! They're trying to surround us, and then ride in on us, attacking from all sides at once! By God, does that Seng really think we'll stand still for him?"

But the ballet had begun, and no one was allowed to stand still. The choreographer sent the Sikhs and Spahis on their great chargers to confront the Chinese right flank, while the Queen's Dragoons on their even huger mounts charged the main Chinese front, and the Fifteenth Punjabis, on foot, attacked at bayonet-point a battery the Chinese were moving up on the left, and the French infantry went for the town of Chang-chia-wan itself. It was wild and beautiful and awful, and it was over in minutes, the Dragoons streaming through Prince Seng's line in pursuit of fleeing Mongols, the rest of the cast milling about, toy soldiers on toy horses, lots of red coats and gold braid and sweeping plumes and helmets glinting in the sunlight, but the clangor only faint in the distance, and no blood. No blood to be seen.

The ordnance officer was yelling in Donald's ear that it had been a textbook battle, and the beribboned Provost Marshal, Captain Con of the Third Buffs, was galloping up on a sweating horse, shouting that it had been too damned easy, it was going to be bloody hard to keep the men down, they were still too full of spunk.

Spunk? Donald looked down at the dreamlike scene. *Spunk?*

"Going to bust out somehow or t'other!" cried the Provost Marshal. "Best they give the town over to plunder. Make it legal, so t' speak. It's going to happen anyhow!"

He dashed off, his horse whinnying.

"Punishment for enemy treachery," the ordnance officer intoned. "Treacherous of that Seng to take prisoners after the protocol was agreed upon."

"Punishment?" Donald said sharply. "Far as I know, not

a single citizen in that little town has any guilt!"

The officer shrugged. "Fortunes of war."

Anger flushed under Donald's skin like another kind of blood, hot and bubbling. He turned away and spurred his horse. He'd go back to his tent and wait there until it was all over, until Lord Elgin sent for him again. Lord Elgin, who detested war the more, the more he saw of it. But the tents were gone. The tent city had been struck, and soldiers were loading it onto a long line of carts, cursing the luck that kept them here while their mates were down there enjoying themselves in that little town given over to plunder.

The line of carts began to move, the men belaboring the mules that drew them. "Get on there, yer mucking loafer!" Maybe there'd still be time, maybe there'd still be something left to loot, some woman left to rape, some house left to burn down. "Get on, blast yer mucking hide!"

There was nothing Donald could do but follow the men and the carts.

When he was still too far away from the little town to see more than bellying gray smoke and leaping red flame, the sounds came to him clearly: the roar of fire, the crash and smash of wood, the cries of agony and desperate fear, the riotous screech of mindless glee. He dismounted and leaned against his horse's flank, anger burning in him gray and red like the burning town.

"Come and help!" a man shouted, grabbing his arm, jerking him forward, forcing him into a run; a uniformed man with a round, white collar instead of tabs—a padre. Wordlessly, he ran, dragging Donald with him, his free hand dangling a strange-looking instrument. They leaped over the shattered remains of the wooden gate that, before this day of disaster, had shut the town into safety. They were in a street, an alley, crawling with people as a hive crawls with bees. Soldiers yelling hoarsely, grabbing, snatching, smashing. Soldiers

30

laughing madly, draped in silks and furs. Soldiers clutching armfuls of anything, precious or base—there was no time to examine, to pick and choose. Soldiers cursing, driving the butts of their weapons against whatever they could not carry. Soldiers smashing in doors, dragging cowering people out from behind them, rushing in to search and break and tear apart. Soldiers calling merrily to each other, setting fires. Soldiers pulling screaming women along by the legs or hands or waists or hair, whatever was handiest. Soldiers fighting each other to get at the women, helping each other to hold them down, stumbling over other soldiers humped on spreadeagled women.

The padre darted and dodged and bumped his way through the bedlam, dragging Donald behind him. At last they staggered through a doorway into a large, dim room that seemed to contain many bodies, writhing and retching, moaning and groaning on the floor.

It wasn't the sight of the bodies that stopped Donald short, his stomach roiling. It was the smell—the overpowering smell of opium. But the padre gave him no time. He thrust him down to sit on the floor and pushed a girl into his arms.

"Hold her. Like this." He pulled the girl around until she was half-reclining in Donald's arms, her back against his chest. "Hold her tight. Don't let her struggle."

He inserted a tube into the girl's mouth, ignoring her gagging, and began to push it down her throat, muttering through his concentration:

"Surgeon'll be along in a minute. I got him to let me have a stomach pump first. I think I'm doing it right."

The girl's mouth and hands were smeared with opium. Open tins of the black, gluey stuff lay all about.

"They've tried to poison themselves with it," the padre murmured, never stopping his work over the girl. "To escape dishonor. Look out! You're letting her slip! Ah—"

31

The last was a cry of satisfaction as the girl began to retch violently. He pulled the tube from her throat, drawing forth a great spew of black vomit.

"She'll do now."

He pushed her gently aside, left her lying in her own vomit, and urged Donald on to the next woman. An old one. Must be eighty, Donald thought with horror.

"Oh, God!" he groaned aloud.

"You may well call on God!" the padre said grimly, shoving the ancient into Donald's arms, beginning to work on her. After a moment of tense silence: "I'm afraid this one's gone."

The surgeon came with an orderly and another stomach pump and they went on working, the two teams of them, fast and grim and silent, in a blur of revolting sights and smells and sounds that seemed to Donald after a while to meld into a single continuous, filthy, stinking upheaval.

After a very long time the surgeon said, "That's all, I think. Fifty, I made it? Three old women. Two children. One baby. The rest young girls."

"That's right." The padre turned to Donald. "Thank you, man. We saved them all but three."

Aching in every muscle, sick to his stomach, sicker to his heart, Donald turned away. Saved them for what? For the ravening beasts outside?

But outside it was quiet now. The savage day was over. Moonlight lay gently on the ravaged town. Only a few men still roved the littered alley seeking some overlooked crumb. Their figures were fitfully lit by two or three fires that still burned, but they too were dying down. The whole world seemed gentle, exhausted by the day's ferocity.

Donald walked, stumbling over men who lay snoring and snorting in the open. He came to a small stream. Stripping off the clothes that would never be clean again, he stepped into the icy water and washed himself, shivering, accepting the paralyzing cold as justice, retribution, penance, for he too was English and must bear guilt for this day's sin.

Camped under the walls of Peking, the armies waited. There was no sign from within the city. Outside it, the commanders could not make up their minds. Thirty-nine prisoners had been taken, including Bowlby, the *Times* correspondent, who had decided to accompany Harry Parkes. They might be under torture. They might be dying. Their lives might depend on rescue from outside. On the other hand, it might be the opposite: action from outside might mean the instant death of the prisoners.

Spies were recruited from among the Chinese living around the city. Day after day, Donald sat in the cold and flapping command tent, translating questions and answers, talking, talking, his throat raw and his mouth dry. Parkes, the spies said, was in the prison of the Board of Punishments, being interviewed daily by Prince Seng. At the beginning of each interview, Seng had him forced to his knees and his head banged on the ground in a compulsory kowtow. The other prisoners were in other jails. Nineteen of them had been forced to kneel in a courtyard at the Summer Palace for three days, without food or water, their hands tied behind them with wetted ropes. The ropes had shrunk as they dried. The men's hands had swelled to twice their normal size and turned black.

What did a man's hands look like that had swelled to twice normal size and turned black? Donald tried to work up enough spittle to swallow the bitter lump in his throat. He thought of Elgin. How was he dealing with his detestation? Not only war now, and killing, and rape and loot. Torture, too. No one had seen Elgin, it was said, since the armies moved away from Chang-chia-wan, leaving the little town to die of its wounds.

On the fourteenth day, the generals decided to march to the Summer Palace, where the nineteen men had been tor-

33

tured. Donald, listening to the discussion in the command tent, thought that the real reason for the march was to give the men something to do. They were knocking about, getting jerky from idleness. Another Pei-tang, another Chang-chia-wan, was not desirable.

The Summer Palace, the spies said, lay directly north of the walled rectangle of the Imperial City. It was a sacred place, they said, reserved to the Emperor and his cohorts. It was said to be huge, many hundreds of *li*; Donald worked it out at eighty square miles. A man-made fairyland of parks and forests and hills and dales and lakes, it contained two hundred buildings, of which thirty were imperial palaces and the rest pagodas, pavilions, temples, storage houses, and quarters for the eunuchs who cared for the place. An unbelievable place, the spies whispered. Full of treasure. A heaven on earth for the Son of Heaven.

Donald rode alone to the Summer Palace, in the wake of the armies. It was an early October day, the sun high in a pale sky, the breeze cold but light and soft, not strong enough to carry with it the fine sand of the Gobi Desert that could seep under the tightest-buttoned cuffs and collars and plague the body with itchy grit. A day of days, serene and silent, no one to talk and yammer, to hammer at Donald with "What did he say?" and "Tell him that . . ." Donald's mind floated dreamily as his body slouched in the saddle, as the reins drooped and the horse gratefully sank its head and walked quietly along.

But then it shied and edged into the shallow ditch that bordered the path. A high-wheeled Peking cart was thundering toward them, drawn by a lathered, rolling-eyed pony galloping as fast as it could under the whip that its driver was applying. Donald stared in astonishment as the cart approached. The driver wasn't Chinese—he was English, in the uniform of the Queen's Dragoons. The cart didn't contain

34

cabbages or fruit or sacks of wheat; it was piled high with a shaky mountain of—furniture? ornaments? porcelains? a jeweled screen?

The cart rushed by, leaving behind, like a ship's wake, a rippling stream of brilliant, shimmering color. What the devil was it? *Silk?*

Donald looked back at the cart in time to see something fall from it: the end of the bolt of silk. The beginning of it must have caught on a bush or something, and it had unrolled itself as the cart rushed along, to lay down on the humble earth a fairy-tale path that led, no doubt, to the fairy-tale palace of which the spies had whispered.

But the lovely path did not last long. Another cart rushed by, and another, and another, tearing and tattering the silk under their iron-rimmed wheels.

Every cart was piled high. Every driver was English, in uniform, plying the whip as heavily as he could to rush away with what he had got.

The Summer Palace was being looted.

Donald cautiously edged his horse forward in the shallow ditch. Around a bend or two, he came to a great circular courtyard that had been barred by iron gates that now gaped open. The courtyard was alive with men, their arms full of burdens, hurrying in and out of a magnificent building whose facade, Donald thought, must be made of hand-wrought porcelain tiles. But none of the hundreds rushing about the courtyard were interested in the tiles. They were interested only in movable property. The courtyard was littered with things that had fallen from the piles that they were carrying—beautiful, glittering broken things of gold and silver and precious quartz, torn silks, shattered shards of porcelain. Treasures, scattered and trampled and ignored in the frantic greed of the looters to get more. And more. The supply seemed to be unending. Donald dismounted and wandered into the building—a great hall of magnificent proportions whose walls had been covered with mirrors in gilded frames, every mirror now splintered, shards of glass crackling underfoot. Room after room, gutted, emptied of everything but the shattered remains of what could not be carried off—chandeliers, brocades draped from ceiling to floor, lacquered furniture, pedestals, more mirrors. Upstairs, rooms in which there was still treasure, in which men were grubbing through drawers and commodes and chests of gilded, carved, and jeweled wood, smashing with their musket butts what would not open at once, taking cock shots with their pistols at what would not be moved. In one room, six men going through a chest like pigs at a trough, their heads together, their hands mingling as they dipped and rummaged in the flash of jewels.

Donald wandered away from the frenzy, down a quiet, shady path, into another frenzy in another palace. And another. And another. In one courtyard lay a number of Chinese bodies over which the plunderers tripped and stumbled, stopping to kick and curse them. "Bloody U-nicks!"

In a fascination of horror, Donald fetched his horse and rode on, coming at last to open parkland among knolls and woods and lakes where there were no palaces, no treasures, no jewels, no gold. Here it was quiet and beautiful. On a calm body of water that reflected the sunlight, beside a graceful pavilion whose roof gleamed with breath-stopping richness of deep blue tiles, Donald found a miniature navy drawn up for battle. A hundred or more little ships, perfect miniatures, completely rigged, armed with tiny brass cannon. An Emperor's toy? Had the Emperor and Yehonala been playing at naval battle while their country fell under the barbarian heel?

Beside the pavilion grew a bush in full and splendid flower—great, pink blooms that Donald had never seen before. He picked one. The touch of its petals was smooth and thick, like wax. It was scentless. Pure.

He laid himself down beside the bush in the beneficent sunlight and fell into a dreamless sleep, still holding the flower. When he awoke he felt light-headed, as though the setting sun were not the same one that set in Hong Kong and England, as though it were a special sun that set only for this splendid place, mourning its plundering. His horse was browsing quietly, and at last he rose and mounted and rode slowly back, still holding the flower. The horse's hooves made no sound on the greensward, but they clattered on the granite mosaics of the courtyards and slithered and stamped and cracked over the debris of precious litter.

"And what did *you* get?" someone said.

Donald looked up. It was Lord Elgin, astride a white horse. The sight of him restored something in Donald, raised him out of the dreamlike horror into some range of normalcy.

"This," he said, holding out the flower. "This is what I got."

He smiled, but Lord Elgin remained closed and tight, his eyes cold as ice, his mouth a sharp line. He whirled his horse and rode away, leaving Donald stunned with something that felt like sorrow.

Outside the An Tung Gate, one of the several that pierced Peking's forty-foot-thick wall, thirteen howitzers were drawn up in a semicircle.

Inside the British command tent, the commander cleared his throat and turned to Donald.

"You are to write a letter to the Emperor's brother, Prince Kung. You are to promise him that if that gate"—he jerked a thumb over his shoulder—"is not opened by noon two days hence, the tenth of October, guaranteeing to us and to the French free access to the city, and if, by the same time, the prisoners are not released, you are to promise him that those thirteen guns will open fire."

The words fell into dead silence. The commander glanced coldly around at the men who crowded the tent.

"There is no other way," he said calmly. "We must take the risk. It is already growing very cold. In a month's time the freeze will start. It is too late to call up reinforcements, and we are low on ammunition. Prince Seng's cavalry is still virtually intact. It is now or never. Lord Elgin has spoken to Baron Gros, and they have agreed on this step."

He nodded at Donald across the table.

"That is all."

Donald gathered up the notes he had made and left the tense atmosphere of the command tent. In his own tent he laid out his writing brushes and the slab of ink, spread out a large sheet of paper, and weighted it down at the corners with little sacks of sand. He took up a brush, moistened it, rubbed it gently over the slab of ink, positioned it precisely over the paper at the proper perpendicular angle, and made the first brushstroke of Prince Kung's long Chinese title. He would write the letter perfectly. That was his business. The content of it was not. The content was Lord Elgin's business, the business of the man who detested war and who, it seemed, no longer knew how to handle his detestation.

The time until expiration of the ultimatum passed as slowly as though every minute were an hour. But suddenly it was a quarter of noon on the appointed day. With great ostentation and much clangor the thirteen howitzers had been loaded. They squatted like black monsters from a prehistoric age gathered to menace a city as old as they. Their gunners stood beside them at ramrod attention. On a platform stood an ordnance officer, a small Union Jack raised in one hand, eyes fixed on his watch. At the dot of noon he would lower the flag, giving the signal to fire, if the gate were not opened.

Another little stretch of time passed in utter silence.

The ordnance officer intoned, "Three minutes of noon."

And then the gate creaked slowly open. Little swirls of dust, drawn by the draft, swept to and fro in the aperture. For a while nothing happened. Then the first prisoner stumbled through, looking about him fearfully. His face was gaunt and gray as the dust, his eyes huge and sunken. Men from the surgeon's corps hustled him onto a stretcher and bore him quickly away.

He was followed by seventeen others, staggering uncertainly, filthy, bloodcaked. And finally by Parkes himself, his profile leanly sharpened, his Adam's apple jerking.

"I want it burned to the ground," said Lord Elgin. *"To the ground.* Of thirty-nine prisoners taken, twenty died of neglect and cruelty, among them a civilian, Mr. Bowlby of the *Times.* Such an atrocity cannot go unpunished. But I do not wish to make the Chinese people suffer more than they already do from the vainglory of their masters. I wish only the Emperor to suffer. Therefore I order that his playground, the Summer Palace, all its buildings, everything that is left of it, be burned to the ground."

Baron Gros's interpreter stepped forward.

"Sir, I have instructions to protest your order. The Baron finds it a completely useless act of vandalism."

For an instant, between the intervening heads, Donald caught a glimpse of Lord Elgin's face. His expression was petulant, as though he were about to stamp his foot. When he spoke, his tone was almost shrill.

"Tell your master that my decision is personal—and irrevocable."

Five days later, Donald stood with Parkes outside the great hall of the Board of Ceremonies in Peking, awaiting the arrival of Lord Elgin and Prince Kung for the exchange of ratifications of the Treaty of Tientsin.

Black smoke from the burning buildings and ornamental

woods of the Summer Palace had cast a pall over the city. Grimy bits of soot sifted down on the heads and shoulders of the waiters.

At the appointed time, Prince Kung arrived in a sedan chair borne by six bearers, followed by six mandarins. He was dressed in a long gown of somber gray with a black brocaded jacket, unornamented. His long face with its high cheekbones and deeply slit eyes was expressionless.

Two hours later, the Eighth Earl of Elgin and Kincardine arrived, in a sedan chair borne by eight bearers, followed by an escort of a hundred soldiers. He was dressed in emerald green velvet and ivory lace. He had lost weight and his broad face had become craggy. Its expression was haughty.

As Parkes turned to follow Lord Elgin into the hall, he said to Donald, "Come on." And then, in a tone of surprise, "Aren't you coming?"

"No," Donald said, turning away.

He didn't want to look into Lord Elgin's face again.

He wandered aimlessly down the road. His eyes began to water—it must be the smoke. He reached a corner and saw that, beyond the cleared area around the Board of Ceremonies, packed crowds lined the roadway. Silent, staring, black-eyed, Chinese crowds.

Someone took his arm and turned him around and started to walk him back to the hall.

Hughes.

"Don't you know, boy, you're a devil of a lot more *their* enemy than they be yours?" Then, without pause, in the same gruff tone: "We've all to deal with our problems our own way. Not for you nor me to judge."

With the heels of his hands Donald rubbed the water from his eyes. He wasn't judging. He was just—sad.

Chapter III

1861

IT SEEMED TO Donald that at crisis points in his life he was always standing at windows looking gloomily out over waters—Hong Kong harbor, the Pearl River, and now the thick and silty Whangpoo.

He'd been excited at first when Andrew told him he was to be transferred to Shanghai. Without mentioning that Yin-kwa had suggested it, Andrew said that since opium was now legal, Hong Kong, which had been the main buttress of the smuggling, would no longer be so important. On the other hand Shanghai, at the mouth of the Yangtsze River, would certainly grow in importance, especially as, under the new treaty, three of the Yangtsze River port cities were to be opened up to foreigners as additional Treaty Ports.

"We'll be able to go upriver as far as Hankow—further than any foreigner's been before. Maybe you'll be one of the first to go!" A guffaw and a heavy slap on the back. "Get yourself packed. I'm transferring you to Shanghai."

But it didn't seem that life in Shanghai was going to be much different from life in Hong Kong. His introduction to Shanghai's foreign society had been the same as in Hong Kong—the same grins and backslaps and "Lucky devils!" from Andrew's host of friends. This time Donald had felt cautious instead of joyful, but that hadn't changed anything. The friends hadn't even noticed, for this time there'd been more to congratulate Donald about. Bloody fine to have been personally chosen by Lord Elgin! Bloody fine to have actually been in Peking in his very first few weeks in China! Bloody fine to have been at Lord Elgin's side when he made that statesmanlike decision to burn the Summer Palace. Bloody fine lesson for the Chinese, didn't Donald agree?

He'd been noncommittal. It was impossible, in the sumptuous offices of Carradine & Co., in the long bar of the Shanghai Club, in the stately dining rooms of the Palace Hotel—impossible in any of those places, and impossible too at home with Andrew, to say what war was like, to speak of the tall mud walls of the conquered forts behind which two thousand dead men sheltered, of the little dead town of Chang-chia-wan, of the puffed-up dead hands of the prisoners, of their haunted eyes, of the detestation that had finally overwhelmed Lord Elgin. Impossible.

So he'd been noncommittal in the extreme, but even that Andrew's friends hadn't noticed, for there'd been so much to crow about: the new treaty, the new indemnity that the Chinese were to pay—eighteen million dollars!—the new Treaty Ports, the new "concessions" in the Treaty Ports, territory to be ceded to foreigners where foreign laws would prevail. And, of course, the new legality of opium, and the new arrogance that the new legality gave the opium traders.

It wasn't until the end of the first week that Andrew had introduced him to Wei Jin-see. With quickened heartbeat he had looked searchingly at Yin-kwa's adopted son, married to

Yin-kwa's only and beloved daughter. Surprisingly, he didn't seem to be pure Chinese. His eyes were black, but round and deep-set—European eyes. He was perhaps five years older than Donald, with a wide, jovial smile that did not extend to those European eyes. The eyes were shuttered. Donald extended a hand, but Jin-see pretended not to see it, shook his own hands together in the Chinese style of greeting, and then, in excellent English, excused himself—he was very busy at the moment.

Donald looked after him, coldness descending on his heart. Andrew said in an annoyed tone:

"Elusive beggar! If not for Yin-kwa, I'd get rid of him. . . . His father was an Englishman. Died in the 1842 war. I knew him slightly."

And since then, nothing. Donald had seen Jin-see several times and they had talked, genially and trivially. Whatever Jin-see's essence was, it was carefully concealed behind those shuttered eyes.

Donald turned away from the window. Perhaps there was no essence to Jin-see other than joviality. Perhaps he had been wrong in believing that Yin-kwa's visit on Jackass Point held some promise that Jin-see would fulfill. Or perhaps some twisty Chinese test had been administered and he had failed it and the promise had been quietly withdrawn.

Whatever—it was time to think once more of persuading Andrew to let him go. Carradine & Co. in Shanghai did a little token business in silk and porcelain, but its main job was importing opium—lots and lots of opium. And he was more determined than ever that he wouldn't be an opium trader, legal or otherwise. By God, what a botch he'd made of the start of his career! Letting Andrew hoodwink him completely and—what hurt more in a kind of way—hoodwinking himself into letting Yin-kwa renew the hope that Andrew had destroyed. Well . . . He sank into his chair at the desk and stared down at the blank white blotter. Nothing to be done now but learn his lesson and make the best of it until he could find some way of getting out.

A shadow fell across the blotter. Donald looked up. Jin-see was leaning aginst the windowsill, smiling. Not his usual wide smile; a small smile, a slight lifting of the lips. And when he spoke there was no hint of joviality in his tone.

"Will you have dinner with me on Thursday night?"

"Thursday?" Donald faltered, trying to adjust to this astonishing new aspect of Jin-see.

"Yes. Will you?"

"I'd like to very much."

"Good. At my home. I'll send a sedan chair for you at seven o'clock."

The next moment he was gone, as quickly and quietly as he had come.

Donald found himself once again at the window. Dinner with Jin-see? And at his *home*? It was unheard of. Chinese and foreigners met socially only in restaurants on formal occasions.

The Whangpoo's waters seemed not quite so thick and muddy. The craft on them sailed or steamed or were rowed about briskly, going somewhere, coming from somewhere. There was life here—and hope.

The sedan chair coolies bore Donald through the evening streets, dodging and weaving through the crowds that grew greater every day. Crowds of Chinese peasants, ragged, hungry, wandering about, openmouthed, bewildered. Refugees created by the marches of the Tai-ping rebels who for years had woven back and forth across the Yangtsze Valley, battling the imperial troops. Now they were moving south and east toward the rich coastal cities, driving before them thousands upon thousands of refugees. What a country! At the top, the Emperor and his thirteen official wives and his concubine-empress Yehonala, spinning out his fairy-tale life in his fairy-tale palaces. At the bottom, the homeless, starving refugees. In between, the restless, heaving mobs of rebels laying waste the land. The English swarming into the Treaty Ports, pushing opium in at every crack. The Chinese too, now, hastening to grow poppies. By God, doom was descending! If something very good and very immediate didn't come out of this dinner with Jin-see, he'd slip onto a ship and go home. To the devil with Andrew!

The chair coolies were thudding along a curving roadway that ran around the ancient walled city of which Yin-kwa had spoken. The walls and the arrow towers were long gone, but traces of the gates still remained. The foreigners called it the "Chinese City" in contrast to the foreign enclaves that were growing up around it: to the north, the English and American "concessions" that, combined, formed the International Settlement; to the south, the French Concession—"French Town," they called it. The chair coolies swung to their right, into the Chinese City, into a maze of narrow, crooked alleys so crowded that it seemed they could not pass at all. But they dodged and weaved, shouting "make way, make way," and suddenly a tall wooden gate was opening and they were taking the chair through it, out of the chaos of the alleys, into another world.

Donald stepped out of the chair to look around him wonderingly. A wide, quiet, marble-paved courtyard, with little glossy-leaved trees in tubs and dozens of colored lanterns hanging from the high walls. Across the courtyard, a low house with a doorway like a huge moon, circular and gilded. Another, larger house, from which a servant came hurrying, bowing and smiling, beckoning Donald to follow. They entered the house and went through many passages, Donald catching glimpses of silken carpets, rich woods, brocade

45

hangings, jade and porcelain ornaments—the panoply of wealth, but muted, unobtrusive. They entered a room that was in sharp contrast: an almost shabby room, much lived in, with comfortably upholstered foreign-style sofas and armchairs and, in a corner, a small round dining table.

Jin-see rose from one of the armchairs. He was dressed in a soft, loose robe, quite different from the stiff brocade he wore in the office. He was smiling the small smile.

"I hope you won't mind joining us in our family quarters. They're far more comfortable than the rest of the house."

Heart beating fast, Donald said, "I'm delighted."

Jin-see gestured: "And this is my wife, Olan."

She rose from the depths of an armchair, the only Chinese woman Donald had so far seen to whom the phrase "porcelain doll" could genuinely be applied. She was exquisite, her face almost ethereal in the purity of its line and color, her shining black hair, caught up in a knob at the nape of her neck, seeming too heavy for the delicacy of her bone structure. She was dressed in a simple dark gown that seemed to float about her as she stepped forward to bow. Speechless with admiration, Donald bowed back.

Jin-see said, his tone warm and friendly, "Lovely, isn't she? She speaks no English. I'm sure she'd like it if we spoke Chinese."

"Of course!"

Donald bowed again. Two or three times he'd tried to speak to Jin-see in Chinese, but Jin-see had shied away.

"And this . . . " Laughing, Jin-see turned toward the door from behind which came a loud patter of running feet. ". . . this is our daughter."

A little girl burst into the room, all bright black eyes and bouncing pigtails. She was making for her father when she caught sight of Donald and stopped instantaneously in the middle of the room, like a small, startled animal.

"We named her Chu-li," Jin-see said, "but a month or two ago she heard the name Julie in English, and ever since she's insisted that her name be changed to that."

The child glanced at her father, then back to Donald.

"Julie," she said firmly.

"Julie," he said, smiling.

She came to Donald confidingly and raised her arms to be lifted onto his lap. He held her lightly on his knee. God! Three days ago his only thought had been how to get away from Andrew! Half an hour ago he'd sworn to slip out on the first ship! And now . . .

Dinner passed in a haze. The food was marvelous—none of those fancy restaurant touches that, Donald now realized, foreigners mistook for good Chinese eating. Olan was gracious, Jin-see easy, the child bright and talkative. Conversation flowed. But still it seemed long until Olan rose and said good night and took the child's hand and left the room. Tea was placed on the table—an exquisite porcelain pot of jasmine-scented tea—and the servants too left. Jin-see poured, placed one of the small handleless cups before Donald, and sat for a moment in silence, brooding over his own cup in which a tiny jasmine flower floated. Donald sipped tea to ease the constriction in his throat.

"Donald." Jin-see spoke softly and evenly, using the name as though they had been friends for a long time.

Donald said, "Yes?" and glanced at him but saw nothing—his eyes were still shuttered. He said, still staring into his cup:

"My father-in-law Yin-kwa went to see you on Jackass Point for a reason that I now propose to explain to you. If you don't want to hear it, say so."

"I want to hear it," Donald said, keeping his voice steady.

"Very well." Jin-see nodded almost absently. He picked up his cup and turned it in his long, slim fingers. "I must tell

47

you first a little history. Yin-kwa comes from a very old merchant family. His great-great-great-grandfather was one of only ten merchants who were authorized by the Emperor to trade with the foreigners when the foreign traders first came to China two hundred years ago."

He sipped tea. Then:

"Merchants may be very rich, but in the Confucian hierarchy they are very low down—much below scholars, below farmers, only slightly above beggars and soldiers. Nevertheless, if China is ever to become a partner in the comity of nations, it is the merchants who will drag her out of the fantasy world of the emperors, out of the Confucian backwaters, into reality. For, as Yin-kwa says, it is the merchants who know the nature of the barbarian. We have been dealing with him for two hundred years. We know how to minimize the enormous disadvantages that China suffers in relation to the foreigners."

He paused a moment. Then:

"Does that make sense to you?"

"It does."

Donald's heart was beating so hard that he felt the pulse in his throat. *This* was the kind of thing he had envisaged when Andrew used the word "princely"!

"Good," said Jin-see quietly. "Because the proposal Yin-kwa had in mind when he visited you, the proposal I'm making to you now, is this: that you and I join in forming a trading company that will set an example to Chinese and foreigners alike of achieving counterbalance between Chinese and foreign interests—wait!" He held up a hand as Donald opened his mouth. "Let me explain what I mean."

He sat forward, sweeping the teacups aside.

"Take, for instance, shipping facilities. More and more foreign ships are coming into the Treaty Ports—more and bigger. No Chinese port has facilities for ships of that size and number. If we sit back and let the foreigners build up our port facilities, we'll be handing them still another huge advantage. We, the Chinese, must provide and control those facilities—wharves, dockyards, warehouses, labor. D'you see what I mean? Take building. The influx of foreigners and Chinese into the Treaty Ports and the growth of trade are going to create a huge building boom. We, the Chinese, must seize control of building materials—bricks, lumber, mortar, labor. Take food. The need of food in the growing cities is going to soar—not only staples, but items like white sugar, machine-ground wheat for foreign-style bread. What about factories for refining sugar and wheat flour? And beyond those things—what about transportation? Those small steam packets can well replace junks in the huge internal river system and along the coast—"

Donald could no longer restrain himself. He burst into speech:

"By God, Jin-see, that's why I came to China! That's the kind of thing I thought I'd be doing when Andrew told me he was going to make me his heir!"

Suddenly he collapsed like a pricked balloon.

"But I've no money! I couldn't invest any capital!"

Jin-see laughed.

"We don't need capital from you. Yin-kwa had control of my father's fortune and he turned it over to me when he launched me as compradore of Carradine's in Shanghai. I've ample capital and if we need more Yin-kwa will provide it. What we need from you isn't capital—it's evidence that an Englishman is cooperating on an equal basis with a Chinese. An Englishman who doesn't think, like your uncle and his cohorts, that the proper way of dealing with the Chinese is to browbeat them. Who has taken the trouble to learn our language excellently. Who is known to hate opium. Who has even tried to save the lives of fugitive rebels."

He laughed as Donald's mouth dropped open.

"There's very little that Yin-kwa's spy network doesn't pick up. I'll tell you a little secret—Andrew's Number One Boy Chong supplements his income by passing on tidbits of information."

He leaned forward, suddenly very sober:

"Will you do it?"

As soberly, Donald said, "Yes."

"It will mean both of us resigning from Carradine & Co., and that will mean you'll no longer be Andrew's heir."

"Almost from the day I arrived in Hong Kong I've been thinking of how to get out of being Andrew's heir."

Jin-see laughed, and Donald, looking at him across the table, saw that the shutters had fallen from his eyes. He could look right through Jin-see's eyes, and what he saw in the depths beyond were youth and eagerness and a joyous expectancy. Suddenly they were laughing together, laughing as though the world were dew-new and dawn-promising, as though there were no one in it whose blood flowed as young and red and strong as theirs. Spontaneously, Donald extended a hand, and this time Jin-see took it. They shook hands across the table in an access of pleasure in each other.

JIN-SEE

George Tyson : His Wife
1763 - 1845
England

Three sons

Charlie * _ _ _ _ _ _ _ m. _ _ _ _ _ _ _ Ling-ling
b. 1803   b. 1813
England   Canton
d. 1842   d. 1842
Chapoo   Chapoo

Wei = His Wife
b. unknown
d. 1842
Ningpo

Two sons

Jin-see   Two daughters
b. 1832   b. 1835 & 1838
Macao   d. 1842
                 Chapoo

* The Red Barbarian

Chapter IV

1861

AT THREE O'CLOCK in the morning, the gateman roused the sleepy chair-bearers as his master and the English visitor shook hands in the middle of the courtyard, laughing, clapping each other's backs. His master was in a fine mood!

But when the bearers had swung the chair out of the compound, his master turned and walked slowly toward the low house with the golden moon door. The gateman hurried across the courtyard to slide the door open and stand beside it, bowing respectfully, as his master entered. Something important must have happened. Instead of seeking his bed at this late hour, his master was going to report to his ancestors.

Inside the little house, Jin-see struck a match to an oil lamp. The room wavered into sight. Walls and floor of rich, polished woods. In the middle of the floor, a large, square, white cushion. At the end of the room, the ancestral altar, a tall, narrow carved-wood table on which stood two pewter candlesticks, a pewter vase for incense sticks, and a single soul tablet, a small one, perhaps two by four inches, of pure white marble, engraved and gold-inlaid with the character WEI. The name of Jin-see's grandfather, his mother's father, which he himself had taken.

Jin-see knelt and bowed his forehead to the floor. Then he rose and went to the white cushion, sat down upon it, cross-legged, bowed his head, closed his eyes, and set himself deliberately to slow the racing of his blood.

At last, when his mind was still and empty and he could feel the quiet beat of his heart, he conjured up the face of his grandfather as he had last seen it when he was ten years old. A long, thin face mazed with wrinkles; desperately anxious eyes; tight lips calipered between lines of worry.

"Be careful, Jin-see," the lips whispered. "Don't show your face outside the house. Anyone can tell from one look at you that you have English blood. They'll harm you, and they'll try to harm your mother, for they'll know that she lay with an Englishman."

It had been impossible to hide indoors forever, like the two little sisters who cowered obediently behind the shutters. But outside there were the hating faces, the hating, screaming voices.

"English devil child!"

"Devil offspring of a whore mother and an English devil!"

And there were the slaps and shakings, the stones clunking against his head and shoulders, the spittle splashing in his eyes.

"Why do they hate me?" he shouted at his mother when she dragged him indoors, panting and heaving from his efforts to hit back at those who hit him. She folded him in her arms as he fought and kicked against her too, and her voice was hoarse with weeping.

"Because your father is English, my poor little Jin-see, and the English are making war against us, with many fire ships that can hurl their fire a great distance and destroy whole cities in a few minutes, and kill many thousands of our people."

"I hate my father!"

"Oh no, Jin-see! No, no, no! I love him! If I were to lose every drop of blood in my body, each drop as it oozed out would say, 'I love him!' "

"Why isn't he here to take care of us?"

"Because your grandfather took us away from him. He thought your father was going to take us to England forever, so he brought us here to Ningpo and the war caught us."

The war. The war.

The cold and terrifying day when he awoke to find his mother and sisters gone—gone to Chapoo for safety, his grandfather said, under the protection of a Tartar general.

"But I couldn't send you with them, Jin-see. I couldn't bear the thought that I might lose you in the debris of war."

And those days alone with his grandfather—still the breath-held crouchings in corners, the fearful warnings: "Don't show your face! They'll know you have English blood!"

And at last the worst day of all, the most terrible: the day his grandfather too disappeared and there was no one but a strange foreigner with a swiveling cocked eye, the missionary who had eventually brought him back to Hong Kong and to Yin-kwa.

Jin-see shivered violently and sat up, shaking off the waking nightmare. He knew now what had happened. When he was fifteen Yin-kwa had told him the whole story of the war, of how his grandfather, his mother, his sisters, and finally

53

his English father—all of them except himself—had died in it. At the end of the story Yin-kwa had said, "And so, of course, I adopted you, for I loved your father like a brother."

Strange. To him, his father had seemed a figment made up to fit Yin-kwa's story, not a flesh-and-blood person whom one could love like a brother—or like a father. Had he loved his father before he hated him? Before those terrible Ningpo years when his heart had been a lump of burning ice, forever cold with fear and hot with fury? It seemed to him now that those years had blotted out everything that went before, that life had begun in the beautiful courtyards of Yin-kwa's home, that love had begun with beautiful Olan when he was ten and she was seven.

Yet there was a wispy memory. A laughing man sailing away on a ship. When this memory came to him, sometimes dreaming, sometimes awake, it always seemed to Jin-see that he was straining to keep the man in sight, but a sunbeam came to blur his vision, and when he could see again desolation swept him, for the ship was far away and the man gone from view. That man had been his father. Had he loved him then?

And now? He had resisted Yin-kwa's wish that he and Donald enter into partnership. He disliked all Englishmen. He could tolerate them only by the evasive kind of joviality at which he had become expert. He had resisted Yin-kwa, though he had seen Donald's anxiety and sensed his longing, until Yin-kwa wrote commandingly: "Do as I say, for I am not mistaken in Donald."

So he had invited Donald to dinner, still reserving to himself the right not to put Yin-kwa's proposal to him. But he had found himself liking Donald, and Olan had liked him too, and Julie had taken to him hugely—bright little Julie, whose instincts could be trusted, even at the age of five. A likable

54

Englishman. The first Englishman he had ever liked. The first time he had ever had a term of reference by which to measure the wispy figure who had disappeared in the brightness of a sunbeam, by which to endow with substance the image of Yin-kwa's tale.

Jin-see rose and went to the altar. A small click, and a drawer hidden in the carvings slid open. In the drawer lay another tablet, the second of the pair Yin-kwa had given him when he and Olan left Yin-kwa's household to start their life in Shanghai. An exact match of the first, except that this one was carved in English letters with the name CHARLIE.

Jin-see set the tablet upon the altar beside Wei's. Lit an incense stick in the lamp's flame and blew on it until it glowed and musky smoke was swirling. Slipped it into the pewter vase. Laid himself face down on the floor, outstretched his arms toward the altar, and struck his forehead to the boards three times.

Then he went again to sit cross-legged on the cushion. He felt very calm and very stoic. The battle was over, the thorny resistance that had prickled for so long in his breast to the filial duty Yin-kwa had laid upon him—the "life-duty," Yin-kwa had called it. He had accepted it now, and he began methodically to review it.

"Jin-see," Yin-kwa had said, "in the beginning your father and I helped to spread the smuggling of opium. Hardly anyone knew, at that time, how evil opium is. When we finally realized the nature of opium, we withdrew from the trade. Your father died shortly after, but I made a vow in his name and mine. If everyone who hates opium turns his back on it, who will be there to reverse the tide when the time comes? I will be there, I vowed. I, or my sons, or Charlie's son, or their sons. It will take a long time to finish off opium. A hundred years? Longer? It will be the life-duty of many lifetimes."

55

Especially mine, Jin-see had thought, for mine was the English father.

"I became Carradine's compradore," Yin-kwa went on, "and I stuck to him tight. He can't rid himself of me, though he'd like to. I chose Carradine because he is the biggest of the British smugglers, the most arrogant, the most offensive, as his father was before him. It is against Carradine that a telling blow must be struck, when the time comes. If I cannot strike it myself, you will do it, Jin-see, for his father was your father's murderer."

Jin-see had bowed his fifteen-year-old head.

"While opium is being smuggled," Yin-kwa said, "it is uncontrollable. The only way of controlling it would be to sink the smugglers' ships and cutters and launches. Can you imagine our old war junks doing that? But once opium is made legal and everyone can trade it, grow it, sell it, Chinese as well as British—once that happens—and it will happen; the British want it thus, and they will have their way. . . ."

Yin-kwa's clever eyes stared into space, seeing his visions.

There was, first of all, the trading company that would begin to equalize Chinese disadvantages in the face of the foreign commercial invasion.

"My grandfather foresaw this time when the foreign traders would come into our very heartland, and that is why he sent me to the swivel-eyed missionary to learn English, and that is why I have seen to it that my sons and you, Jin-see, all know English."

There was the Chinese Opium Merchants Guild that, once opium was legal, would control all buying, selling, and transport of opium, foreign and domestic, throughout China, and thus would be the only customer of the British opium importers.

"Can you see it, Jin-see? Instead of selling to uncounted

numbers of customers all along the smuggling routes, they'll be able to sell only to the Guild—and we will control the Guild."

There was the development of a domestic opium good enough to compete with Patna opium.

"Domestic opium will be very plentiful and very cheap. The only advantage of British opium will be its extraordinary quality. If we can develop an opium as good as theirs and keep it in reserve to flood the market at dirt-cheap prices at a crucial moment . . . "

And there was the Chinese national anti-opium movement that would be created and made strong throughout China, would one day join with the British anti-opium societies in a huge wave of indignation that would sweep away opium, turn full circle, and restore the purity of the days before opium smuggling began.

Jin-see sighed and sagged on the cushion. Was a hundred years long enough?

The false dawn was breaking as Jin-see slipped from the house of his ancestors back into the house of the living.

In the great bed Olan lay asleep, her lovely face silvered in the first faint light. Beloved Olan, with whose love his real life had started. Olan of the Fairies. The fairies had brought her, Yin-kwa said, and she could still hear them when they called to her. Sometimes her spirit went to stay with them for a while, leaving her body to sleep, still and white and cold. At those times, the tension in Jin-see mounted until he felt he would twang in a high wind.

But her spirit always returned to her, and she was always happy then, with only one regret: that as yet they had no son. Though that was not a real regret, for she had consulted her seers who told her not to fear, the son would come. Jin-

57

see was beginning to wonder whether he should consult one of the English doctors. Was something wrong with her? Perhaps, even, with him?

But to consult an English doctor would be a farfetched and extraordinary measure.

She was awake, looking up at him with soft and dreamy eyes. Desire for her swept him, desire so great and urgent that it was somehow mystic, having to do with the white tablets on the ancestral altar, the duty he owed the ancestors to give them sons.

He bent to her and she stretched her arms to enfold him.

Afterward, he lay awhile in the wonderland between wakefulness and sleep, the fragrance of her hair all around him, wishing to prolong the moment, but slowly sliding into sleep. Her hand on his cheek held him back. He slitted an eye and saw her, sitting up in bed, the first full light of dawn illuminating her beauty. She was smiling. She spoke so softly that his sleep-besieged ears hardly heard her.

"I've conceived him. Our son."

He fell off the cliff of sleep, smiling. It would indeed be right and fitting if, on this night when he had at last acknowledged his father, he and Olan had made his father's grandson.

Chapter V

1862

ONALD SAT AT the dining table in Jin-see's family room, shuffling through a stack of papers—the statements of the first six months' operation of Jinsey Mathes. He was absorbed, eyes aglow with satisfaction. Jin-see watched him, smiling. What a difference from the man who had arrived in Shanghai a year ago on *Falcon*! That man had been tense and wary, regarding with a cautious eye the friends Andrew pressed on him, shaking their hands briefly, muttering monosyllabic replies to the questions and remarks they showered on him. Andrew had hovered watchfully over him. Jin-see had written Yin-kwa that he feared Donald would never have the courage to break with Andrew, in answer to which Yin-kwa had written, "Do as I say, for I am not mistaken in Donald."

And Donald *had* had the courage. Had gone with Jin-see into Andrew's office and handed him his letter of resignation. Had stood quietly, whitefaced but steady, through Andrew's explosion, saying firmly whenever Andrew paused for breath, "You never told me that you trade opium. I will *not* be an opium trader."

Finally they'd left Andrew in midbellow, his eyes popping from his puffy, crimson face—the lechery and the drink were beginning to show. The next day, Jinsey Mathes had been born. And now, look at Donald! Easy and joyful, delighting Olan with his courtesy and his near-perfect Chinese, delighting Julie with his playfulness, and even more with his seriousness—he knew when to take her seriously. She adored him.

And delighting Jin-see himself in a strange, tantalizing way. Was Donald's smile like Charlie's? His courtesy? His simplicity? His . . . Englishness? There were English and English, after all. Some need not be treated with evasive joviality. Some could be treated as friends. Could be liked. Perhaps, one day, loved. As perhaps Jin-see had loved his father Charlie?

Donald looked up from the papers.

"It's going fine! No froth. Everything rock solid. Building, engineering, machinery—the kinds of things that will automatically spawn more business. We've done well, but we've also been lucky. We started at just the right time."

They had! The times were fine for business. When the Hsien Feng Emperor died of the dissipations in which his Empress was said to have encouraged him, she had connived with the Emperor's brother, Prince Kung, to become coregent for her six-year-old son, the new Emperor. They made a shrewd pair. Warfare against the foreigners hadn't worked. It was time to try cooperation. A few antiforeign princes had been discreetly executed. Prince Seng had been set to fighting rebels instead of foreigners. With the suppression of rebellions, the refugees had begun to return to their farmlands. A new stability had started to emerge. Trade had boomed.

But Donald was no longer thinking about Jinsey Mathes. He had piled the papers neatly in the center of the table, and now he turned to Jin-see with a small frown.

Jin-see braced himself. It was coming.

"Jin-see," Donald said thoughtfully, "there's something I'd like to clear up. Last night at the Club Andrew said, specially loud to make sure I heard, that you're going to be chairman of some new organization, the Chinese Opium Merchants Guild. It's ridiculous, of course, but I'd just like to hear you say that Andrew's wrong."

Jin-see drew a long breath.

"He's not wrong. Yin-kwa is the general chairman of the Chinese Opium Merchants Guild. I am chairman of the Shanghai branch. Yin-kwa's sons, or his delegates, are chairmen of the branches in the other Treaty Ports."

"You're not serious!"

"I am."

"But—that's *treachery*, Jin-see!"

"Listen, Donald—"

"Listen to *what*?" Donald rose, white and shaking. "What explanation can there be that isn't a bloody lie? I'm finished with you, Jin-see. By God, I've finished with China! I'm pulling out of Jinsey Mathes and going home!"

He swung around and strode to the door.

Jin-see was there before him.

"Will you sit down and listen?"

They glared at each other. At last, with a shrug, Donald returned to his seat at the table and sat staring icily out of the window.

Jin-see leaned against the wall behind him and spoke as quietly as his thudding heart would permit.

"D'you remember, Donald, when Yin-kwa visited you on

61

Jackass Point, he said to you, 'Should the British be allowed to debauch our people, and should no Chinese even try to control them?' "

"Yes." Donald's voice dripped acid. "I wondered then what the devil he meant, since he's Andrew's opium-trading partner, and I'm still wondering!"

"Well, think about it. In the opium trade, one man's restraint means nothing. If he turns his back on opium, there are a dozen others waiting to take his place. That's why Yinkwa didn't quit opium. That's why he stuck with Andrew, the biggest of the opium smugglers."

"You're talking rubbish," Donald muttered.

"Not at all." Jin-see came around and sat at the table. "As long as opium was being smuggled, nobody could control the British smugglers. They bought opium legally in India and brought it here and delivered it at a thousand smuggling points, and nobody could interfere with them, least of all the poor old bungling Chinese navy. But now that opium is legal *we* can control the British traders. We, the Chinese merchants. Because the Chinese Opium Merchants Guild *will be their only customer.*"

"What?" Donald looked at Jin-see, startled.

"That's right." Jin-see gave him a tentative smile. "They can bring opium from India to the Treaty Ports, and that's as far as they can get. They won't be able to sell an ounce of opium except to the Guild because every opium dealer in the whole of China will be a member of the Guild."

"But—" Donald frowned. "What about domestic opium? The Chinese farmers are growing poppies too."

"And the Guild will handle their opium too. The Guild will handle *all* opium. Andrew and his friends, and the British government, and the British-Indian government, were all crowing when the new treaties were ratified and opium became legal. But actually, they were killing their own golden goose. Domestic opium will soon be plentiful and much cheaper than Indian. Imports are going to tumble within the next few years. They might be wiped out completely if we could produce an opium as good as Patna, but we can't yet, and there'll always be rich people who'll demand Patna."

"You sound as though you're *competing* with the British, not controlling them!"

"We *are* competing with them." Jin-see leaned forward. "We're going to take the opium market away from them, except for top-quality opium, and one day we'll be able to produce that too, and then we'll take that market as well. Don't you see, Donald? In the long run, we can stop our own farmers from growing poppies. In the long run we can abolish opium within China as long as opium isn't continually being brought in from outside. The essential thing is to stop the British from bringing it in. That's what Yin-kwa has been planning all these years."

Donald sighed, a sound that was almost a groan. Jin-see looked into his troubled eyes and thought, Not Yin-kwa's plan. *Our* plan. *My* plan. My life-duty. My filial duty to my father, whose body rests in the Bay of Hangchow, whose soul tablet lies upon my altar.

His heart lightened and he grinned at Donald, feeling his eyes begin to shine, seeing with enormous relief an answering spark in Donald's.

"It's *crazy!*" Donald said, shaking his head. "Let me try and get it straight. Obviously, the Guild is not going to be suppressing opium. They'll be dealing enthusiastically."

"Yes. The purpose of the Guild is to control the British traders. That's just the first step."

"Are *you* going to trade opium?"

"No."

"How can you be chairman of the Guild and not trade opium?"

"Easily. I'll tell everybody that I'm not trading."

"And they'll believe you?"

"Of course not. They'll believe that I'm secretly financing one of them to trade on my behalf."

"Why would you do that?"

"Because of you, of course."

"*Me?*"

"Yes!" Jin-see laughed. "Everybody knows you hate opium, that you left Andrew because of opium. Now you and I are partners. If I were to be seen to trade opium I'd make you lose a tremendous amount of face, and naturally I wouldn't do that. Naturally I'd pretend not to trade opium, while getting someone else to do it for me in greatest secrecy. The proper Chinese way of seeing to it that nobody loses face. The Chinese will think it so proper that I'll bet nobody'll even try to find out who I'm using to trade for me."

"You'll be devious and dishonest, but they'll all think you're doing the right thing?"

"The Chinese will, certainly. Of course, not Andrew and his friends. They'll laugh and say it serves you bloody well right—you left Andrew because he's an opium trader, only to find yourself snugly tucked up with another one, and a damned twisty Chinese one at that."

Donald shrugged. "As long as *you're* not betraying me." His voice trailed off. Then, with a laugh: "How long's all this going to take, anyway?"

"A hundred years."

"What? Yin-kwa'll be long gone, and you too!"

"My son will carry on. And then my son's son."

"You have no son!"

"I . . . Shhh . . . "

Jin-see held up a finger. They both turned their heads to

listen. Someone was scurrying down the corridor outside.

Jin-see's heart began to beat heavily.

The Old Woman crouched in a corner of the bedroom, watching. They called her the Old Woman because she was gray and wrinkled, though she was not much older than Olan. She had been Olan's little servant when they were children and had taken care of her ever since. When Olan's spirit went to the fairies, she it was who sat beside the still body, rubbing the cold extremities, forcing water between the clenched teeth, calling to the spirit to return. She loved Olan perhaps more even than Yin-kwa or Jin-see, for her love was dumb and encompassed the whole of her being.

Now she watched anxiously as the midwife worked over Olan. Olan had not yet fulfilled her duty. She had not yet produced a son. Let this one be a son!

In a short while, simultaneously, the baby let out its first yell and the midwife cried, "It is a son!"

The Old Woman slipped quickly to the door. She must be the first to carry the news to Jin-see. Her beloved Olan was vindicated! She had produced a son! The Old Woman hurried along the passages to the door of the family room where Jin-see sat with the Englishman. She flung the door open. It was almost dark, but she could make out Jin-see's raised head against the lighter square of the window.

In her cracked voice she cried out to him as loud as she could, "You have a son!"

A great burst of joy and triumph flowed like a swift river through Jin-see. A son! A son! He rose and got a bottle and glasses from a cupboard, poured wine, and held out a glass to Donald, his hand shaking a little with the bubbling of his excitement.

"Donald, let us toast the birth of my son."

Donald was gaping.

"Just now? He's just been born? You didn't say anything!"

"In case it was another daughter, although Olan has been sure from the first that it was a son. You see, I do have a son to carry on after me. A hundred years isn't as crazy as it sounds. Donald, I haven't tricked you in any way. What I've told you today is the whole truth, as Yin-kwa planned it, as his sons and I and my son and my son's son will try to carry it out. Won't you stay, Donald? Stay in China. Stay with me in Jinsey Mathes."

Donald rose to his feet, his face stiffening as he tried to conceal the depths of his emotion. He took the glass and raised it.

"To Jinsey Mathes. And to your son."

When Donald left, Jin-see went quickly through the passages to the room in which Olan had borne his son. They had tidied everything up. The Old Woman and the midwife stood on either side of the bed, silently admiring the baby, who lay quietly on Olan's breast. When Jin-see entered, they turned to leave, casting smiling glances at him, claiming a share in the joy of the occasion. He had his rightful due now, what every man must have, a son to perform the rituals of the past, to make sons for the future, to ensure the continuance of the family.

Alone, Jin-see stood beside the bed, his heart thudding steadily, the blood rushing buoyantly through his veins. Olan was deeply asleep. Perhaps she had gone to her fairies for a while. Beloved Olan, a child herself, an enchanting, moonstruck child in the body of a lovely woman. The baby lay on her breast, wrapped in red silk, his tiny face crumpled and red as the silk, eyes tightly closed, breaths light as the beat of butterfly wings.

The Son. The Grandson. The Englishman Charlie's grandson. No—not that. His father's grandson.

He looked entirely Chinese. It was early to say, but it seemed that he would never be called English devil child. And he would have the most Chinese of names. Jin-see had thought of a name for him, the thought flickering in and out of his mind, for, even as he laughed at himself, he was afraid that if he entertained it fully, malignant spirits might notice and inflict bad luck on Olan's pregnancy. But now the son was born and he could think openly of his name, even pronounce it aloud.

Ta-lung. Great Dragon.

The wonderful name lay on the air. He placed his hand lightly on the baby's black-haired head, feeling that he might burst with the joy and solemnity of the moment.

Chapter VI

1864

THE CUSTOMS SHED stood on the bank of the Whang-poo River, on the waterfront road that the foreigners had named the Bund. It was huge and cavernous and dim and redolent of a thousand things, predominantly the heavy oil that coated machine parts, and opium.

A frowning clerk led Jin-see between piled crates and boxes and gunnysacks to the place where the opium chests were stacked. Square wooden chests, strongly made, each weighing about a picul—133 pounds—and containing forty balls of opium. The chests had different marks and numbers, indicating different shippers and purchasers, but they had all come from Patna through Calcutta.

The clerk took from his file a wad of papers, the bills of lading for the shipments. He said to Jin-see resentfully:

"I don't know why you are giving us the trouble of having all these chests recounted. We are very busy here, but very careful. We do not make mistakes."

"I'm sure you don't," Jin-see said mildly, "but the shippers may have. There are supposed to be 1,030 chests here. The import duty is thirty taels of silver per chest. That amounts to 30,900 taels, over 50,000 dollars. You know how opium is traded. The Guild buys the bills of lading from the importers and pays the duty direct to Customs. Any mistake would cost the Guild merchants, not the importers. As chairman of the Guild I'd be failing in my responsibility if I paid out 30,900 taels without counting the chests."

The clerk shrugged and called two coolies over to move the chests, separating them according to their marks and numbers so that Jin-see could check them against the bills of lading. There were five bills of lading, in the names of Dent, Sassoon, Hardoon, Elias, and David—except for Dent, all newcomers to the opium trade. There was no bill of lading for Carradine. Andrew still shipped in his own white-sailed clippers, despising the smelly, noisy, steel-hulled commercial steamers on which any cheap-jack could buy space. And Andrew still imported in thousands of chests, not the couple of hundred covered by each of the bills of lading Jin-see held.

The counting took a long time. When it was over at last and the coolies dismissed, the clerk had regained his good humor.

"I'm sorry I was ill-tempered," he said to Jin-see. "I thought that you doubted our efficiency. We are proud of our Customs Service."

Jin-see smiled. "Justly so. It is admirable."

It was, in fact, the best thing to come out of the Unequal Treaties. The Chinese Maritime Customs Service, headed by Robert Hart, was putting order into the old chaotic system of collecting revenues and producing greater revenues than ever before. But, as with most of the other "good" things that came out of the treaties, there was a catch: the new revenues were being seized upon by the foreigners to secure the loans they were making to Peking. But Jin-see smiled at the proud little clerk. He was efficient and hardworking, as he should be, and let the rest go over his head, as it should. In the ballooning business world of Shanghai, efficient clerks were jewels of great price and their energies should not be distracted by matters they could do nothing about.

The clerk, gratified by Jin-see's smile, took a step closer.

"Sir, is it true what I heard, that when they negotiated the treaties, our Chinese envoys wanted to set the duty at sixty taels per chest?"

"Yes. They hoped to make opium so expensive that fewer people could afford it."

"It was the British, then, who set the duty at thirty taels?"

"Yes."

"You know, sir, that these 1,030 chests bring the total imported in the last year to 100,000 chests?"

"I know. It all goes through the Guild."

The clerk shook his head slowly and sadly.

Jin-see took comfort from the little man's simple and sincere mourning for the growth of the opium trade, but his heart grew heavier as he made his way toward the exit. In the wildest of the smuggling days, perhaps sixty thousand chests a year had come into China. Now, a hundred thousand, plus rapidly increasing domestic production. How long was it going to take to accomplish the life-duty? Was it possible to accomplish it at all? Opium was entrenched deeper than ever, the members of the Guild rejoicing in their growing riches, and with them millions of others—the farmers growing poppies, the middlemen, the wholesalers and retailers, the boilers who prepared opium for smoking, the owners of dens and divans, the makers of pipes and all the paraphernalia of smoking, the hangers-on. A livelihood from opium was no longer an exciting departure from tradition. It was becoming a tradition in itself.

"Hello," a voice said in English.

Jin-see turned. Robert Dent, son of Lancelot Dent, who, in Yin-kwa's day, had been second only to Andrew's father in the ferocity of his smuggling activities.

Jin-see put on a calm and confident smile.

"You've been counting chests, I suppose," Dent said.

Jin-see nodded. "Have to make sure the Guild is getting its money's worth."

"You've got us by the balls, haven't you?"

Jin-see's heart thudded heavily. Were the English feeling a pinch? With an effort to keep his smile intact, he said:

"No Chinese would attack the parts you mention!"

Dent guffawed good-humoredly.

"You know damned well what I mean! Old Lord Palmerston was a God-blasted fool to let Andrew's father persuade him that legalizing opium in China would provide an everlastingly profitable trade for India. Patna opium! Best in the world! An inexhaustible market for it in China! God Almighty! I made ten times more out of opium when I smuggled it than I do now, with your damned Guild controlling everything and local poppies being grown all over."

Jin-see said gently: "You're not importing much, I see. Out of the thousand-odd chests over there, only a couple of hundred are yours."

"I can see the writing on the wall as well as the next man. Anybody who continues to rely on opium is a fool. My son started up a line of machinery, and now we've got an engineering department going. Just made a bid for the new bridge across the Soochow Creek."

"That's fine!" For a moment Jin-see's smile became genuine. "Fine for you. Fine for China."

"Aye." Dent came closer and his voice dropped confidentially. "It's not just local opium and falling prices that make me want to get out of opium. The trade's been cheapened by

71

these new importers. Sassoon, Hardoon, Elias. Middle East-
erners with British passports. Upstarts, aping their betters.
Calling themselves opium traders! They're nothing but job-
bers. Buy small lots, ship them in on commercial freighters,
get the best price they can, buy a bit more. By God, I remember the days when my father bought opium by the clipper-
load at the Calcutta auctions!"

Jin-see went on smiling. They *were* feeling a pinch, these
old-timers who thought there was a cream in opium trading,
and they were it!

Dent lowered his voice still further:

"But the time for clipper-loads is well past, though Carradine's still doing it. Buying clipper-loads. And he hasn't even
tried to modernize his fleet. All sailing ships still. I've been
wondering"—his voice became indistinct—"drop him a
hint . . . "

Jin-see raised his eyebrows.

"You mean the *Guild* drop him a hint? Why should we? In
any case, he wouldn't listen. Carradine's is a *princely* house!"

Dent gave him a look between a glare and a grin.

"On the other hand," Jin-see murmured, "you're a com-
patriot of his, and I understand your father was his father's
friend—"

"*Rival,*" Dent interrupted. "Hated each other. Carradine
wouldn't listen to me!"

"There's nothing to be done then, is there?"

Dent suddenly lost his good humor.

"You should have let Donald Mathes alone! If he'd still been
with Andrew it would've been different! But you had to grab
him. You've got *that* poor fool by the balls, you have!"

Jin-see said smoothly, his smile still undisturbed, "There's
no need to blackguard Donald. The Guild has nothing to do
with Jinsey Mathes and Donald has nothing to do with the
Guild."

"And I suppose *you're* all simon-pure too, not dealing in opium?"

"That's right, I'm not."

Dent snorted. "If Donald believes that, he's the only one who does! Everybody knows you're dealing through a dummy. You're a cold one, you are! Tough as nails under those prissy Chinese manners! Poor damned Donald!"

He swung around and marched off.

Jin-see waited for him to get out of sight, the blood humming in his veins.

Behind him, the clerk said, "Sir, you are glad. Something the Englishman said made you glad."

Jin-see turned to him, smiling. "Yes. And the Customs is a fine service. And you're a fine clerk."

The clerk beamed.

At home, Julie was waiting just inside the gate.

As soon as she saw him she exclaimed, like the clerk:

"You are glad, Father!"

He nodded and her eyes sparkled for a moment, then abruptly filled with tears. The corners of her mouth turned down. She looked like a woebegone waif. He laughed. She was waiting to tell him her version of something before any one else could tell him theirs.

She was eight years old now and too tall to be swung up in his arms, so he took her hand and walked her along beside him.

"What did you do today, Julie?"

She hesitated for the space of ten paces. Then, hastily, in a small squeaky voice, as she saw Olan's Old Woman wrathfully approaching:

"I smacked my brother."

"She *hit* him," the Old Woman shouted furiously. "She hit him so hard he flew across the room!"

73

"What!"

Jin-see opened his eyes wide and stared down at the child. Her tears became real and began to flow swiftly, pouring in great round drops down her face. She clutched him around the waist and hid her face against his stomach. He waved the Old Woman away, sat down on a bench, and held her between his knees.

"Why did you hit your brother?"

At first she couldn't answer for sobbing, and then she turned stubborn and wouldn't answer, but he stared her down, overpowering her willfulness. At last:

"Because I *hate* him!"

"Why do you hate him? He's your brother!"

This time she answered at once, the floodgates bursting, the furious words pouring out.

"Because you showed him to our ancestors and you never showed me! Because you're going to educate him, but you're going to leave me like a dunce, not knowing a single character, not knowing even how to hold a writing brush! My mother says I'm going to be married so I only need to know how to run a house and cook and sew and rubbish like that! But I'm not going to be married! Not ever! I want to learn to read and write and figure! I want to *be educated!*"

The tears had disappeared. Her eyes, brilliant with anger, glared at him out of her blotched face.

She should have been a son! The life-duty needed someone with ardor like hers! Great Dragon—his heart faltered. The boy was only two years old, but up to now he had shown no traits to merit his wonderful name. He was quiet and obedient and intelligent, but . . .

"*Do you hear me?*" Julie shouted.

He drew her to him and held her against his heart, rocking her gently.

74

"I hear you. I will educate you. Tomorrow I'll get a tutor for you."

She gave a long, trembling sigh, and he felt her tight little body relax.

"I'll get you an English tutor too, so you can talk to Donald in his own language. Would you like that?"

She nodded vigorously, her hair moving silkily against his arm.

They went into the family room hand in hand. Great Dragon was sitting on Olan's lap. There was a big bump on his forehead, on which Olan had spread the black ointment that was supposed to draw out poisons. Julie ran and hugged and kissed her mother and her brother, repentance as intense as anger had been.

"I'm sorry! I'm sorry!"

"What for?"

Olan had forgotten already. She held Julie to her, cheek to cheek. Watching them, Jin-see thought how different they were, and yet the same. Julie had her mother's beauty, but in her it was awry and not beautiful; yet she sparkled and rippled with intelligence and fire, and in her own way she was lovely.

The boy, squeezed between the mother and the daughter, sat unprotesting, gazing quietly at his father.

When dinner was over, a servant came to fetch Julie to bed, but Jin-see said: "I will take her." She ran to him, glowing, and took his hand. They walked out of the room and down the passage, but not to her bedroom. They left the house by a side door and began to cross the courtyard. Jin-see felt the child's hand tighten in his and he glanced down at her. Her eyes were round and solemn.

The gateman, as always, hurried to slide open the golden

moon door of the ancestors' house. They went in. Jin-see lit the lamp. The child stood silent, gazing slowly around, taking in everything—the polished woods, the white cushion, the carved altar, the candles, the incense bowl, the two white soul tablets glowing in the lamplight. She went slowly to the altar and touched them with a fingertip.

"These are my ancestors?"

Her whisper fluted.

He nodded and went to stand beside her.

"This one"—he took up Charlie's tablet—"is the tablet of your grandfather, my father, who was an Englishman. His name was Charlie." He took up the other tablet. "This is the tablet of your great-grandfather, my mother's father, whose name was Wei, the same as ours. No one knew his other name because he was the only survivor of a shipwreck when he was very small and didn't know his own name." He put the tablet back in its place. "We have other ancestors, of course, but unfortunately we don't know who they are because my father came from England, and because of the shipwreck."

She was listening as though her ears had grown out on stalks. When he fell silent, she said:

"Now I know who my ancestors are, but they don't know me."

"I will present you," he said.

He showed her how to light an incense stick and put it into the bowl. Then he knelt and drew her down beside him.

"This is my daughter," he said loudly, raising his face to the altar. "Your descendant. Her name is Julie, a name she chose for herself, which is suitable because it has an English sound to it. She is full of spirit and has a fine mind. For that reason I will educate her as though she were a son. Even though she is but a girl, you will be proud of her one day."

She said in a piercing whisper: "Tell them I'm not going to be married."

He raised his face again to the altar.

"Today, at her age of eight years old, Julie does not wish to marry. If she is still of the same mind when she comes to the age of marriage, I will not force her."

The child's head was bowed and she was trembling slightly. After a moment, he held her hands together and showed her how to make a kowtow.

Chapter VII

1868

I T WAS AN unpretentious wooden door, two steps up from
a crowded alley in the Chinese City. Above the door hung
a painted sign, one of dozens of similar ones that protruded dangerously from flanges over the heads of the pedestrians, a black-on-white sign that read in plain Chinese
characters: THE OPIUM MERCHANTS GUILD.

On one side of the door was a noodle shop that was constantly crowded with people slurping up noodles out of bowls
that small half-naked boys rushed about carrying from per-
spiring cooks to waiting customers.

On the other side of the door was an opium shop, a retail
establishment where raw opium was boiled to prepare it for
smoking, then packed into individual tins or into large jars
from which it was sold by weight in sticky, tinned-paper
packages.

Sales were made by a fat, blowsy woman who presided over

a large cast-iron scale. Beside her on the counter were the weights—fanciful little bronze figures, half duck, half rooster, the largest an inch high, weighing about six ounces, the smallest tiny, weighing half an ounce. According to the customer's desire, the woman placed a weight in the left-hand pan of the scale, then spooned opium into the right-hand pan until the indicators of the scale, which were shaped like ducks' beaks, came together exactly. No one got a tittle more than he paid for, nor a tittle less, for buyers and woman watched each other closely.

A few wealthy buyers came in for whole tins, choosing from among the different colored wrappings. Patna opium was wrapped in white paper. Of the domestic opiums, the best came from the northern provinces and were wrapped in red or orange.

Beggars crouched outside the shop looking like heaps of filthy rags—opium smokers on their last legs, dying their slow deaths. If someone threw them a copper they scuffled for it with feeble viciousness; the one who managed to snag it crawled or humped himself into the shop as quickly as he could to buy out of another jar over which the blowsy woman presided, a jar containing dottle scraped from the pipes of the rich. Servants in wealthy homes and in divans did not overlook this small but steady source of income.

Jin-see stood at the curb watching the opium shop. Sales were brisk. The customers came in a constant stream. It was easy to tell which were smokers buying for themselves. The color of their skin was anywhere from mud gray to transparent-pale; their build from thin to skeletal; their mien from dazed to trancelike. Those who were buying for a parent or a husband lacked the eerie look of smokers, but the women were all thin and hungry-looking and the children frail, some so small that they could hardly reach the money over the counter to the blowsy woman.

Jin-see's stare was impenetrable. The woman, looking up for a moment, saw him and shivered a little, and made a superstitious sign against him. But Jin-see did not see her. He was seeing the life-duty that would encompass his own life and Great Dragon's, and that of Great Dragon's sons, and before it was accomplished millions would have died of opium, many millions.

Jin-see turned away from the puzzled eyes of the blowsy woman and entered the door. It opened on a narrow flight of steps that led to the rooms above the noodle and opium shops, and the rooms above the shops on either side of those. The space was large, filled with rows of desks at which people worked concentratedly. The Opium Merchants Guild was a very busy place.

As Jin-see came up the steps, his chief clerk hurried to meet him.

"Sir, the members are all here."

"Good. Have we received the replies to our letter?"

"All, except from Carradine. Carradine sent a messenger asking if he could see you at noon today."

"And you said?"

"That you would see him."

"Good."

Jin-see went quickly into his private office, averting his head to keep the clerk from seeing the anthracite gleam of his eyes. Carradine was hooked! Today the life-duty would be advanced a great step. And more than that. Touching the mystic realm of remotest memory, the death of the English father who had disappeared in the brightness of a sunbeam would be avenged.

Jin-see sat at his desk and composed himself as he had when he sat on the white cushion in his ancestors' house the night he had put his father's soul tablet on the altar. Closed his eyes.

Stilled the thudding of his heart. Slowed the racing of his blood.

When he was calm, he rose and went into the meeting room. It was large enough to seat comfortably the hundred and four members of the Shanghai branch of the Guild, the men without whose cognizance and consent no opium could be bought or sold or transported in the entire region served by the port of Shanghai.

There was a murmur of greeting as Jin-see bowed and took his place behind the table. The members of the Guild were smiling. They too knew that Carradine was hooked. They hated Carradine. As long as they had had to depend on him for opium, they had swallowed his insults with jolly laughs. But they didn't need him any longer.

Jin-see began the meeting.

Had the arrangements made at the last meeting been fully carried out?

Yes. Everyone spoke up. Supplies of domestic opium had been moved from up-country warehouses to Shanghai. The Shanghai warehouses of the Guild members were full to bursting. Inspection conveyed the impression that every Guild merchant was heavily overstocked. And inspections had been made. Dent had visited several of the merchants and asked to see their warehouses. So had Sassoon and Hardoon and Elias.

And the answers to the letter the Guild had sent out?

The chief clerk took over. First, he read aloud the letter that had gone on the Guild's letterhead to each of the British importers:

"We beg to inform you that because of good work by our farmers and fine weather in the interior, this season's production of domestic opium has been unexpectedly huge. Therefore, most regretfully, we find ourselves unable for the time being to take delivery of our orders for Indian opium. It would be a great kindness on your part to delay delivery for about six months."

To this letter every one of the British importers had sent an answer, grouchy or gracious, agreeing to delay delivery— everyone but Carradine.

"Carradine," Jin-see informed the meeting, "has asked to see me today." He waited for the exclamations to die down, then bowed toward the center of the room. "Ching si-sang, will you refresh my memory as to what happened when you went to see him?"

An old man—skimpy white beard, skimpy white hair tied in an old-fashioned queue—got to his feet and looked around, swallowing a chuckle. Everyone sat back, smiling.

"It was five months ago," the old man said. "As you suggested, Wei Jin-see, I pretended to be nervous. I looked around his office as though to be sure no one could overhear. I went close to his desk. I bent forward. . . ."

Like an actor, the old man bent forward, a strained and worried look on his face.

"I whispered. . . ."

He raised a hand as though to shield his mouth from sight. A gust of laughter swept the room. Delighted, the old man went on:

"I asked him, if I were to put him in the way of making an extraordinary profit, would he share the profit with me? He laughed in his vulgar way and asked if I was proposing a swindle. I hung my head. . . ."

The old man hung his head. This time the laughter rose to a gale and the old man beamed. He was enjoying himself hugely.

"I hung my head and said, well, not really a *swindle*. I had some special information. Every year I make advance contracts with farmers whose poppy crops look good. This year

I had just returned from my usual tour up-country and I had seen nothing at all good. This year it looked like domestic opium would be very poor. The Guild, I said, was keeping it secret, because if the British knew, they would raise the prices of Indian opium. I said if he would buy a great quantity in Calcutta and have it here in a few months' time, the Guild warehouses would be almost empty and he would make a great killing. He slapped my back—I nearly fell over—and said there were no crooks like old crooks, and he'd give me ten percent discount."

The old man paused, but this time there was no laughter, for his smile had faded and his clever eyes were grave. When he spoke again his voice was very quiet.

"Before I went into his office, Carradine kept me waiting for an hour although I had made an appointment. Then he did not come out himself to fetch me—he sent an office boy to say I could go in. I called him Mr. Carradine, and he called me 'old Ching' and 'old rascal.' "

Heads were shaking all around the room. Ching si-sang was the oldest member of the Guild. He was always addressed as "si-sang"—firstborn—to show respect for his age. And although he enjoyed making people laugh, he was no buffoon. Next to Wei Jin-see himself, he had perhaps the most acute mind of those present, and the greatest determination. Those who knew him well did not trifle with him.

Jin-see said: "Thank you, Ching si-sang. You did well. I will report to all of you after my meeting with Carradine."

At a quarter to noon, Jin-see went to his window to watch for Carradine's arrival. In the narrow alleys of the Chinese City people walked or were carried in sedan chairs, but Carradine would come in his carriage that would take up most of the street's width and he would not care—those whom it obstructed could go another way or wait until he left. Some of the new British traders had learned to show the Chinese a modicum of good manners, but to those like Carradine all Chinese were inferior and contemptible, easily flouted by loud curses, easily terrified by the rattling of sabers.

Since the day seven years ago when Jin-see and Donald had handed Andrew their resignations, Jin-see had not seen much of him, but each time he saw him, Andrew had deteriorated a little more. The once-classic nose marred by the red stars of broken veins. The eyes faded. The cheeks puffy. The waist thickened. The stomach bulging. He was over sixty now and still chasing wild chickens. No woman whom he called his own, no son whom he acknowledged, though Hong Kong and the port cities must be peopled by his bastards. A man of no respect and no dignity, a man having nothing but a blown-up image of himself, which was about to be pricked, and wealth, which was about to be lost.

Jin-see stared out the window, waiting for Carradine in the cold certitude of what was about to happen to him.

The carriage came into the street and pulled up before the wooden door. A liveried footman jumped down to lower the step of the carriage and respectfully offer Carradine his arm. The beggars outside the opium shop surged forward, then hunkered back as the footman kicked at them.

Andrew stepped out of the carriage. From above, Jin-see saw that he was balding. The fringe of hair around the bald spot had been carefully arranged to hide it. Andrew disappeared into the doorway and moments later Jin-see heard his footfall on the stairs, heavy and uneven. The door burst open and Andrew stumbled into the room, weaving drunkenly, face engorged, holding out the Guild's letter in one hand, flicking it roughly with the fingers of the other, roaring before he was properly in the room:

"What the bloody hell is this, Jin-see?"

Jin-see sat down behind his desk and gestured toward the

chair opposite, but Andrew stayed where he was, fury like a pulsing aura around him.

"What the hell does this mean?"

"What it says," Jin-see answered quietly. "The Guild's warehouses are overflowing with domestic opium. Until we've moved some of it, it's impossible for us to take delivery of Indian opium. We have neither the space to store it nor the money to pay for it. We've asked for six months' grace. We're not cancelling our orders—just asking for a postponement. All the importers have agreed, except yourself."

"By God, what's it to them? Dent and the other old-timers are practically out of opium now, dabbling in machinery and textiles and devil knows what. Those new traders, those bloody Sassoons and Hardoons and mucking-doons, they're nothing but peddlers! The piddling lots they buy can be bonded in Customs till delivery's taken. But *me*, Jin-see!" He glared and panted and pounded his chest. "By God, you know mucking well that I buy thousands of chests at a time, and I ship on my own clippers! I've got *twelve thousand* chests right now afloat. *Falcon, Sylph, Jamesina*—all of my beautiful ships, at sea right now full of opium! And you ask me to delay delivery for six months? Are you *mad*?"

His voice, rasping with anger and drunkenness, resounded throughout the office. Jin-see rose to shut the door, the blood tingling in his veins. It was worse—or better—than he'd thought! Twelve thousand chests! He went back to sit behind his desk and spoke softly into the sodden face before him.

"Were *you* mad, Carradine? Twelve thousand chests? Four million dollars' worth? Nearly all your capital, for a single shipment of opium, all at sea at the same time? Were *you* mad?"

"Of course not! I don't believe your bloody warehouses are full! That bloody old Ching said—"

"Ah!" Jin-see smiled and sat back as though everything had been explained. "Old Ching said! Poor, senile old Ching went on a trip up-country before the poppies were even planted, and came back crying that the crop was going to be terrible. Is that what he told you? And you believed him?"

Carradine took a step forward and grabbed at the back of a chair to keep from staggering. His face was frozen in a mottle of red blotches against sickly white.

"Do sit down," Jin-see murmured. "Can I offer you something? Tea? Brandy?"

Carradine clambered around the chair like a blind man and sank into the seat.

"I'm so sorry," Jin-see said pleasantly. "You really should have checked Ching's story before investing all that money. But of course, if you had checked, the other importers would have found out and cut themselves in on the profit you imagined you were going to make."

"I'll sue!" Carradine muttered hoarsely. "Under the treaties, we're immune from Chinese law, don't forget! I'll sue you in the British Consular Court!"

Jin-see shrugged. "You can try. But even before the British Consul I doubt you'd have a leg to stand on, because you don't have orders from us for anything like twelve thousand chests. Couple of hundred is more like it. The rest you bought on spec, based on the story Ching told you. Perhaps you could get him put in jail for a month or two for telling you fairy tales."

There was silence, broken by Carradine's gasping breaths. Then:

"You're ruining me, Jin-see. I'll be *ruined*."

"Oh, it can't be as bad as that!" Jin-see spoke encouragingly. "As you said, the longtime opium traders have all got other things going. None of them is dependent on opium anymore. Dent's got a contract for bridges over the Soochow

86

Creek. Butterfield's starting a shipping line with steamers going up the Yangtsze as far as Hankow. Surely you've got something else going too?"

"God damn you!" Carradine leaped to his feet, grabbing the edge of the desk to keep from falling. "You know bloody well I haven't! Why the hell should I have? Opium was good enough for my father, and it's good enough for me!"

Jin-see raised his eyebrows.

"You're a long way behind the times, Carradine. Opium stopped being good enough for any English trader the minute it was legalized and the Chinese were able to produce it too. Opium's opium, you know. When a smoker's dying for a pipe, he doesn't hold out for Patna, he smokes whatever he can get. And in the end all smokers get to the point where they're dying for a pipe. The British share of the market's tumbling. A hundred thousand chests four years ago. Maybe twenty thousand this year." He shook his head wonderingly. "And you bought twelve thousand on old Ching's say-so!"

With a roar, Carradine lunged at him across the desk. Jin-see merely pushed back his chair as two of the Guild's guards burst into the room, burly men whose normal duty was to accompany cartloads of chests being moved from place to place to prevent plunder. They did not lay hands on Carradine but stationed themselves ominously on either side of him. With a prodigious effort, Carradine contained his soaring anger and backed off Jin-see's desk, the color fleeing his face, leaving it pasty like wet flour. His eyes darted frantically from Jin-see to the guards and back again. Jin-see smiled icily, reading in them the tumultuous flow of Carradine's thoughts. How he longed to go for Jin-see again, to smash his fist into his face! But if he did, the guards would lay hands on him, and nothing could be more galling than being manhandled by Chinese coolies! Not only that, the guards would throw him out into the alley, and then it would all be over. He'd never get in again to see Jin-see. To ask for mercy.

Jin-see watched Carradine swallow his overweening pride, watched him lick his lips and twist them into an ingratiating smile.

"You took Donald away from me, Jin-see. When he left, I was too old to start branching out by myself."

"Too old at fifty-five? Dent was no younger. But then, of course, Dent has a son."

"God damn it!" Carradine's voice blared again and he heaved himself forward in his chair. "*Donald* was supposed to take over from me! *Donald* was my heir—"

The roar stopped abruptly. Gasping with the effort of cutting himself short, Carradine buried his face in his hands.

Jin-see eyed him coldly. Would Carradine be able to bring himself to ask for mercy? It would be less despicable if he didn't. But Carradine's voice came from between his hands, muffled, almost inaudible.

"Will you take delivery of a thousand chests at least?"

Jin-see stared over his bowed head. Was that Yin-kwa standing in the distance? And beyond him, was that the mistily remembered English father?

"Please," said Carradine. "Please. Without that, I'm penniless."

Jin-see sighed.

"Very well. I'll personally advance the money until the Guild's cash position is liquid again. Three hundred dollars a chest?"

It was, Jin-see knew, what Carradine had paid at Calcutta. Carradine nodded briefly, face still hidden. Jin-see took a checkbook from his desk, wrote a draft for three hundred thousand dollars, brushed in his signature, and affixed his personal chop. He laid the draft before Carradine, keeping a finger on it.

"There's one condition. That you close down your offices

in China and go back to England. There's enough here"—
with the tip of his finger he moved the draft an inch—"for
you to buy a small place in some village and live your life out
quietly."

Carradine raised his head just enough to stare at the draft
on the edge of the desk before him.

"D'you accept?" Jin-see said. "There's really nothing else
you can do."

When Carradine did not speak, Jin-see picked up the draft,
held it between his fingers as though about to tear it.

"Wait a minute," Carradine mumbled thickly. "What'll I
do with the rest of the shipment?"

"Put it up for auction. The Dutch might take it for the East
Indies, or the French for Indo-China. Or some other Britisher
for Malaya and Singapore."

"A quantity like that?" Carradine's eyes, once so startlingly blue, now almost colorless, peered up at Jin-see. "I'd
get no more than ten cents on the dollar! With that three
hundred thousand I could carry on my Hong Kong office at
least, sell the rest of the shipment slowly. . . ."

With a small smile, Jin-see tore a little nick in the draft.
Carradine shot out a shaking hand.

"I accept! Give it to me!"

Jin-see gave it to him. It fluttered slightly in his trembling
fingers. He sat staring at it as though hypnotized. After a little, Jin-see came around the desk, helped him to his feet,
pointed him toward the door, and watched him go through
it, his steps uncertain, as though he were entering a strange
land. As indeed he was—a land in which there was no princely
house of Carradine, no Shanghai Club with the longest bar
in the world, no sycophants willing to bend an elbow with
him at any time across that bar, no liveried servants, no carriage and horses—indeed, no Andrew Carradine, for that old
codger in the village pub was not he.

Shrill cries from the street distracted Jin-see, and he went

89

to the window. Carradine's carriage was covered with a living blanket of happy children. Squealing with joy, they climbed all over it, scratching the gleaming paintwork, pulling the ears of the patient horses, tying knots in the reins. The liveried coachman and footman stood by, smiling benevolently. By whatever osmosis they had learned it, they knew that their master was finished. When he came stumbling out the door, they let him climb into the carriage without help and went lazily, taking their time, to shoo the children playfully away.

It was a week later that Donald said:

"Jin-see, Andrew's sailed for England on *Falcon*, leaving Carradine & Co. in a god-awful mess. He cleaned out the bank accounts, even the cashbox. There's no money to pay bills or accounts, not even salaries for this month. The British Consul's appointed a receiver."

Jin-see pushed away the papers on which he was working and sat back.

"Before you ask—yes, it was my doing. I bankrupted him."

"How?"

"By an elaborate trick that I planned very carefully and got all the opium merchants to help me execute."

"Why?"

"For many reasons. He was the last of the big opium importers. He had plenty of time to diversify like Dent and the others into businesses that would benefit China as well as himself. He didn't. He clung to opium and to his image of himself as the Great Opium Trader. He was a drunken, boastful, browbeating bully. He was the epitome of the kind of Englishman who's most offensive to the Chinese."

Donald said nothing. They were sitting, not looking at each other, facing the windows. Jinsey Mathes's offices had been much enlarged in the last few years, but they still shared a room, a big one overlooking the Bund and the river. In the daytime they had a front-row view of the foreign warships, English and French and one American, anchored in a majestic row in the middle of the river, guardians and ever-present reminders of foreign dominance in this Chinese city. But now it was nearly dark. The warships were no more than black blobs on the faint sheen of the water, and the glass of the windows was a mirror, reflecting their two heads.

Jin-see said evenly: "There was another reason. I rounded out a piece of history when I ruined Andrew and forced him to leave China. I completed a circle. Andrew's father—your grandfather, William Carradine—killed my father."

In the glass of the windows, Donald's reflected head jerked sharply. He said, "What?" his tone rising uncertainly.

"In 1842," Jin-see said. "During the first of the opium wars. British troops had just taken the town of Chapoo on the Bay of Hangchow. While they were still securing it, your grandfather was already having chests of opium moved into a pagoda on the beach: the Carradines were always on the heels of the British armies with opium to offer in the conquered cities at cheap introductory prices. My father went into the pagoda. He had just found my mother and my sisters, dead, and he was searching for me. He saw movement at the top of the pagoda and climbed up, thinking it might be me. It was your grandfather. He attacked my father with a fighting iron. They both fell five stories to their deaths."

The reflection of Donald's head in the glass was motionless, but his heavy breathing was audible.

"My father was English," Jin-see said. "He and Yin-kwa were partners—opium smugglers, on a much smaller scale than the Carradines. But it was my father who first thought of anchoring hulks in the Bay of Canton to serve as floating warehouses for opium, which gave the smuggling a big boost. That was what started your grandfather hating my father. He hated him more and more over the years. It was irrational. He'd had syphilis most of his life: in the end, when he killed my father, Yin-kwa says he was quite mad. After my father's death, Yin-kwa adopted me. His plan to abolish opium—his obsession—is . . . atonement. For his and my father's sin in helping to enslave the Chinese to opium. The life-duty, he calls it."

There was a long silence. Jin-see waited, watching Donald's reflection in the glass, feeling the high beat of his heart. This was the moment Yin-kwa had foreseen when he wrote, "I am not mistaken in Donald."

At last Donald stirred.

"All Andrew ever told me was that he knew your father slightly. . . . Well, if you're atoning for your father's sin, I should be atoning for my grandfather's, and Andrew's."

He turned away from the window to face Jin-see. He was pale and, in that solemn moment, stunningly handsome, the blue eyes direct and frank, giving and sharing. Jin-see swallowed a balloon that swelled in his throat. Indeed, Yin-kwa had not been mistaken in Donald!

He said huskily: "That's what Yin-kwa thought when he chose you—that when you knew the whole story you'd want a share in the life-duty too. I'm sorry the story's had to be eked out to you bit by bit."

"If you'd told it to me all in one chunk in the beginning, I don't suppose I'd have believed it. I certainly wouldn't have *understood* it. Funny to think how absolutely green I was when Yin-kwa came to see me that night on Jackass Point! If it's taken all these years for me to understand what Yin-kwa said that night, I can see that the life-duty could well take a hundred years. What does Yin-kwa think that I should do?"

"There're many anti-opium societies in England, not one of them strong enough to put pressure on Parliament. Before opium can be abolished in China, the clause in the Unequal

Treaties that makes opium legal has to be abrogated, and only Parliament can do that. Yin-kwa thought that in due course you'd go home to England and organize the anti-opium societies to persuade Parliament."

Donald smiled slowly: "Does Yin-kwa think I could do that? You know, I feel quite honored."

The office boy came clattering into the room. At Carradine & Co., the office boys had been clad in uniform and trained to slip around soundlessly. At Jinsey Mathes, time and money were not wasted on such elegancies. This office boy wore crumpled blue cotton trousers, a once-white singlet, wooden clogs. He was not at all embarrassed by the noise he made. He clacked about lighting lamps, peering into the teapot on Jin-see's desk, refilling it from the big brass kettle he had brought with him. He didn't vouchsafe his employers a glance—they might not have existed as far as he was concerned.

When he had clacked out of the room again, Donald laughed wryly.

"That's the way to take life. Do your job and to the devil with everybody else. He's smarter than I am."

He rubbed his hands hard over his face.

"It's ridiculous, but somehow I feel bad about Andrew. My mother was his sister. My father was a big Lancashire mill-owner, though they lived most of the time in London. They both died in an accident while I was at Oxford. I hardly knew them. First I had a nursemaid, then a tutor, who took me to the drawing room at stated times to see them. My father was always taking his shiny gold watch out of his fob pocket, glaring at it, and tapping it while he glared across at my mother. My mother was beautiful—a lovely, feminine Andrew. You know how handsome he was! Once I hugged her, and she kept very still and said, 'Darling, you're making a great mess of my hair!' I never dared to touch her again. I

93

just adored her from afar. And then there was boarding school. And then there was Oxford. And then the accident. And then Andrew. I was never so happy as in those years when I looked up to Andrew like a prince, when I thought it the most unbelievable luck to be his heir."

"You should get married," Jin-see said after a while. "What you need is a family."

Donald laughed, a little sadly, but lightly enough.

"I haven't yet met a woman who's put me in mind of marriage. As I remember, the girls in London and Oxford were nice girls, but it seems that as soon as English girls come to China they change. They suddenly find out that they're much more precious than they'd ever thought before. That there're 'natives' to be looked down upon. That there're servants to be bullied. You won't catch me marrying one of those! Perhaps when I get home."

He turned suddenly.

"Jin-see, let's give it another fifteen or sixteen years. Jinsey Mathes is seven years old now, and we're ten times bigger than when we started. In another fifteen years we'll be a huge commercial department store—sell 'em anything from a complete spinning and weaving mill to a railway line to a shipping company. You'll be twenty times a millionaire and I'll be that at least once—and I'll need it! Organizing attacks on Parliament takes money. And I'll be forty-seven or forty-eight years old—a good age for that sort of thing, mature enough to get respect but far from doddering. And Great Dragon will be old enough to take over from me."

Jin-see interrupted quietly. "Great Dragon is going to be a mandarin. I've just engaged a very famous retired mandarin to be his tutor."

"What? *Why?* He's got a readymade career in Jinsey Mathes!"

"By the time Parliament is persuaded to abrogate the opium clauses in the treaties, Great Dragon will be a highly trained mandarin in Peking, knowing English very well—the natural choice, I hope, to be put in charge of the Chinese government's correspondence with Parliament concerning the abrogation."

After a moment Donald said: "I see. I forget that it's a *life*-duty. Yours and your son's, and my son's too if I ever have one."

"Or your daughter's," Jin-see said, smiling, thinking of Julie.

Chapter VIII

1872

IT WAS NOT YET NOON, but Jinsey Mathes, like all firms throughout China, was closing for a week of celebration. Tomorrow was New Year's Day, the first day of the first moon of the eleventh year of Tung Chih.

Although his reign was beginning its eleventh year, the Tung Chih Emperor himself was only sixteen years old. His mother, the Dowager Empress, and his uncle, Prince Kung, still governed on his behalf. It was rumored that he was a profligate like his father. It was rumored that his mother indulged him. But no one paid any attention to that. His mother was growing ever more forceful, ever more skillful at exercising power, and trade was booming.

Jin-see and Donald sat in their office to receive the good wishes of their staff, who were coming in in groups of two or three, holding the red envelopes that the cashier had just handed them, each containing a bonus of three months' salary: Jinsey Mathes had had an excellent year. The last to come in was the office boy in what might have been the same crumpled blue trousers and clogs he'd worn that day four years ago. He seemed overwhelmed by what he had found in his red envelope. He went down on his knees and kowtowed to both Jin-see and Donald.

When he'd gone, Donald exclaimed: "I think that's the first time he's paid me any attention!"

Jin-see laughed. "He was the last one—we can leave now."

They shrugged on their coats and went down to the street. A little crowd had gathered to inspect the new vehicles that were awaiting them—"jin-rickshaws," imported from Japan. In the new year they were going to start a factory for making an improved model of the rickshaws, with ball bearings to render them really smooth-running on Shanghai's macadam roads.

They stood on the curb beside their rickshaws and wished each other a happy New Year, shaking their own hands together in the Chinese gesture. Donald handed Jin-see a tiny red-wrapped parcel, his traditional New Year gift to Julie: a golden sovereign.

"Give her a big hug for me. And Olan—how's she? When's the baby due?"

"About two months. She's fine."

But as he stepped into his rickshaw, the familiar worry twitched at Jin-see's heart. Olan seemed better than ever physically, but her rhythms had changed. They were no longer able to tell with certainty when her spirit was with her and when not. She no longer slipped into catatonic sleep. She remained awake and smiled and moved about and did as she was told, mindlessly. The Old Woman was in despair. She could no longer watch over an unmoving body and chant for its spirit to return. The spirit appeared to be in the body, but often it was not, and there was nothing the Old Woman could do but follow the body about and mourn silently.

This was Olan's third pregnancy. It had been ten years since Great Dragon's birth, and Jin-see had not given a thought to the possibility that she might become pregnant again. She was thirty-seven years old—not too old, but the pregnancy was affecting her strangely. Perhaps he should ask Donald about English doctors.

The day was very fine and Jin-see's rickshaw coolie, who had also received a bonus, had decided to give his master a treat by taking him home the long way around. He had proceeded north along the Bund and turned into Nanking Road, the ironclad wooden wheels of the rickshaw revolving roughly even though they were running on macadam. Indeed, ball bearings would be a great improvement!

The macadam ended where the two foreign concessions ended, at the Race Course. There was talk of enlarging the foreign concessions—the foreign worlds set down on Chinese soil in which the Chinese had no authority, athough those Chinese who lived within their boundaries were obliged to pay the fees and taxes assessed by the foreigners, obliged to abide by their rules and regulations or be arrested by their police, tried in their courts, and jailed in their jails.

The crowds hurrying along the streets—all Chinese; foreigners didn't walk, they rode in carriages—looked happy today because of the holiday, but their everyday look was anxious and angry, sometimes murderously so. Who could help hating a man who, much better fed and clothed than you, disdainfully spurned you while strutting your earth on the strength of treaties that his infinitely superior armaments had forced upon you? Hatred was the permanent legacy of the Unequal Treaties.

Still, despite the cankered wounds, there was much to be proud of. The great buildings, the factories, the shipping on the river, the city itself, its hustle and bustle. Enormous wealth was represented, more Chinese than foreign, though the foreign wealth was ostentatiously splendid and the Chinese wealth, for the most part, was hidden away behind the high walls of family compounds like Jin-see's own. The "compradore system" had worked, was working. In the Treaty Ports at least, the compradores had dragged China out of the fantasy world of the Sons of Heaven into the comity of nations.

But—Jin-see smiled sardonically—merchants had honor only in their own world. In other, more esoteric Chinese worlds, merchants were still very low down in the hierarchy. Li si-sang, the retired mandarin he'd engaged as Great Dragon's teacher, had consented to employment by Jin-see only because Jin-see was so rich and he so poor and Jin-see had tempted him with offers of much money, which he had accepted, for which reason he resented Jin-see all the more. Jin-see had installed him with his young daughter in a little house built for them in his compound. They lived in the house and took his money and neither troubled to hide the fact that they felt demeaned.

Julie had been horrified when she learned how much Jin-see was paying Li si-sang.

"That's *ten times* what you pay Miss Crachett! And she's as good a teacher as Li si-sang. Donald says my English is very good, and Great Dragon's even better because he started when he was only two."

"Miss Crachett is teaching you a language. Li si-sang is teaching Great Dragon a *career*—a great career. How to be a good mandarin."

"What about my other tutors? You're not paying them much either, and they're teaching *me* a career—how to be a good businesswoman."

He glanced at her sideways, and she wriggled around to face him, anticipating him.

"Father, you promised! You promised *in front of our ances-*

99

tors that you wouldn't force me to marry! There're two kinds of Chinese wives—unpaid servants, or idle women with nothing to do but eat and gossip and smoke opium. I am not going to marry."

"Your mother—" he began.

"Mother is special!" Her voice became tender. "You and I both know, Father, that Mother is a little mad. Perhaps more than a little. And anyway, a husband like you is one in several million. So it's no good using Mother and you as an example of how good marriage can be." Her smile became mischievous. "The only person I might want to marry would be Donald, and he's old enough to be my father, so that's no good either. Besides, if I married I'd take a great chunk of dowry out of our family into somebody else's, and that would be stupid."

She snuggled up to him. "Seriously, Father—with Great Dragon going to be a mandarin, have you thought who's going to look after the family fortunes when you're old? You're not going to be young forever. Don't you see, Father? *I'm* the only one to succeed you."

He laughed and gave her sleek pigtail a tug—but she was right.

"Don't laugh at me, Father!" Suddenly there were tears in her eyes. "You're always planning for Great Dragon. You humor me, but you *plan* for him."

He said, a little blankly: "But he's the one who'll inherit the life-duty." Didn't she know he loved her more than anyone except Olan?

She said, the tears in her voice as well: "Is the life-duty only for men? Can't I have a part in it too?"

He stared at her speculatively. She could, of course. She was right that he should train someone in the management of the family money, to take over from him in case of need. And she was certainly clever enough.

"All right," he said. "I'll tell you what. When Great Dragon becomes a mandarin his salary will be minuscule, and half the time he won't be able to collect it. He'll need a lot of support from the family. I'll set up a family *hong*—a company. At first it'll handle a kind of trust fund for Great Dragon. Perhaps later I'll feed more through it—investments and so forth. I'll let you be the office manager of the *hong*. Would you like that?"

She turned very pale, and then bright pink. The tears welled more thickly. "I'd *love* it!"

He grinned at her and caressed her hair.

"Then you'll have it. I'll *plan* for it. . . . There's one more plan I have that you can't object to because you won't marry. I want to marry Great Dragon to Li si-sang's daughter."

"What!" She sat bolt upright. "But she's a stuck-up prig, Father!"

"She's only nine. Let's hope she'll improve. Her father was not only a great mandarin—he was honest too. That's why he's so poor! He had a great deal of prestige in Peking, which will reflect on his daughter, and in turn on her husband, and that'll give Great Dragon a fine start in Peking."

"Li si-sang won't let her marry Great Dragon. He's the son of a *merchant*!"

"He'll be a mandarin by the time they marry."

"Poor Great Dragon! What a fate! But he'll make a wonderful mandarin. He's so good and—and . . . *prim*."

He laughed again. It was a good description. At ten years old, Great Dragon already had something of Li si-sang's manner.

The rickshaw's wheels were rumbling and shaking on the ancient cobblestones of the Chinese City. Something more than ball bearings was needed to improve the vehicle. Something to clad the wheel rims other than iron. Rubber?

Jin-see was thinking of rubber when the rickshaw coolie put down the shafts outside the tall blank gate of his courtyard. The gate was flung open and the gateman appeared, beckoning urgently. Behind him, the Old Woman came into view, hobbling as quickly as she could, she too beckoning. Behind her, a bevy of servants crowded, awed looks on their faces.

Olan.

Something had happened to Olan.

Jin-see swept past the Old Woman into the house, past more big-eyed servants, past Great Dragon, squatting on his heels outside the bedroom door, whitefaced, at last into the bedroom. It was a mess of sheets, towels, cloths, basins, kettles, and pans of steaming water. Olan lay in the bed, pale as a ghost, eyes closed, breathing in gasps. Julie stood on one side of the bed holding her mother's hand, pale too, but composed and alert. The midwife bent over Olan, her loose sleeves pinned over her shoulders, her muscular arms bare. She was rhythmically pressing Olan's swollen belly, sweat standing out on her forehead as she worked.

Jin-see stepped through the impedimenta to the foot of the bed. Keeping his voice calm and even, he asked the woman:

"Can you manage this? If not, say so. Nobody will blame you, but I want the truth."

The woman had been a midwife for many years, her mother before her, and her grandmother too. The admission came from her slowly and reluctantly:

"I don't know. It's two months before time, and the baby seems to be wrong way around."

Olan moaned and her body trembled in a long shudder.

Jin-see went swiftly to his study, sat at his desk, and began to scribble a note. His valet was at his side before he finished. He handed him the note.

"Take the rickshaw. Tell the coolie to run as fast as he can.

102

Find Donald and give him this. If he is not at home, ask his Number One Boy where he is, but *find him*. The letter asks him to come at once and bring an English doctor."

Before the servant had left the courtyard, the murmur was fleeing around the house. An English doctor! Nobody in the house had even seen one! The mysteries they were said to perform were at least dangerous if not outright evil. . . . When Jin-see went back into the bedroom, the midwife glared at him, then sighed and wiped the sweat from her brow onto her forearm and went on massaging Olan's belly.

They waited.

The Old Woman came with a broom and swept around the bed and across the floor and out the door. She would sweep all the way through the corridors, through the front door, out into the courtyard. She was sweeping away the evil that had befallen. Jin-see did not stop her. It gave her comfort, and perhaps it would do some good.

Olan moaned again and shuddered, her body convulsing as she pushed uselessly to try and give the child birth. Julie dribbled a little water into her mouth, but her teeth were tightly clenched and the water trickled over her chin and soaked the pillow.

Jin-see left the room, almost tripping over Great Dragon, who still crouched on his heels outside the door. In the courtyard, the gateman hurried to slide open the moon door. Jin-see entered the ancestors' house and lit the taper. The soul tablets glowed on the altar, drawing to themselves all the light there was. Jin-see knelt on the white cushion.

Don't let her die.

I have loved her from the beginning, from that moment in the Hong Kong Governor's office when the swivel-eyed foreign missionary brought me back from Ningpo to return me to my father, not knowing he was dead, and Yin-kwa said,

"Charlie's son is my son," and Olan jumped off his lap and looked into my face with her brilliant smile and said, "Jin-see?"

From that moment I have loved her.

Don't let her die.

Don't let her die.

He heard the gate open and the rumble of carriage wheels in the courtyard, and he rose and blew out the taper and hurried outside.

Donald and another man were jumping from the carriage.

Donald said: "This is Dr. Macpherson. We were at the same dinner party, where your servant found us. We came at once."

Jin-see said: "Thank you. Come quickly."

In the bedroom, the midwife stood aside and gave place to the doctor. He took off his coat, rolled up his shirt sleeves, washed his hands in a basin of hot water that Julie brought him, took instruments out of his bag, and ranged them on a towel. Then, slowly and carefully but strongly, he began to work over Olan. His hands moved and his instruments flashed as he picked them up and put them down. After a time he grunted in a satisfied way and nodded at the midwife, who bent to help him, seeming to know without being told what he wished her to do. Suddenly, between their four hands, Jin-see glimpsed a tiny leg. A moment later the doctor grunted again, this time in a sharp, surprised way. Then—"Ah, here's the head." There was a tiny, mewling cry. The midwife took the baby from the doctor's hands, turning her back toward Jin-see.

Olan gave a great shudder and her head fell to one side. She opened her eyes for a moment and looked at Jin-see, and it seemed to him that she smiled. Then she cuddled down on the pillows like a child. He put a hand on her cheek. It was soft and warm and dewy, and it seemed to him that she moved a little to press her head against his hand. The sweet and trusting movement rushed from his hand to his heart, and his heart began to beat again, expanding and contracting, shedding the rigidity that had paralyzed it. He knew that the others were leaving the room—the midwife with the baby, the Old Woman, Julie, finally the doctor. He was alone with Olan. She was alive. She was breathing. Her cheek was soft and warm and dewy, pressed against his hand. His heart beat steadily. His spirit settled back into his body.

After a while, the Old Woman came back into the room, and then Donald, tiptoeing. Jin-see smiled at Donald, surprised that the smile, loosening his mouth after the hours in which he had held it so tautly, made his lips sore. Donald did not smile in answer. His face was grave, and there were deep shadow-wells beneath his eyes. Was it a trick of the lamplight?

Donald said softly: "Macpherson's waiting for you in the family room. He wants to talk to you."

Yes, of course, the doctor. He must thank him. Ask him to send a bill. Jin-see followed Donald into the family room.

The doctor was sitting at the table. There were many things on the table. The cook, not knowing what refreshment to serve an English doctor, had served everything: tea, Chinese wine, foreign wine, beer, whisky, brandy. Jin-see saw the bottles clearly, as in a still life. The doctor had a glass in his hand. He was holding it tightly: his knuckles were white and the glass shuddered a little, slopping the liquid about. The doctor's craggy face was stern and frowning.

The clinging strands of nightmare tightened once again on Jin-see's mind. Too loud, he said:

"Is there something wrong with my wife?"

"It's not your wife," the doctor said abruptly. "She'll be all right in a few days. It's the baby. A girl. About six weeks premature, and a breech birth. She's sickly, of course. And"— he looked squarely at Jin-see—"she's deformed. The entire left leg is missing. The left foot is attached directly to the pelvis."

"What?" Jin-see muttered vaguely, relief so great in his heart that for a moment he felt nothing. Olan was all right. The baby—but he couldn't think of the baby now.

The doctor was saying gravely: "I myself have never before seen such a deformity, but I've heard of one exactly like it from an old colleague in Edinburgh. He told me that for an instant he was tempted to let the baby die. He didn't, of course. Seventeen years later, he went to a concert and heard a wonderful harpist. Looked for her name in the program. It was the baby he had let live. She had a long dress on."

The doctor harrumphed and picked up his coat.

"Unprofessional to tell you that, but my colleague is dead, and you have a tragedy on your hands. Wanted you to know that it needn't turn out badly. I'll stop in tomorrow to see how your wife's doing, and the baby."

In the courtyard, Donald looked keenly at Jin-see.

"I can stay, if you like."

"I'll be all right."

"You sure?"

"I'm sure!"

Strange. They were so solicitous, and he was so glad, so singingly glad, because Olan was not going to die.

He went back to sit at Olan's bedside. She slept quietly, curled on her pillows. He could not tell whether her spirit was with her or with the fairies. They had not brought the baby back. Where was she? It didn't matter. Olan . . .

When it was nearing dawn and the light from the window had turned silvery, he floated to the surface of dreams and knew that Julie was beside him.

"Father, wake up. A messenger from Canton has just arrived. My grandfather is dying."

He rose slowly, his heart racing, his mind stumbling. Yin-kwa was dying. It was dawn on the first day of the new year. Yin-kwa's beloved daughter Olan had passed through the crucible and would live. His newest granddaughter, the poor little crippled baby, would live too. But Yin-kwa was dying.

"Hurry, Father," Julie whispered. "The messenger came in grandfather's fastest ship. You must go at once."

"The baby . . ." he said.

She shook her head. "I'll take care of everything. Go, Father."

The first firecrackers of the new year began exploding in the alleys outside, a merry sound.

The long line moved slowly forward as the mourners, one by one, entered the anteroom of Yin-kwa's ancestors' house to kowtow before his splendid coffin. For twenty days they would come to pay respects to Yin-kwa's body, before it was moved to the Temple of the Queen of Heaven to await burial on the day that the seers would appoint. As each mourner entered, the professional lamenters wailed out their dirge anew, beating their breasts and tearing at their hair. The mourners were the most important men in Canton. The lamenters must do proper honor both to them and to the man they mourned.

Jin-see, his ears beginning to ring, slipped out of the anteroom and began to pace through Yin-kwa's lovely courtyards.

Yin-kwa had clung to life, waiting for his arrival. The fast ship had made the journey from Shanghai to Canton in only six days, and he had rushed from the port to Yin-kwa's bedside, had stood with Yin-kwa's sons, watching the thin, motionless body beneath the coverlets, the aristocratic face, the skin still tight-stretched and unwrinkled, the nose hawklike between the sinking cheeks. The face had not betrayed anything, not age, nor joy, nor sorrow, nor love, nor hatred. Only the eyes had spoken the words of Yin-kwa's spirit, and now they were closed, the lids lightly trembling, so the face was no more than a mask.

But after a time the eyes had opened and looked in turn at each of the sons, a deep look that said, "I have loved you." Beyond Jin-see, the eyes had flickered, and Jin-see knew that they were looking for Olan, whom Yin-kwa loved more than any other. He bent forward and spoke distinctly: "Olan is in childbed with your youngest granddaughter." Yin-kwa had smiled then, a slight flattening of the eyes, a tiny, effortful lift of the corners of the lips. And then the eyes had closed slowly and they had left him, each in turn prostrating himself three times in the deep kowtows of farewell. He had gone in the night with no one near him but his one and only wife, slipped away, at what exact moment even she did not know, to join his ancestors. On Jin-see's altar there were only two soul tablets, but on Yin-kwa's there were many. Yin-kwa was but the newest and youngest of many ancestors who still lived with their descendants in these gracious courtyards.

Jin-see reached the last of the courtyards: the courtyard of the women, in the middle of which was a reflecting pool. He had played here with Olan in those wonderful post-Ningpo years, before he'd grown too old for the women's court and been banished. His beautiful mother had played here too, in her time, the mother he remembered only with tear-swollen eyes in dim Ningpo hideaways. "No, no, Jin-see, I love your father! If I were to lose every drop of blood in my body, each drop as it oozed out would say 'I love him!'" And so did he, Jin-see, love Olan. The blood coursing through his veins hummed, "I love her." The blood pumping from his heart throbbed a song to the man whose body lay in the splendid coffin. "I will care for her. I will guard her with my life. I will let no harm come to her. I thank you for her. I thank you for myself—for my own life. I thank you."

A shadow fell across the reflecting pool and he looked up. It was Yin-kwa's wife, Olan's mother. Like himself, she was dressed in mourning white with sackcloth tied around her waist. She had never been possessed of beauty, but she had always been beautiful with the calm certainty of her husband's fidelity. Yin-kwa had never taken concubines. Now, she was pale but peaceful: her husband's body lay in its coffin, but his spirit was still with her.

She put a hand on Jin-see's arm.

"Husband of my daughter, go home. There is no need for you to wait the twenty days of lamentation. My husband would not want it, while our daughter waits and longs for you."

He smiled at her. "Thank you. I will go."

"The child?" she asked. "Our newest granddaughter?"

He hesitated. But he could not tell her now of the child's deformity. Later, one day . . .

"She is well," he said.

Olan's mother smiled.

When Jin-see walked into his family room, Olan was sitting at the table, a glass of tea and a plate of cakes before her. She stretched her hand to him and he went quickly to take it, his heart welling with love and gratitude because she was alive.

"We were waiting for you," she said, smiling.

"We?"

He looked around and saw with astonishment that Donald was sitting on the sofa beside Julie.

There was something in their faces.

He said softly: "What's gone wrong?"

Julie rose and came to him gravely.

"The baby is dead."

He thought how good it was that he hadn't told Olan's

mother of the deformity. Now they need never tell her. They need only say that the child had died.

"My mother killed her," Julie said very softly.

His heart gave a great leap and then dropped like a stone in his breast. He felt that he was suffocating.

Olan, whose hand he was still holding, moved her fingers.

"Jin-see, you're hurting me."

Hurting her . . .

He turned to her slowly, afraid, afraid.

"Olan, did you harm the baby?"

"No!" She smiled like an angel. She was so beautiful. So beautiful. "I *saved* the baby! She had only one leg, Jin-see. Can you imagine what pain that would have caused her as she grew up and realized that she was different from other children, that she'd never be the same, that nobody would ever want to marry her, that her life would be no life at all? Our poor little crippled daughter!"

Great tears welled into the beautiful black eyes, slid down the ivory cheeks, and dripped onto the table.

"I was so sad, Jin-see! For two days I cried. Julie tried to make me stop, she tried to make me eat and drink, but I could not. The tears kept coming. Then"—the brilliant smile reappeared—"I had a wonderful idea. I sent for the cabinet-maker and asked him to carve a tiny wooden leg. I sent the Old Woman to buy opium. I dipped my little finger into the opium and scooped up some of it and gave it to the baby to suck. In just a little while she left for the other world. And there she's going to be happy!"

Olan laughed. Drawing her hand from Jin-see's, she clapped it lightly against the other, making a tapping sound that echoed weirdly in the silence of the room.

"I had the gardener dig a hole in the field behind the house, and I put our daughter into a silk box, and I called Julie and Great Dragon and all the servants, and we buried her in the hole. And then we piled brush on top of the grave and made a fire, and I burned the wooden leg, for its spirit to go with the spirit of our daughter to the other world. Every year, on her anniversary, I will burn another leg, each year a little bigger one, and she will grow up in the other world with both her legs, whole and beautiful and happy. Wasn't that a wonderful idea, Jin-see? Are you glad, Jin-see?"

He took her in his arms and pressed her against him, staring bleakly over her head.

"I'm glad," he said.

Afterward, when Julie had taken her mother to bed, Donald said:

"Macpherson knows. I hoped to keep it from him, but his carriage driver heard it from the servants. He feels he ought to report it."

"What!" Jin-see's eyes flashed. "It's got nothing to do with the police!"

"Macpherson feels it's his duty, since Olan was his patient and so was the baby. But he realizes the situation and agreed to do nothing until you came back."

Jin-see groaned aloud. Olan in a police court. Olan in an asylum. By the great green turtle, how to appease Macpherson?

"Would he accept a—present?"

"Not he," said Donald. "Some of the other doctors might, but not Macpherson."

"What would satisfy him? There must be something that would satisfy him, otherwise he wouldn't have agreed to wait for me to get back."

"I think he'd be satisfied if he could be sure that she'd never have the chance to do such a thing again."

"I want to be sure of that myself!"

Jin-see sank his face into his hands. There was only one

way of being sure of that, and sure that Olan herself would be forever safe from the police, from the hunters.

The hands cupped over his face gave his voice an eerie quality.

"The field in which she buried the baby is part of my property. I'll build a house for her in that field, with a courtyard that will encompass the grave. She'll live there for the rest of her life. I'll see that she never leaves it again. Will that satisfy Macpherson?"

"It'll satisfy Macpherson," Donald said gruffly.

After that they sat in silence. Behind Jin-see's closed eyes the house and courtyard took shape. A small house—an exquisite little house with roof tiles of sapphire blue. Its own staff of servants under the Old Woman. A large courtyard enclosed by high walls, the little grave at the far end, a reflecting pool in the middle. And a single gate, to which only he and Julie would have keys.

A locked gate, to keep Olan within her jeweled prison, to separate Olan from him. He could never again risk Olan having another child.

Chapter IX

1884

"THEY CALL THEMSELVES *I-ho chuan*," Jin-see said.

Donald laughed. "How the devil does that translate? *'I-ho'*—'righteousness'—and 'harmony'? *Chuan?* Isn't that the word for the shadow-boxing that warriors used to perform before combat to harmonize mind and muscle? Well, how about 'Righteous and Harmonious Boxers'?"

"Good! It has just the touch of mystery that the Chinese name implies. Have you ever heard of them?"

"No. Are they rebels?"

"They're a secret society based in north China that's against everybody, especially foreigners and foreign missionaries, and Chinese who convert to Christianity and thus forsake the ancient gods."

"How the devil did Olan get in touch with them?"

Jin-see raised his hands in a helpless gesture.

"On account of our crippled daughter. Every year Olan has

faithfully burned a wooden leg for her, each time a little bigger one. This year the child would be twelve, and Olan's been getting more and more anxious to be assured that she really is growing up with both her legs in the other world. She consulted all sorts of clairvoyants and seers, and finally found this Righteous and Harmonious Boxer. He seems to be a kind of fund-raiser for his society. There's not much money in the north, and they're trying to milk the coastal cities. He's certainly found a rich source in Olan! She's pouring money out to him."

Jin-see went to stand at the window, staring out over the river.

"I should stop it, I suppose. The man's a charlatan. But she's so happy. She calls him her 'magician.' He shows her visions of our daughter in the other world, with both her legs, laughing and playing. She says the child is beautiful and happy. It's hypnosis, of course. Olan must be one of the easiest subjects in the world to hypnotize!"

"Well, he doesn't seem to be doing her any real harm."

"Not as far as that goes, but there're other things. She says he recites incantations and clenches his teeth and foams at the mouth and becomes possessed of spirits that, he claims, protect him against knives and bullets. And he won't talk to me. Told Olan I would disturb his magic, and he would not be able anymore to show her visions of our daughter. Of course, she begged me not to try and see him."

"Well . . ."

Donald came to join Jin-see at the window. Together they gazed silently across the river at the smoke-belching factories that crowded the Pootung waterfront. The day was darkening, and touches of red flame flickered here and there in the fulminating black of the smoke.

Jin-see shivered.

"I hate the dusk. The day dying, and the night not yet come to life."

Donald said slowly: "In England the dusk is very long, especially in the summer."

They fell silent, each suppressing the spark of emotion that passed between them. For the first time since the decision was taken, they had referred, albeit indirectly, to Donald's impending departure. The years they had allotted to their partnership had passed, *Like a lifetime*, thought Jin-see, *like a flash*. . . . They had both known that the time for decision had come. One day Donald said casually:

"When I go, what will we do with Jinsey Mathes?"

And Jin-see: "Turn it into a limited company. Retain shares and draw dividends."

"Yes, Gilbert & Chang are the best corporation lawyers, I suppose."

"When will you leave?"

"Oh, when Great Dragon gets married."

Which, Jin-see thought now, would give them a few more months. Li si-sang was balking. It had taken him a long time and a considerable sum of money to become used to the idea of his daughter being betrothed to a merchant's son, even though he himself had trained that son to be a highly competent mandarin. And now he'd found something else to balk at.

The office boy came clacking in. He had a little pot on his belly now, and his cheeks were thin instead of smooth and round. He was married and had five children. His employers had been duly notified of each birth so that they could instruct the cashier to hand out the appropriate red envelope. Whenever he heard of a lottery or get-rich-quick scheme, he asked Donald to share a ticket with him. He thought Donald was lucky. "What'll you do with the money if we win?" Donald had asked him once. "Take another wife," he'd replied seriously.

Now he said laconically:

"There's an old man outside asking for you."

"Ah!" Jin-see rose. "I'll fetch him in myself. Bring tea—the porcelain teapot and the best cups."

"Who's that?" Donald asked.

"Li si-sang. I've asked him to come here to talk to you. He's got a new objection to the marriage."

"What am I supposed to say to him! I'm a merchant too!"

"Yes, but a *foreign* one. That puts you out of the Confucian hierarchy."

"What's his objection?"

Jin-see grinned. "I'll let him tell you. You wouldn't believe it if I told you!"

A minute later, Jin-see bowed Li si-sang into the room. He was a little old man who might once have been quite tall but was now so bent that his head, with its high-domed forehead and wispy beard, seemed disproportionately long. He looked exactly like pictures of revered scholars in old scroll paintings—and that, of course, was what he was, Jin-see reminded himself sternly as Li si-sang bowed distantly to Donald and seated himself in the armchair Jin-see placed for him, as though Jin-see were the office boy performing a duty.

Jin-see poured tea and ceremoniously handed the old man a cup. He took it without acknowledgment and held it delicately in long, gnarled fingers, staring austerely into space. Jin-see made urgent signs at Donald, who spread his hands, raised his eyebrows, and at last shrugged and cleared his throat.

"Si-sang, Wei Jin-see has asked me to discuss with you the important subject of the marriage of your gracious daughter to his unworthy son, your pupil."

The old man turned to face Donald and talked to him directly as though Jin-see were not present.

"The marriage to which I was foolish enough to consent! I must withdraw my consent! The marriage is impossible if Wei Jin-see continues to insist that his son accept a position that Prince Kung has offered on some new board in Peking that

116

the foreigners propose be created to deal exclusively with *their* affairs!"

Donald glanced inquiringly at Jin-see, who kept his expression inscrutable. He tried again:

"Forgive me, but I am an ignorant foreigner. The new board is only a proposal as yet, but assuming it is established, what makes Prince Kung's offer unacceptable?"

Li si-sang huffed indignantly, arching his scrawny neck like an angry old rooster.

"Do you not think it undignified for a government to devote an entire board exclusively to the affairs of foreign barbarians? Yet Prince Kung is in favor of such a proposal! But worst of all, of course, is his behavior over many years. When the Hsien Feng Emperor died, it was quite proper for Prince Kung, his brother, to become regent for his six-year-old son, the Tung Chih Emperor, but it was *not proper* for him to allow the Empress to become coregent. Then, when the Tung Chih Emperor died at the age of nineteen—of certain depraved practices in which the Empress is said to have encouraged him—Prince Kung allowed her to do a terrible thing. The young Emperor had died without issue. With the connivance of Prince Kung, the Empress adopted her sister's child, four years old, as the son of herself and the Hsien Feng Emperor, and put him on the throne as the Kuang Hsu Emperor!"

Donald was looking bemused.

"Sir, I am confused. It was nepotism, perhaps, but . . ."

"Don't you see?" The old man's voice was squeaky with exasperation. "She substituted her nephew for her son! Her nephew is of the same generation as her son! He cannot perform the ancestral rites for him! She has left her son with no one to perform the rites for him! And Prince Kung connived in this—this *crime*, so that he and she can continue to rule as coregents!"

Glaring and harrumphing, the old man turned away to sip

noisily at his tea. Donald glanced at Jin-see with raised eyebrows, suppressing what was clearly a great desire to laugh. Slowly and carefully, he bent toward Li si-sang.

"Now I understand. You have made it very clear. Indeed, that was a crime against dynastic law. But it was a long time ago—nine years? The Kuang Hsu Emperor is almost of an age to rule himself. And the Empress has removed Prince Kung as coregent and relegated him to the lowly position of training young mandarins for undignified work like serving foreigners in this proposed new board."

A half-hour later, Li si-sang reluctantly agreed to allow the marriage to take place when Great Dragon had passed his final examination.

Jin-see spoke for the first time: "He is in Hangchow now for the semifinal. The final will be in about six months' time?"

Li si-sang nodded stiffly.

They escorted him down to the street and installed him in Jin-see's rickshaw. The coolie respectfully tucked a rug around his knees and, falling in with Jin-see's reverent demeanor, bowed to his passenger before he took up the shafts.

Donald drew a deep breath as the rickshaw went off.

"Talk about the fantasies of the dynastic world!"

They stood on the curb, laughing companionably. Behind them stood the six-story pile that was now completely owned by Jinsey Mathes and occupied by Jinsey Mathes subsidiaries: the import/export company, the engineering company, Cathay Real Estate, Shanghai/Hangchow Shipping. *All cut and dried*, Jin-see thought, his laughter subsiding. Each department under the management of competent men who resented interference from the owners. No more, the heart-swelling excitement of the early years when he and Donald had pored over plans and proposals!

Both of them silent now, they began to walk toward the Chinese City, cutting across the tangled traffic of the Bund to the grassy verge that lay along the river's edge like a narrow park, from which, every few hundred yards, flights of stone steps led down to the debris-laden water. There was a real park at the north end of the Bund, with a broad sweep of sandy path curving around the juncture of the Whangpoo River and the Soochow Creek, and benches on which parkgoers could sit to watch the endless flow of river traffic. Somewhere in the park was a waterfall running down an artificial hillock, splashing onto a cast-iron umbrella held up by a cast-iron boy to shield a coy little cast-iron girl. The water dripped over the edge of the umbrella into a pool in which fat red carp swam about. Jin-see knew these things about the park because Donald had happened once to describe them. He himself had never been in it: a notice on its gate warned that dogs and Chinese were not allowed. It was called the Public Gardens, but only in the sense of the Unequal Treaties: public to foreigners. The life of the Treaty Ports was governed by "Treaty Rights," which had replaced law and societal concepts.

Someone stepped directly in front of Donald, forcing him and Jin-see to stop. An Englishman, balding, heavy red jowls, bloodshot eyes. He stared at Donald with tipsy anger.

"Bloody upstart! *Andrew* brought you out, and look at you now! Working with Chinks, hobnobbing with them! And rich as Croesus, blast you!"

"Good evening," Donald said politely, stepping around the man.

Jin-see stepped around his other side.

"Didn't think anyone remembered Andrew after all these years."

Donald laughed shortly. "Those whose drinks he used to pay for at the Club, they remember him. The point of that wasn't really Andrew, though—it was 'rich as Croesus.' "

They walked on in silence. They had a destination: Yang

King Pang, the creek that divided the International Settlement from French Town, a malodorous ditch bordered by garbage-strewn alleys, between which the water meandered sluggishly, hardly recognizable as water under the thick layer of green scum that undulated on top of it.

There was talk of once again enlarging the foreign concessions by adding to French Town the strip of land that lay between Yang King Pang and the Chinese City. In that case, the two foreign municipalities would pay the cost of filling in the creek and replacing it with a boulevard, the middle of which would be the permanent border between the Settlement and French Town. Until then, the border remained unclear. In the hope of escaping payment of taxes and license fees to one or other of the municipalities, mean little opium shops and dens had concentrated in the creekside alleys. Yang King Pang was the poor man's opium heaven.

They had agreed that before Donald left for England, he must go down into Yang King Pang to complete the picture he had of opium in China, to equip himself as fully as possible for the assault on Parliament. He knew how the opium trade operated: domestic opium now the mainstay of the market, but twenty thousand chests of Patna still imported every year by the Sassoons and Hardoons, wealthy now, handsomely dressed, driving in carriages. He knew prices and profit margins, import and local taxes, license fees—the whole structure that opium occupied in the Chinese economy. He knew that there might now be in China upward of a hundred million opium smokers; nobody had ever tried a count. He knew that moderate smokers of a pipe a day were expected to have no more than twenty years between their first pipe and their last; that habitual smokers of eight or ten pipes a day had no more than three or four years to live; that smokers spent two-thirds of their wages on opium and thus sacrificed their families' health and lives as well as their own.

He had even smoked a little opium himself. Laid himself on a soft couch in a plush divan, waited while a lovely girl prepared a pipe, held it for him over the lamp flame while he inhaled, then chided him prettily for not inhaling deeply enough—he was wasting his money if he didn't enjoy his opium to the full. She would prepare him another pipe and this time . . . He had escaped with difficulty, got out of the divan to breathe the fresh air with no more than a headache.

All these things he knew, but he had never been down into the Yang King Pang opium heaven.

Now, when they reached the bridge that spanned the creek over which most people scurried quickly, Jin-see said: "Well?" and Donald said: "Let's go," and Jin-see turned to lead him down a narrow path beside the bridge into the dark alleys.

It was very quiet and it smelled very bad. Tumbledown shacks clung to each other, wall to wall, roof to roof. Figures scuttled furtively past them, or pressed against the walls to let them by. A woman leaned against a wall, weeping softly, scrubbing at her eyes with the heels of her hands. A few scabby-headed waifs sprawled in the light of a lantern playing a game with picture cards from cigarette tins. Even they were quiet, talking in hoarse whispers as they snatched cards from each other, until one of them looked up and saw Jin-see and Donald. Then they all looked up, gaped for a moment, leapt to their feet, came running, hands outstretched, whining pitifully for coppers. The sudden noise was shocking. Jin-see muttered:

"Don't put your hand into your pocket."

Donald said: "But—"

And Jin-see interrupted sharply: "Don't."

They walked on, avoiding the children's clutching hands. The smell of opium that had been part of the amalgam of smells began to dominate, to float almost tangibly upon the air. Jin-see touched Donald's elbow and they turned into one

121

of the dark huts. Immediately, the opium smell became choking. Jin-see held Donald's arm.

"Don't move until you can see."

Vision came back quickly, for it was not totally dark inside the hut. Smoky oil lamps made spots of light that revealed the interior like the black and gray of a badly exposed photograph.

Shadowy figures lay upon low bunks that lined the crumbling walls and, overflowing the bunks, upon the mud floor—lay slackly, sprawled out, unmoving, lost in their doomed euphoria. The unsteady yellow light glinted on their upturned faces, waxlike and ghostly, on their blank and senseless eyes. It was eerily silent. Euphoria was silent. There were soft sputterings and sighs, but mainly there was only dreaming silence. A ragged young man, acolyte of the silent sacrament, padded barefoot among the dreamers, preparing the sacramental pipes. Quick with much practice, he wasted no movement, dipping a long needle into a tin of opium, twirling it to extract a bead of the black stuff, heating the bead over a lamp, fitting it into the pipe, putting the pipe into the dreamer's hand. The dreamer performed his slow ritual, struggling up onto an elbow, tilting the pipe over a lamp flame, sucking hot air through the bead of opium, sucking it deep, deep into his lungs, holding it a bursting while, releasing it at last in long plumes of vapor that jetted from his nostrils, then sinking back into phantasm. At Donald's feet a dreamer lay on the brink of dissolution, a frail skeleton covered with papery skin. To him the acolyte was tender, clasping his dying hands around the pipe, holding it steady for his dying lips to suck the fume into his dying lungs.

The gray haze swirled slowly, and the rotten, sweetish smell crept about its sly invasion.

"Oh God!" Donald muttered, and Jin-see tugged at his arm.

"Come on. That's enough."

They stumbled back into the alley.

The children were there, waiting. Their numbers had swelled. Their whine started up immediately, and their hands stretched out, clutching.

"Don't," Jin-see said, but it was too late. Donald had already put a hand into his pocket. At once the children began to fight each other viciously, trying to be nearest to Donald, to be the first when he took his hand from his pocket. But he kept his hand tight in his pocket and called out sharply to them to stop. They paid no attention, jostling him, turning their fight against him, wanting him to fall, wanting his height within their reach.

Jin see took coins from his own pocket, shouted to draw the children's attention, showed them the coins, and flung them behind him into the darkness. All but three of the children rushed to retrieve the coins. Those three stuck with Donald, their bodies tense as wire leaning against him, their fierce eyes fixed on the hand in his pocket.

Jin-see took Donald's arm and jerked him away from the children, rushed him toward the bridge. The children followed, screaming curses. Jin-see hauled Donald up onto the bridge, and the children assembled on the path below as though an invisible barrier kept them at the limit of their territory, glaring up with old, old eyes, mouthing furious curses.

"Oh God, Jin-see," Donald panted, leaning against the railing of the bridge.

"They're the children of opium smokers," Jin-see said softly, looking down at them. "Dead smokers. Perhaps they were waiting outside the dens for their fathers, who didn't come out again. Perhaps they were abandoned elsewhere and found their way here, like to like. They live down there in the alleys. They forage and steal and beg and bully and somehow manage to stay alive."

He took three more coins from his pocket and tossed them

to the children, precisely, one to each. They caught them and at once slid off into the darkness.

"Oh God!" Donald breathed. "Oh God!"

"You just saw China, Donald," Jin-see said evenly, feeling the words squeezed out of him by the weight of his emotion. "Not Hong Kong. Not the International Settlement or French Town. China. Strange, isn't it? You've lived in China for twenty-four years and you just saw China for the first time."

He put an arm around Donald's shoulders and drew him away from the railing.

When they reached Jin-see's compound, they were both calmer. The gateman let them in, and they crossed the outer courtyard to the narrow passage beside the ancestors' house that led to Olan's courtyard. Jin-see unlocked the gate and they entered.

The courtyard was of shell-pink marble. At the far end, a little shell pink house that sheltered the baby's grave and the golden bowls that stood before it, filled with incense sticks and flowers. In the middle, an oval-shaped reflecting pool. Masses of glossily tended trees and bushes to disguise the high, enclosing walls. Colored fairy lights hanging from stanchions hidden among the greenery. A lovely, peaceful place.

They crossed the courtyard to the glass-enclosed porch of Olan's house. A twinkling pattern of light shifted over the panes as they approached it, but it was empty when they entered. A round table was laid for dinner, and a potbellied stove glowed in a corner, shedding warmth over rich paneling, silken carpets, brocaded drapes, deep armchairs.

Jin-see poured wine and they drank deeply, with relief and release of tension, standing with their backs to the fire.

"Olan's happy here," Jin-see said abruptly. "She doesn't seem to notice that she never leaves the courtyard. Julie spends a lot of time with her. Great Dragon comes in every day for his midday meal. I spend every evening here. The Old Woman sleeps in the same room with her. She has the grave to tend. She doesn't seem to need anything else."

"Macpherson asks about her every now and then. He's a very cold fish, but he has a special feeling for her."

An inner door opened, and Olan came through.

"Donald!" The brilliant smile flashed. "It's so long since I saw you! And"—she came close, turning her face up to Jin-see's—"my husband."

As always when she came close, his breath caught in his throat. The years of seclusion had hardly touched her. She was a little thin, perhaps, her face a little more finely drawn; and tonight there was something special about her, something that glowed and sparkled.

Suddenly he knew what it was.

"Olan, is your magician here?"

Alarm leapt into her eyes. "You mustn't try to see him, Jin-see!"

He stared at her, passing his tongue over his lips.

"You mustn't, Jin-see! Please! He showed me such lovely pictures today—our daughter, so beautiful, so happy . . ."

There was a flare of light in the courtyard, and she sighed with relief.

"He's gone. Julie's opening the gate for him."

Jin-see strode quickly to the windows.

Julie, a torch in one hand, was unlocking the gate. The magician was standing beside her. A very tall man, towering over Julie. Thin and bony. Long, stringy hair and beard. Unkempt. Dirty. Wild-looking. And so extraordinarily tall.

Olan's magician.

Chapter X

Spring

1885

JIN-SEE SMILED as he watched Donald seat himself in one of the great ironwood armchairs that stood on the dais. Donald must be hating this!

The Wedding Witness, whose signature and chop would certify the marriage papers, called out loudly:

"The New Man and the New Woman will greet"—he stumbled over the English name—"Mister Donald Mathes."

Great Dragon and Ching-mei stepped forward, knelt before Donald, bowed their foreheads to the floor, stood up, and repeated the procedure twice more. Each of the relatives and old friends of the wedding couple's parents were entitled to three kowtows. Great Dragon and Ching-mei had already made numberless kowtows, and there was still a long line waiting their turn.

Donald rose, and an old couple took his place. The Wedding Witness intoned:

"The New Man and the New Woman will greet . . ."

Donald came threading his way through the crowd toward Jin-see.

"You might have left me out of *that*!"

Jin-see laughed wryly. "I'd have liked to leave the whole thing out! I wanted a quiet wedding at home. They'll be living in Peking—we don't need to pat the backs of all these people. But Li si-sang insisted."

"How many guests are there?"

"About a thousand five hundred. I've hired the entire restaurant. Five floors."

"Good God!"

"And we're not yet half through with the wedding. There's the toasting and the dinner to be got through after this. That poor girl is close to exhaustion."

Ching-mei was indeed drooping, her pink and red wedding silks beginning to look bedraggled. Julie, who had acted for Olan in shopping for the bride's trousseau, had told Jin-see that the costume consisted of a total of fourteen pieces, starting with the breastband that flattened Ching-mei's chest. Though she didn't need the breastband at all, Julie confided. She was scrawny. But she had insisted on everything she could possibly insist on. Jin-see, of course, was paying the bills.

Great Dragon, in his long brocade gown with frog-buttons of gold, was also looking pale, but he continued to kneel and bow and rise and kneel again with precision—and a bit of pomposity? Jin-see sighed. Perhaps what seemed pompous to merchants was simply dignified to mandarins. When one's sleeves were so long that they covered the hands completely, one was obliged to slide them up with that important-looking mandarin gesture in order to use one's hands at all. Great Dragon's sleeves were as yet no longer than knuckle-length, but Jin-see could easily imagine him making that gesture.

127

On Great Dragon's fifteenth birthday he had taken him into the ancestors' house and formally confided the life-duty to him, when he himself should no longer be able to carry it. Great Dragon had accepted the responsibility with calm solemnity; it was Julie who had turned pale and blushed and cried "I *love* it!" when he told her that she would have a part in it too. Jin-see sighed again. At least Great Dragon was a thoroughly good man, as well as intelligent and highly trained. And handsome too. He felt an unexpected twinge. He himself had hated the round, foreign-shaped eyes he'd inherited, but now, looking at Great Dragon's flat, Chinese eyes, he felt a strange kind of sorrow. Had part of the endowment of their ancestors been lost? Would the English blood show up again in a grandchild? Strangely, for a moment, Jin-see urgently hoped so. Perhaps it had showed up in Julie, in the asymmetry of her mother's classic Chinese features, in her aversion to a Chinese marriage, in her remarkable affinity for Donald.

The kowtowing was at last over. The bride and groom had withdrawn to change their clothes for the fourth time that day. One set of garments for the early morning ritual of giving thanks to their ancestors. A second set for each to sit alone and eat a last meal as an unmarried person. A third set for the kowtowing. And now a fourth set for the toasting and the dinner. Li si-sang and Ching-mei had been prepared to forgo nothing.

The guests were seated ten to a table—a hundred and fifty tables spread in every corner of the huge restaurant. Waiters had begun to serve dinner before the bride and groom reappeared. Places were reserved for them at the head table, where Jin-see sat with Julie between him and Donald, Li si-sang opposite. But before they would be allowed to eat a mouthful, the bride and groom would have to tour the restaurant, drinking a toast with the guests at each table.

"*Every* table?" Donald almost gasped.

Jin-see glanced sardonically at Li si-sang and shrugged.

"There's cold tea in those cognac bottles that the waiters are carrying behind them."

"Even so! A hundred and fifty drinks of cold tea! That could be *worse*!"

"Most people will let them off with just a sip."

At that moment a noisy young man, already drunk, snatched the glass of cold tea from Ching-mei's hand and gave her a glass of brandy that he poured from the bottle on his table.

"No cheating! Drink a real drink with me! If you don't, I'll know you despise me! Drink up!"

The drunken voice rang loudly and silence fell as all the guests looked around. Ching-mei stared at the glass as though hypnotized. Great Dragon, unable to interfere without insulting a guest, stood stock still. It was a moment for the bride's mother or mother-in-law to save. But this bride had no mother, and her mother-in-law sat in a velvet prison dreaming of another daughter in another world.

In the tense quiet, Julie rose and crossed the room, took the glass from Ching-mei's hand, and smiled sweetly at the young man.

"I will drink for my sister."

She raised the glass to him, forcing him to raise his to her. They drained their glasses.

Ching-mei, whose eyes had been modestly downcast all day, was glaring at Julie with hatred. Julie, putting the glass upside down on the table to signify its emptiness, gave her back a complicated look: amusement, a little scorn, a little warmth.

"By God!" Donald said in Jin-see's ear. "If I weren't old enough to be her father, I'd ask her to marry me!"

Jin-see smiled faintly. "She'd accept."

"What's wrong with you, Jin-see? She's twenty-eight or twenty-nine, isn't she? Why isn't she married yet?"

"She doesn't want to be—except to you, she once told me when she was sixteen."

"She's too good, too wonderful, to be just . . . her mother's keeper."

"She's not going to be that. As soon as Jinsey Mathes is converted, I'm going to open a family *hong* to manage my income and investments, and to see that Great Dragon gets the support he'll need when he goes to Peking. Julie will be the office manager of the *hong*. I promised her that when she was sixteen and decided she couldn't marry you because you were too old for her."

Julie slipped back into her place between them, weaving a little.

"That was a *lot* of brandy!"

"Eat. Sop it up."

Donald piled food into her bowl. She began to eat, giggling tipsily. They watched her, her father and Donald, both smiling fondly.

Then Donald rose.

"Well, I'll go now."

They had planned it like that. Donald was booked on a ship that would sail at midnight. His baggage was already aboard. There would be no dramatic moment of good-bye, just a casual parting as though they would see each other in the morning, as they had in the mornings of nearly twenty-five years.

Jin-see said: "Take care."

Donald said: "I will. You too."

And to Julie: "Bye-bye, little Julie."

A moment later he was politely pushing his way between the crowded tables. Jin-see stared after him, his eyes dry and sandy. The tall, erect, slim, neat, blond-headed, unchange-

130

ably English figure reached the door. Went through it. Was lost to sight. Through the doorway, it seemed to Jin-see, something was rushing after Donald, some essence of himself that was being sucked out of him to go with Donald, for it was Donald's.

Beside him, Julie put down her bowl and wiped her fingers across her eyes.

A month later, on a muggy April evening, Jin-see let himself into Olan's courtyard, started toward the covered porch, then turned back impatiently. It was too warm to be indoors with the potbellied stove. He needed cool and space. He began to pace around the reflecting pool seeking in the water its usual soothing calm. But tonight the surface of the pool mirrored a monochrome of the sullen, gun-metal sky that might have been a mirror of his own spirit.

The vacuum Donald had left was great and painful. To sit in the new boardroom of Jinsey Mathes & Co. Ltd. listening to others' proposals was painful and dull and boring. It was fine to see Julie happily going off each morning to the office of the new family *hong*, but painful to stay away from it himself, in case a suggestion of supervision might spoil her long-delayed joy. And the chairmanship of the Opium Merchants Guild was becoming increasingly painful. The merchants grew fatter and more complacent day by day, taking it for granted that the empire of opium would go on forever, bringing their sons and grandsons into the Guild like a dynastic succession. And since Donald's departure, a new strain had been added. For twenty-five years the merchants had believed that Jin-see was trading opium through a dummy, one of their own number, and nobody had troubled to try and find out who, for it was right and proper for Jin-see to be saving Donald's face. But now Donald was gone and eyebrows were being raised. Why should Jin-see not come forth and trade openly?

131

It wouldn't be long now before somebody began to wonder whether, in fact, Jin-see had ever traded opium at all. The caldron was heating up, starting to bubble. And the life-duty far from accomplishment!

Jin-see turned to see Olan coming toward him through the mauve light of the heavy clouds that hid the setting sun. She walked lightly, her loose hair cascading. The Old Woman spent hours brushing it, and it gleamed mysteriously, like black gold.

Olan, at least, was forever a delight. In the first years of her seclusion he had ached for her in every part of his being. The great bed had seemed a wilderness. The image of her across the courtyard in another bed, chaste and unrumpled, had tormented him. Time after time, impelled by demons, he had leaped up to pace across the courtyard, to stand in the moonlight by the locked gate, the key trembling in his fingers, ready to spring from his hand and turn itself in the lock. And time after time he had returned alone to his sweated sheets. In those days his heart had overflowed fiercely with bitterness and sorrow. But now, as she came to him, it overflowed sweetly with love. He had ceased to desire her. He only loved her now.

She took his hand and drew him to a bench, and sat beside him.

"Our son and our daughter-in-law came to have their meal with me at noon."

His awareness heightened. Why should she mention it specially? They did the same every day.

Her eyes were puzzled. "Are they married, Jin-see? I seem to remember that they came once in wedding garments and kowtowed to me, but perhaps I was mistaken. I don't always remember things properly."

"You remembered this properly," he said gently. "They are married. What made you think they might not be?"

"Because they haven't shared a pillow."

His blood prickled. He said carefully:

"What makes you think they haven't?"

"I don't know," she said, and smiled. "But they haven't."

He rose again to pace around the pool. Great Dragon and Ching-mei had Li si-sang's house to themselves. He had moved out to stay with relatives. What was there to prevent consummation of the marriage? It was true that Great Dragon had hardly had opportunity fo find out what sex was about—he'd have had to be foxier than he was to get away long enough from Li si-sang's mandarin-sharp supervision. But Jin-see, for that reason, had lectured him specifically, and he certainly knew the basics. Could it be that sex was too earthy for prissy missy Ching-mei? A little load of guilt weighed down Jin-see's heart. He had meant only for Ching-mei to bring to Great Dragon the prestige that would mean so much to his career. Well, if prissy missy didn't like sex, Great Dragon would simply take a concubine. He wouldn't be prevented by love, as Jin-see had been prevented.

He turned away from the pool and walked back to where Olan was sitting. He would go away. Take a holiday. Do what he'd planned for so many years—go up north to find a place where the great Patna poppy would grow as well as in Patna.

"Olan, will you mind if I go away for a while?"

"Where will you go?"

"To the north. Shensi. Shansi."

"Where the Yellow River turns to go to the sea?"

He was astonished. "Yes."

She nodded slowly. "I remember, the year before we were married, the Yellow River turned itself around as though to hold Shansi in the bend of its elbow. Do you remember?"

He remembered, of course. By some freak of nature, the river had suddenly forced a new path to the sea, emptying itself into the Gulf of Pei-chi-li at a point four degrees of lat-

133

itude north of its old mouth. The change of course had ruined the Grand Canal, thrown sixty thousand canal workers
out of work, and destroyed thousands of peasant farms.

Olan was speaking softly.

"The river chose Shansi. Shansi is a chosen place. I feel an
omen. You must go to Shansi, Jin-see, and do there whatever it is that you must do."

Chapter XI

Summer

1885

JIN-SEE STOOD at the rail of the river steamer watching the sun rise over the vast, misty expanse of water. Here, in the enormous mouth of the Long River, there was no land at all to be seen. The river's official name was Yangtsze-kiang, River of the Yang Kingdom, which had existed in this delta three thousand years ago. But to the Chinese it was simply the Long River, running three thousand five hundred miles from its source in the Tibetan highlands, through fierce, snow-capped gorges thirteen thousand feet deep, to the broad flat-lands, and at last to its great delta in the East China Sea. A beautiful, majestic, turbulent, calm, chaotic, peaceful river that had watered the heartland of China since the beginning of time.

In the silvery light of dawn, the unending life of the river was slowly revealing itself. In the distance, a long line of empty junks bobbed high in the water behind a launch that towed them against the river, black smoke huffing from its funnel. Nearby, other junks loomed out of the mist, heavily laden, low in the water, their sails speeding them on the current down to the sea. Long, narrow fishing boats rocked on the water, cormorants crowding their gunwales, shouldering each other, plunging the moment they saw a fish, forever frustrated, for the metal ring around their snaky necks prevented them from swallowing, and the fisherman invariably deprived them of their catch. Yet they persisted, plunging, surfacing, surrendering to the man.

The wind whistled in Jin-see's ears. The air was so fresh and clean that it nipped at the soft skin inside his nostrils. It was wonderful! For the next seven days, until the ship reached Hankow, he would be peacefully suspended in time. The ship's passengers were all English, most of them young, on their first tour of duty to learn the ropes in one of the Treaty Ports on the river. They would leave him strictly alone. To the captain and purser they would grumble: what was a Chinaman doing on a British ship? The captain and purser, knowing that Jin-see was aboard because he was a director of the shipping company, because he was rich enough to buy and sell them all, and besides had some kind of twisty Chinese hold on the shipping agent, would commiserate and curse the bloody mess-ups that Head Office was forever making. Jin-see smiled to himself. Last night when he came aboard he'd asked the purser for a separate table in the saloon, and when the purser hastened to grant his request, he had gravely thanked him, tongue in cheek. By the great green turtle, seven whole days of peace and quiet!

A voice beside him said in accented Chinese:

"Good morning, Wei Jin-see."

His heart sank. For a moment he was desperately tempted to ignore the greeting, but he couldn't avoid whoever it was for seven days. Better face the man down immediately. He turned coldly.

The man was an Englishman, a small-scale opium dealer called Ah-fet by the members of the Opium Merchants Guild. His name was Alfred Pratt: "Alfred" sounded like "Ah-fet" to the opium merchants, and the nickname had stuck. He was one of the few Englishmen who could speak Chinese, quite fluently although his pronunciation was bad. It was bad in English too, Jin-see had found. He had a choppy accent, like the English sergeants in the police force of the International Settlement, who were only reluctantly acknowledged as compatriots by most Shanghai Englishmen. The Sassoons and Hardoons didn't acknowledge them at all—they couldn't afford to, for they themselves were on shaky social ground. The opium merchants, amused by these delicate gradations in a people who, by their standards, were all uncouth, besides having offensive bodily odors, were inclined to like Ah-fet the more because the Sassoons and Hardoons disdained him. He was a diffident little man, snub-nosed and mousy-haired, and he was now smiling apologetically. Jin-see found his hostility diminishing.

"Good morning," he said courteously.

Pratt nodded and smiled again, and then leaned on the rail without another word, watching the life of the river. After a few minutes, with a little bow, he went below. It almost seemed that he had come on deck only to check on Jin-see and had been satisfied merely to find him there.

But when Jin-see went to the saloon for breakfast, Pratt was sitting at his table. The purser hurried over.

"You won't mind, sir? The other tables are full."

The places at the other tables had been spread out to make them look full. But Jin-see knew that the cocky young Englishmen would be no more polite to Pratt than they would to him, and he nodded to the purser.

"It's all right."

At the table, Pratt rose and bowed.

"I apologize for intruding on your privacy," he said in Chinese.

"Not at all."

They sat down. The steward brought menus. When they had ordered and the steward had gone, Pratt began to speak.

"I was glad to find you aboard. I thought I saw you last night, but I wasn't sure."

Jin-see unfolded his napkin, beginning to regret his courtesy. The steward brought tea in a heavy shipboard teapot. Pratt poured for both of them into the thick cups. Jin-see shuddered at the strong, black brew. Pratt put four spoonfuls of sugar into his cup, added milk, stirred, and sipped with evident satisfaction.

"Ahhh . . . one thing all Englishmen share in common is a love of tea."

Jin-see, reaching silently for a piece of toast, felt Pratt's gaze flick toward him. He said nothing, and Pratt went on.

"Not much else, though, that an Englishman of my class can share with his countrymen. Difficult for people of my class to rise out of it in England. That's why my mother sent me here. Heard that Shanghai was booming, with chances for everybody. Hoped that I could do better for myself than I ever could at home, and eventually maybe send for her and my young brother. Dad died years ago."

He sipped again at his tea. With growing exasperation Jin-see munched on cold toast. Why had he not nipped this in the bud on deck this morning?

"That was ten years ago, when I was eighteen," Pratt said through a mouthful of toast and tea. "I soon found I couldn't get any kind of decent job here, no more than in England. Finally got a job as tally-man in a rice warehouse. The owners hired me because I didn't know Chinese then, and they

138

thought I couldn't plot thievery with the coolies."

He laughed a little. Jin-see, close to explosion, looked up and saw in his eyes, not the smug look of a man with a captive audience, but an anxious, almost pleading look. Was he leading up to something? Jin-see swallowed the sharp words that had been on the tip of his tongue and silently took another piece of toast.

Pratt went on. "I was in that warehouse five years. Took me that long to save up a sackful of rice. You know how a few grains of rice trickle out every time the coolies shift the sacks with those big hooks? Well, I swept up all those trickles and hoarded them until I had a sackful. Then I sold it and bought opium. Quickest way I knew of making money. *Only way I* could make money quick. But when I finally had enough to send for my mother and brother, my brother wasn't interested and my mother had died." His voice dropped to a mumble. "Anyway, she probably wouldn't have liked to come on money earned through opium."

There was a pause. Jin-see waited. Pratt drank tea. It had grown lukewarm, and he put down his cup with an absentminded grimace.

"I started to learn Chinese while I was at the warehouse. I'm still taking lessons. My pronunciation's no good, I know. My teacher's in despair. His name is Tong Shao-yi."

He said the name slowly and distinctly, then breathed a tiny sigh and fell silent.

A little buzz started up in Jin-see's mind. Recently the opium merchants had begun to talk about a man who was organizing the anti-opium societies. Up to now their efforts had been negligible: a few poorly attended public meetings, a few apostles standing outside divans exhorting smokers to go home. But this man was coordinating their random efforts. He was beginning to make an impact. He was beginning to be a nuisance. A man called Tong Shao-yi.

Jin-see said: "I have heard that name."

Suddenly low-voiced words began to tumble out of Pratt's mouth.

"Tong Shao-yi's asked me many times to speak to you about financing a national anti-opium movement. I said: 'Why the devil should the chairman of the Opium Merchants Guild be interested in anti-opium activities?' He said he thought you would be. He said he'd studied you carefully and he thought you weren't dealing in opium, that you'd never dealt in opium. He said if he approached you himself he'd spoil his chances because you're playing some deep game and you'd be obliged to throw him out, just for the look of the thing. That's why he wanted me to approach you. When I saw you come aboard last night I thought I'd make a try. But of course you're not interested! How could you be? I'm sorry . . . I'll leave . . . I'm sorry to have bothered you."

In confusion, he began to rise.

"As a matter of fact," Jin-see said, "I *am* interested."

That night, staring up at the complicated network of pipes that covered the ceiling of his cabin, Jin-see reviewed his day-long discussion with Pratt.

It seemed that the key to the whole situation would be confirmation of Great Dragon's appointment to the new Board of Foreign Affairs, the Wai-wu Pu. If he were confirmed, he would move at once to Peking and could bring Tong Shao-yi to Prince Kung's attention. Tong Shao-yi, Pratt said, was a natural leader, a charming man, a wonderful speaker. Once introduced to the Prince, he would surely capture his attention. Besides, no one in a position like Prince Kung's could afford to ignore a cause like Tong Shao-yi's. And although the Dowager Empress had demoted Prince Kung, he was still her brother-in-law and must have her ear. With a little judicious maneuvering, he might bring Tong Shao-yi to *her* attention.

In England, Donald had joined the Executive Committee for the Suppression of the Opium Trade, the coordinating body of the English anti-opium societies. Contact between Peking and the Committee would obviously be a "foreign affair," the business of the Wai-wu Pu, and—since it was most unlikely that anybody in the Wai-wu Pu would be better versed in English than Great Dragon—of Great Dragon himself.

Put all these things together, and it was possible to imagine a Chinese National Anti-Opium Movement led by Tong Shao-yi, under the patronage of the Dowager Empress herself, joining in a huge wave of patriotic feeling with the English Executive Committee under the leadership of Donald, sweeping away the opium clauses in the treaties.

Jin-see turned over, smiling. That was a long way off yet. In the meantime, Pratt would return to Shanghai after finishing his business in Hankow and open an account for Tong Shao-yi with funds that Jin-see would make available. Tong Shao-yi would at once quit teaching and devote himself to organizing the anti-opium crusade. Since this would at once increase his nuisance value to the Guild, Pratt would hire bodyguards to be with him constantly.

Jin-see rolled out of his bunk. Sleep was too far away. He found his writing brush and paper and started a letter to Julie. She should instruct the *hong*'s bank manager to hand certain funds in cash to an Englishman named Alfred Pratt who would call on him with Jin-see's business card. The transaction to be entirely secret.

Jin-see sat under a tree in the central square of a sun-baked village spread out on a plateau on the north bank of the Yellow River. Pratt had turned out to be a gold mine. When he learned why Jin-see was traveling to the north, he had said he knew a place in the Shansi mountains where poppies grew extravagantly well. Following Pratt's directions, Jin-see had traveled by junk northward from Hankow, through a maze of waterways, to the town of Chengchow, thence by pony cart to a point on the south bank of the Yellow River, across the river by flat-bottomed boat, and by cart again to Number Three Village. The village headman had received with pleasure the message Jin-see had given him from "Ah-fet" and had gone off at once to make further arrangements, leaving Jin-see to wait under the tree.

The village had a warm, dry smell of earth and straw and manure and wood smoke, all mingled together and baked clean by the sun. Small children played in the dust, calling out in their sweet, shrill voices, running in and out of the stark black-and-white patterns of shade and sun. Dogs lolled about lazily. Chickens clucked and pecked in the dirt. The leaves of the persimmon trees rustled as they danced to the tune of the warm breeze. Beyond, the mountains rose among rolling green fields of wheat and millet and thrust their peaks and ridges high into the sky.

Jin-see sat on his bench feeling happy. Presently the headman's wife came with green tea and steamed buns stuffed with pork, which, as Jin-see bit into them, oozed mouthfuls of delicious gravy. She sat down on the bench beside him, a heavy woman with big breasts that had suckled many children. No one in Number Three Village had heard of flattening breastbands. She had an intricate smell, sharp and oddly pleasant. The eyes in her broad face were merry, and she smiled easily.

"You know Ah-fet?"

Jin-see nodded, his mouth full of pork bun juices, and she chuckled.

"He is a very nice man, though a foreigner. He comes here

142

often to inspect our poppies. At first we laughed at him because he speaks so strangely, but soon we came to understand him. Do you know his wife?"

Jin-see shook his head.

"He brought her with him the last time he came. She's Chinese. No more than sixteen or seventeen. She adores him like a god, and it's no wonder! Do you know their story?"

Jin-see shook his head again but he needn't have—she went right on talking.

"Her mother was an opium smoker. Sent her around the streets of Shanghai from the time she was able to walk, selling jasmine flowers, the kind that city women use to ornament their hair. In all weathers, the poor little thing! That was how she came to know Ah-fet. He was working in a rice warehouse, and he used to take her in every day, give her food and money. When she was eleven years old her mother sold her to a brothel. Couldn't have got much for her, a scrawny little half-starved thing she must have been, but enough to buy enough opium to kill herself, I suppose. Anyway, the child never saw her mother again. She actually thought the brothel wasn't bad—at least she didn't have to walk the streets in all weathers, and she got food to eat twice every day. She was there two or three years until Ah-fet found her and bought her out and married her. That's a good story, isn't it?"

"Yes," he said. It was a wonderful story. It sounded just the kind of thing that Pratt would do.

"She's a nice little thing," the woman said. "Filled out well, with all the good food he feeds her. Red cheeks and shiny eyes, and some flesh on her that a man can get hold of."

She patted her own bosom and hips and laughed gaily.

Jin-see laughed too. The woman was comfortable to be with—strong and earthy and . . . unbreakable.

The headman came back with the headmen of Numbers

143

One and Two villages. They would all go together up into the mountains, to show Jin-see the land that Ah-fet had spoken of. It was good land. It was wonderful land!

They walked to the other side of the village, followed by all the children and all the dogs, and perhaps all the chickens too. They came to a circle of bare, flattened earth in the midst of a grove of persimmon trees where four men with four small ponies waited. They mounted and started in single file up a path, the men leading the ponies. The children called goodbye and waved, and suddenly Jin-see could see them no longer, though he could still hear their voices, for they were concealed by dense, damp, sweet-smelling forest. They had entered the foothills of the Chungtiao Mountains.

For four hours they wound upward, the ponies plodding sturdily, the men striding in unbroken rhythm over the pathway that was sometimes covered by a rustling blanket of leaves, sometimes broken by protruding roots, sometimes slippery wet with overflow from hidden streams. It seemed at times that they would never emerge from the cling of the forest, but they always did, coming out suddenly into dipping valleys of narrow terraced fields. Jin-see's ears began to hum. The path grew rockier as they climbed higher, the vegetation sparser. Patches of bare clay showed through the green. The sun came and went, came and went, behind the shoulders of the mountains, and at one moment disappeared altogether. It grew dark quickly. The men stopped to light stubby candles sheltered in oiled-paper lanterns. Little could be seen beyond the small radius of their light, but the ponies seemed to know their way by instinct. It grew very cold.

At last they made a short, sheer climb, crossed a ridge, and descended on the other side. A door opened, shedding light. The ponies stopped. Jin-see slid wearily from his saddle. Someone led him into a candlelit room—mud floor, clay walls heavily blackened by years of smoke from cooking stoves, a

144

scuffed table on which a silent woman was laying food, three-legged wooden stools. They ate quickly, too tired to talk, then stumbled into another dim room that echoed with the snores and snorts of many sleeping men. Faint light came from small clay stoves set under a platform built along one wall. The sleepers lay on the platform, side by side in a long row, warmed by the stoves under them and the collection of quilts covering them.

"Our farmers," muttered one of the headmen. "They come up in squads to take turns at working the crop."

He burrowed among the quilts, extracted one and thrust it into Jin-see's arms, then inserted himself between the sleepers and became part of the lumpy row. The other two headmen had also disappeared. Jin-see waited a moment, smelling the sourness of the soiled quilts, the unwashed men, the pony's sweat that still clung to his clothes, and other things he didn't want to identify. Then he too squirmed onto the platform and was asleep before his head touched the wood.

When he awoke, pale light was trickling through slits high in the walls. The men on either side of him were still snoring. A thousand itches burned all over his body where bedbugs or fleas or lice had feasted. The stench had built up during the night to a density that made breathing difficult. He wriggled off the platform, crossed the mud floor, slid open a door—and stepped out into a magic world.

Mountains towered around him in a great ring, their lofty peaks haloed in the golden light of sunrise, their slopes sweeping steeply down to form a gigantic bowl, the bottom of which was still hidden in the mists of night. He stood on a broad ledge cantilevered halfway between the ridges and the unseen valley. The farmhouse in which they had slept lay in the angle of the ledge and the mountainside, a doll's house, a plaything under the mighty heights. The pass through which they had come the night before clefted sharply

145

down to the ledge, the only entrance into this secret valley. Awestruck, Jin-see turned slowly, gazing. Cold, crisp air rushed sweetly down from the mountaintops, whisking away the night's rancidness, laving him, lifting him toward the soaring peaks. When the first beam of sunlight shot over a ridge and tumbled down the slopes, he moved to the rim of the ledge and looked down. A sheer cliff fell a hundred feet or more to the floor of the valley, and there, extravagantly spread before him, lay a great, soft white carpet. It was as though countless white butterflies had fluttered down from the mountains and settled, wing to wing, hovering gently on the dawn air, to carpet the valley. The poppies were in flower. The entire floor of the valley, fifteen acres or more, was covered with flowering poppies.

He stepped back, holding his breath. "Shansi is a chosen place," Olan had said. Indeed, this valley must have been made by the gods and the spirits and the fairies for their own delectation. The farmers of the three villages had borrowed it from its owners for the pursuit of their livelihood. But if he bought it, if he took it from its owners, he would disturb its ethos, for good or ill. Who knew what the gods and the spirits and the fairies might think of it? "I feel an omen," Olan had said.

He heard a hail. The headman of Number Three Village was stepping out of the farmhouse, stretching, scratching himself, calling out a greeting, his voice echoing.

Jin-see called back. He was being ridiculous. The heights were making him light-headed. It was a valley, more beautiful than others, but made of the same elements. It was what he had come to seek: a place where the great Patna poppy would grow and flourish.

It took a week to haggle out the agreement, Jin-see escalating his offers as slowly and with as much display of reluctance as the headmen lowered their demands. Every morning Jin-see and the headmen would sit over the breakfast table after the farmers had gone down to the field, the headmen swearing that they must have been mad to think that they could sell this marvelous valley! There was nothing like its wonderful soil. No, of course they couldn't sell it! Then they would all go down the steep, narrow steps cut into the rock that led from the farmhouse ledge down to the field, and the headmen would squat on their heels and lovingly pick up handfuls of dirt and let it trickle back through their fingers, saying again and again how good it was. Since the beginning of time this soil had been washed down from the mountains by the rains, been trapped here on the valley floor, the layer thickening every year, till now the richness of it went deep down. Every year, after the opium was harvested, the poppy plants were ploughed back into the soil and a light crop of grasses was grown, and that too was plowed back, so the soil retained its riches and the friability that made it so marvelous for poppies.

Did Jin-see think he could buy for the paltry sum he was offering the product of centuries of loving care? Ai-yah! The headmen snorted indignantly and got to their feet and moved off, not too far nor too fast, and squatted down again to wait for Jin-see to join them. When Jin-see said that he might increase his offer a little, they shook their heads sadly as at an ignoramus. Did he realize how hard it was to grow poppies? Here in the high mountains, the tiny seeds must be sown broadcast in late fall to lie all winter under a blanket of snow. In the spring, when the seeds began to sprout, the real work began and lasted right until the harvest in the summer. When the seedlings formed their first four leaves, they had to be thinned out to a carefully calculated distance of ten inches from each other, far enough apart to allow room for growth, near enough to support each other, for poppies with their fragile

147

root system were easily blown down. The soil had to be mounded to support the base of each plant as it grew taller. The plants had to be inspected constantly for parasites and mildew. Secondary growth had to be pruned out. If it did not rain enough, water had to be diverted to the field from a mountain stream through a complex system of bamboo pipes, an infinitely troublesome job. Did Jin-see really think that, after the many years of hard work they'd put in, he could buy their field for so insignificant a sum?

Jin-see looked up into the sky as though making mental calculations and shook his head and said, well, why not go back to the farmhouse and have a drink on it? He had sent one of the pony drivers down the mountain to buy wine and there were two great clay jars of the best *mao tai* in the court-yard of the farmhouse. So they all climbed back up and sat in the shade and drank, and soon they were laughing rau-cously and slapping their thighs and telling earthy stories and saying to Jin-see that he was a fine fellow—if they sold the valley at all, they'd sell it to him.

And finally one day Jin-see laid aside his wine cup and said that he was about to make his final offer. The headmen sat up alertly. Jin-see cleared his throat, spat discreetly into a bush behind him, shot his sleeves in the mandarin gesture he had so often seen Li si-sang make, began to speak slowly and sol-emnly.

He would pay for the valley a sum halfway between his latest offer and the headmen's latest demand. He would pay cash—currency, or silver bullion, or gold bars. Actual mon-etary value in the hands of every villager to do with as he pleased. Bury it, or spend it, or send his son to the city to learn to read and write and reckon figures so no grasping landlord and no cheating tax collector could ever fool him again.

But the purchase of the valley was not the only proposal

Jin-see had to make. He had a further proposal that would free the villagers from the Opium Merchants Guild, to which, ultimately, their opium was sold every year at prices dictated by the Guild. It would make them independent of the Guild— if, of course, the Guild never got to learn about it.

The farmers of the three villages would keep on growing poppies every year, as before, but for Jin-see, not the Guild, with seeds that Jin-see would provide, seeds of the great Indian poppy, whose capsules grew to a size more than two inches in diameter and produced twice as much opium, of twice the quality of ordinary poppies. In a good year, with the new seeds, this valley would produce four hundred pounds of opium. And Jin-see would buy that opium every year at a cash price ten percent higher than the Guild's price. Ah-fet would be his agent. They knew and trusted Ah-fet.

Jin-see sat back and took up his wine cup and sipped, looking gravely into the distance. The headmen withdrew a little and began to whisper to each other. After a while one of them turned to Jin-see.

"Four hundred pounds?"

"A minimum of four hundred pounds. If the year's production is less I'll pay for four hundred pounds. If it's more, I'll pay for whatever is produced."

More whispering. Then another man turned.

"What guarantee will you give us that you'll pay ten percent more than the Guild?"

Jin-see laughed. "If I don't pay ten percent more, you can just turn around and sell to the Guild, can't you? But one word to the Guild about this, and the whole deal is off."

"What shall we tell the Guild representative?"

"When he comes to see you, does he come up here to the valley?"

"Four hours up the mountain and four hours back? No, he doesn't come up here!"

"Then you can tell him anything. Your crop was ruined by a storm. The soil suddenly went sour. Anything. After a year or two he'll stop coming. It's a long way, and while your two hundred pounds is a lot to you, it's a drop in the bucket to the Guild."

"How did you get seeds of the Indian poppy?"

"I sent a man to India, a half-Indian, son of a Chinese woman who married one of those Indians that the English brought to Shanghai for their police force. He stayed around Patna for some weeks. He told me that the British have a tremendous factory in Patna. Halls for examining and testing the opium juice, for drying it, for balling it—each hall as big as a whole village. A storage hall with shelves going up to the roof, ten times the height of a man, where tons of opium can be stored at one time. My man waited until after the harvest, and then he was able to buy secretly from one of the Indian farmers twenty of the capsules that had been kept for seed."

The headmen were silent, digesting this awesome information. A storage hall ten times the height of a man! Indeed this Wei Jin-see must be clever, getting seeds of a poppy that could fill a hall of that size! Indeed this Wei Jin-see must be clever if he could hope to cheat the Guild!

"You say Ah-fet will be your agent?"

"Yes. Ah-fet will come every year in September. He'll pay you cash for the opium, and you'll deliver by pony-back at the landing place on the Yellow River. He'll take it from there."

More conferring. Then a great burst of guffaws and a great slapping of thighs. Done! The headmen fetched their wine cups and filled them, and refilled Jin-see's.

"Wei Jin-see, if you are cheating us . . ."

"If I am cheating you, may the great green turtle lay her eggs on me!"

He poured his wine out onto the ground.

Another shout of laughter and the serious drinking began.

Such a thing happened only once in a lifetime, and not in every man's lifetime at that!

During the days of bargaining, the poppy flowers had withered and the seedpods had begun to develop, each one at first no more than a tiny, spongy, pale green capsule depending from the end of a long, drooping stalk. But the capsules grew quickly, became darker in color, became fat and resilient, began to look as though they were about to burst.

One of the headmen turned a capsule over to show Jinsee. When the ring mark where the petals had been attached to the capsule turned black, the opium juice would be ready for extraction. The juice, thick and white like latex, lay between the outer skin of the capsule and an inner skin that enclosed the seeds. The capsule must be incised to allow the juice to flow. The incision must be precise: the inner skin must not be pierced or the juice would flow inward and be lost, and the cut must be a long spiral, for a straight cut would allow the juice to run too fast. It would not have time to coagulate and it would drop off the end of the cut and be lost. In a spiral cut the juice had farther to run; it coagulated slowly as it ran and when it reached the end of the cut it was thick enough to cling in a large drop. The drops had to be gathered one by one, all within the four or five days when the juice was ripe, before it dried and was absorbed into the seedpod. If it rained in that period, the drops were washed off and lost. If there were too much wind, the juice coagulated too fast, clotted on the incision itself, blocking the juice still within the capsule. Every year the villagers offered the Earth God twenty-five chickens to keep the weather good for these five precious days.

This year the weather promised to be ideal. Every able person in all three villages worked for the harvest, and they were already arriving, groups walking up the mountain, bringing enough food to last a week, and thick oilcloth for makeshift tents. They were happy and laughing: this was the time of their most lucrative harvest, and the crop this year was very fine.

Every morning the three headmen walked around the field, turning capsules over to inspect the ring marks, and one morning they nodded to each other and to the crowd of villagers. It was time.

Immediately, men and women moved into the field, ranged themselves in long, parallel rows, and began expertly to twirl capsules between their fingers, incising them with tiny, curve-bladed knives. As they worked they moved slowly backward to avoid brushing against incised capsules and wiping off some of the juice that began to ooze the instant the cut was made. Every two hours fresh workers moved in. The work continued ceaselessly until dark, when the light of flickering cook-fires began to dot the periphery of the field and the smell of food began to mingle with the smell of the opium. As each capsule was incised and its drop of opium released, the smell was also released. As the juice oozed, the smell accumulated over the field like an unseen fog, floated upward, invaded the farmhouse, invaded the mountains themselves. The smell of opium was everywhere.

Head aching, Jin-see left his dinner and went outdoors. On his second night in the valley he had extracted a couple of quilts from the motley collection on the communal platform, had shaken them in the light of a lantern—bedbugs fled light— and laid them down on a sandy patch behind the farmhouse. Since then he had slept under the stars, seeing them so close and bright that it seemed impossible he could not touch them if only he were not too sleepy to stretch an arm, and then falling straight into deep and untroubled sleep. But tonight the smell of the oozing opium, growing ever stronger, kept him awake. Toward dawn he rose and went to the edge of

152

the cliff and looked down on the rosy glow of lanterns shining beneath the expanse of orange-colored oilcloth tents. The farmers were already stirring.

At first light the work began again, some of the workers going back to cutting capsules, others to gathering the drops that had coagulated during the night. Where the rows of cutters moved backward, the rows of gatherers moved forward, wiping the drops off onto poppy leaves, leaving behind them the stripped plants. Children followed them, waiting to carry laden poppy leaves to the group of women who were laying them carefully into shallow pans. When the pans were full, other women carried them up to the farmhouse ledge, covered them with porous rice paper, and laid them out to dry. As the moisture evaporated, the latex would darken. By the time it was dry enough to be rolled into balls, it would be black.

Jin-see sat on a stone at the edge of the cliff, fascinated by the ordered pandemonium in the field below—five hundred men and women and children weaving back and forth, around and past each other, up and down the rocky staircase, like an army of ants in ceaseless peregrination. The headman of Number Three Village came to sit beside him.

"Good, isn't it?"

"Wonderful! Next year, for the same amount of work, you'll have more than double the money."

The headman cocked his head shrewdly.

"I heard that they don't produce opium in Europe. Is that because Europeans, like the English in our country, are all bosses? That's what I heard. You can't produce opium unless you have many, many people willing to work like coolies."

"Mmmm." Jin-see glanced at him with respect, and the man laughed.

"I may be only a farmer, but I'm not stupid. Why are you doing this, Wei Jin-see? The others think that you're doing it

153

for profit, but I think that you won't be able to sell the opium you buy from us without the Guild knowing, so you must have some other reason than profit."

"If I have," Jin-see said evenly, "it's *my* motive."

"Yes. Yes. I'm just curious. I just think that if it's not a money-making motive, it must be some kind of *good* motive. It can't be a bad one. Anyway, I wish you luck."

He rose and banged Jin-see on the back and walked away.

Thoughtfully, Jin-see shifted on his stone seat. It was a good omen. An illiterate farmer figuring that out for himself and giving a blessing. A good omen, such as Olan had foreseen.

His gaze fell on a woman in the field below, a girl, who seemed to be in command of the children's work corps. She stood on a rock, watching the gatherers. As soon as a gatherer raised his hand to indicate that he needed to be relieved of a laden poppy leaf, she directed a child to him with an imperious wave of her arm. She was quick and alert, and she was enjoying herself hugely. Looking down on her from above, Jin-see saw the top of her black head, the thick braid of her hair bouncing as she turned her head from side to side. Her body, foreshortened by the angle of his view, seemed strong and sturdy. She looked up suddenly, as though drawn by his gaze. The sunlight fell full on her face—a country girl's face, round and red-cheeked, broad-nosed, not pretty but attractive, full of life. As their eyes met, she flashed him a merry smile.

When the harvest was over and the field that Jin-see had first seen so magnificently clothed was nothing but a mass of stripped and dying plants, Jin-see sat with the headmen in the courtyard of the farmhouse amid the lung-clogging reek of the drying opium, drinking with them, matching them cup for cup. He could relax now. The whole thing had turned out exactly as he and Pratt had planned. When Pratt took delivery of the opium each September, he would move it across the river to Chengchow and store it under a fictitious name in a warehouse known only to Jin-see and himself. Perhaps the opium would never be used. Perhaps it would accumulate in storage until one fine day it could be destroyed and forgotten. But perhaps it would be used one day to flood the market—Patna quality opium at the price of cheap domestic—the final blow to British dominion.

Jin-see found himself getting dizzy. He rose, staggering a little, but the headmen wouldn't let him leave. They dragged him down, forced another cup on him, and another—and then suddenly they were asleep themselves, slumped where they'd been sitting, snorting through open mouths, the wine cups fallen, the wine spilled. Jin-see sat a while longer, staring giddily from one to the other. Then he laughed and rose and stumbled to his quilts behind the farmhouse. Tonight the stars were not so brilliant, for the moon was full. The last full moon of the summer. He wrapped himself in his quilts and lay on his back, the light of the moon shining on him, the strange, bright-dark, ghostly light of the huge pale-gold orb that hung above him like a watcher.

He smiled at the moon, his eyelids drifting closed. That woman in Number Three Village—the headman's wife. She hadn't come up for the harvest. What would she do if she knew how drunk her husband had got tonight? Scold him roundly? Or laugh and get drunk too when he told her of the rich new deal? That was a woman!

A hand touched his shoulder. For a moment he paid no attention, thinking he had imagined it, a part of his drunkenness. But the touch came again and he slit open an eye to see who it might be.

It was the girl who'd been in charge of the children during the harvest, who'd looked up at him with that merry smile. She was standing beside him in a long robe that gleamed in the moonlight. She had combed out her hair and it flowed around her, not glinting gold like Olan's, but thick and black like a fall of dark water. The moon highlighted her broad cheekbones. Her wide mouth was curved in a little smile and her eyes were bright.

He stared up at her. She made a slight movement and her robe fell away, leaving her naked. He saw her from below, the angle of his gaze the reverse of what it had been from the clifftop. Her legs, round and strong like pillars. The thick blackness of the pubic mound. The underside of her breasts, vibrating slightly as though they had a life of their own.

Flesh that a man could get hold of.

As in a dream, he lifted the quilt and she slid in beside him, bending her head so that her hair enveloped him.

In the morning when Jin-see entered the breakfast room, the headmen were already at table. They looked slyly at him, laughing. Jin-see laughed too, feeling happy. Not embarrassed. Not guilty. Simply satisfied, as a man feels who has taken a woman in the night.

The headman of Number Three Village said, chuckling:

"You can have her for free, thrown into our bargain. She's the widow of one of our men, but she came from across the river and has no relatives with us. She ogles us men a lot and it makes our wives angry. Take her with you. She'll be glad to go. She's eager for city things."

They all began to laugh again, and Jin-see said equably:

"I will ask my wife and daughter, and if they are agreeable, I will send for her."

Chapter XII

Fall 1885

THE SHIP WAS being warped to the dock, the debris-laden water slapping against its side and churning thickly under the pilings. Far to the left Jin-see glimpsed the contours of the new and ever-taller, ever-bulkier buildings of the Bund, an imposing skyline. Here in Yangtszepoo, behind the wharves and shipyards, there were tumbledown shacks, algae-clogged ponds, quacking flocks of ducks, the remnants of little farms succumbing to urban life. The contrasts between foreign and Chinese Shanghai were becoming every day more marked.

But the ship was being made fast, and Jin-see's thoughts turned to home. It was good to be going home! He hadn't sent a telegram announcing his arrival and they wouldn't be expecting him, but that was all the better. He would surprise them. Not Olan—she would be calm, perhaps she had guessed he was coming. And Great Dragon would hide surprise, would greet him formally with correct mandarin posture. But Julie would shout with joy and fling her arms around him.

The gangway bumped down, and he descended with the first rush of passengers. At the bottom of the gangway milled the usual crowd of waterfront hangers-on, jockeying to pick up a coin or two by carrying passengers' luggage and snaring carriages for them. A ragged, bright-eyed boy squirmed agilely through the crowd and landed at Jin-see's feet. Grinning ingratiatingly, he wrested the suitcase from Jin-see's hand and sped off in the direction of a carriage that stood a little apart from the others. The driver leaped from his box and flung open the door of his vehicle. In a moment, Jin-see found himself stepping into the carriage. The boy handed his suitcase to the driver and ran off without waiting for his coin.

The carriage door was slammed behind Jin-see, and he found himself closeted in almost complete darkness—the glass upper half of the doors had been painted black—and in stuffiness redolent of myriad breaths breathed by previous occupants. He half turned to let himself out—there must be better carriages than this in the row on the dock!—but the vehicle started abruptly and he was caught off balance. He lurched awkwardly sideways and fell upon the seat that, in a narrow carriage of this kind, called "sedan chair horse cart," was wide enough only for two people.

There *were* two people on it, himself and another.

Adrenaline spurted into his bloodstream in a frantic rush. He jerked forward to snatch at the door latch, and felt his arm clasped in a heavy grip while something cold and hard pricked painfully into the side of his neck. Someone said softly:

"This is a very sharp knife."

He froze, half off the seat, hand still on the door latch. The knife pricked again, more sharply, and he felt the warm drip of his own blood.

"Sit back," the man said. "Slowly."

He slid back into the seat, feeling the man's thick thigh against his left leg. An arm went around his shoulders. He was clamped against a strong body. Garlicky breath whistled by his cheek. The point of the knife shifted from the side of his neck to the front and pricked in below his Adam's apple. The carriage was bumping and rattling over cobblestones, but the knife did not waver.

After a time of shock and sweat, rational thought began to return. Jin-see tried to relax as he did in his ancestors' house, willing himself to calm. When he felt that he could speak normally, he said:

"How much are they paying you?"

For an instant the knife wavered, then the man gave a soft snort and pressed it in again, drawing more blood.

It was a gang job. Payment was being made to the gang as a whole and no individual member of it could hope to make a deal for himself and stay alive. The driver must be a gang member too, and that boy on the wharf. No use asking where they were taking him. He'd find out soon enough, and another question would only provoke another cut. Jin-see remained silent, gathering his forces.

The carriage slowed, turned sharply, stopped. There was the rumble of a gate being closed behind them. The carriage door opened, and a burly man appeared in the opening. He reached in and took a strong grip on Jin-see's arm, pulling him out. The man who had held him in the carriage quickly followed. They stood one on each side of him, the knife now held against his back, in the area of his heart.

They were in a courtyard, like Jin-see's own, but dirty and neglected. The house it served was large and solid, four-storied, but also shabby. It had a small tower with an oriole window from which the oblique beams of the setting sun struck dusty glints.

"Walk," one of the men ordered. They started forward, Jin-see hustled between them. The door of the house opened as they approached, and they passed through into a room that contrasted strongly with the exterior of the house: an opulent room, furnished with blackwood armchairs, marble tables, silken rugs. Porcelains and jades stood on the mantel. The room of a rich man.

The two gang men stepped away, leaving Jin-see to stand alone in the middle of the room. Someone was shuffling in: an old man with sparse white hair spiking up from a darkly speckled scalp, dressed in a shabby house-gown that hung in wrinkles about his thin body. He made his way to one of the blackwood armchairs and lowered himself into it. In the silence, Jin-see imagined that he could hear the old bones creak.

The man looked up and with a shock Jin-see recognized him. Ching si-sang. The merchant who had helped to trick Carradine. He had been old then, seventeen years ago. Now, seeing him for the first time not clothed in stiff brocade, without the round black cap that hid his ugly scalp, without his jade-headed cane, Jin-see realized that he was ancient. Ancient and feeble. But he had those two massive, glowering men at the back of the room, and no doubt others of the gang within call. And he had malevolence. It glinted out of the eyes that had always seemed to hold an amused gleam. It breathed out of the lips that had always chuckled. Was it new? Or had it always been there, lurking unrecognized behind the pleasant, joking manner?

Ching said in a thin voice: "Sit down, Wei Jin-see."

Jin-see bowed and sat in an armchair opposite him. The old man looked him over, eyes feebly aglow.

"Wei Jin-see, I will not offer you tea and sweetmeats and pretend that I am glad to see you, though in a way I am. I am glad to see you here, knowing that you will stand or sit or even kowtow should I command it."

160

He chuckled, his shoulders shaking.

"But I will not do that. I want only to have a talk with you before they"—he gestured at the thugs—"slit your throat. All these years, Wei Jin-see, we at the Guild thought that you were with us, by the water, throwing out nets to catch fish, but all the time you were sitting in a tree laughing at us. You never traded opium, did you? Never, since the beginning of the Guild."

He shook his head admiringly.

"How clever you were! You let us think that you were saving your English friend's face by pretending not to trade opium, while secretly trading through one of us. We respected your need to save his face and we didn't even try to find out who you were using—though many thought that you were using me because I was the one you asked to help you trick Carradine. You can imagine that none of us was very happy when we realized recently that you weren't using anybody."

His anger began to show. It made his voice rasp, and that brought on a rheumy cough. He clutched his chest, struggling to bring up phlegm. At last he spat into a brass spittoon and wiped his lips on a handkerchief. When he looked up again Jin-see felt his skin crawl: it seemed impossible that such old eyes could hold so much hatred.

But his voice was still jocular.

"What are you going to do to make us happy again, Wei Jin-see?"

Jin-see leaned back in his chair and spoke as casually as he could.

"I've been thinking for some time of resigning from the Guild. In fact, I thought that *you* might succeed me as chairman. You're the oldest member—"

"Not me!" The thin lips quirked. "I've retired. I stay home in comfortable old clothes and grumble at my wives and criticize my sons and complain about my daughters and daughters-in-law, and have a thoroughly fine time. But you, Wei Jin-see? If you resigned from the Guild, what would you do? Assuming you had time to do it in."

"Oh, I have plans."

Again the cruel little chuckle that had always seemed so attractive.

"They concern one Tong Shao-yi? Teacher turned crusader, with money that somebody is giving him."

Jin-see considered the grinning, malicious old face. It was pointless to deny it.

"You've found out too about Tong Shao-yi? You've been busy, Ching si-sang. Yes, I'm giving him money. He's excellently qualified to lead the crusade against opium. You realize, of course, that the opium bonanza can't go on forever."

"Why not?" The old voice had sharpened. "It is guaranteed in the treaties."

"The *Unequal* Treaties. And the guarantee is to the *British*, that they may legally import opium into China. Nobody has guaranteed that Chinese farmers may produce opium. When the British guarantee is abrogated, British and Chinese opium alike will be abolished in China. That is why I am financing Tong Shao-yi. And more. I said I had plans. Tong Shao-yi believes it is high time for ways to be developed to help smokers to stop smoking. Medicine that might make withdrawal less painful. Hospitals for those who are suffering withdrawal. The idea is not new. Many years ago High Commissioner Lin Tse-hsu, who was appointed by the Emperor to stop opium smuggling along our southern coast, had the same idea, and my adopted father helped him. As soon as I resign from the Guild—and that was ten minutes ago—I will help Tong Shao-yi."

The old man's head was nodding slowly like that of a child's puppet. His voice, under the stress of his ballooning anger, was almost a hiss.

162

"I will tell you something, Wei Jin-see. Your plans are stupid. *You* are stupid. Opium is part of the life of this country. Millions smoke it and other millions earn their living by it. You cannot deprive all these millions of their pleasure and their livelihood. All these years we spent building up the Guild for our sons and our grandsons. Do you think we will let you and some unimportant teacher interfere with their inheritance?"

The old head was cocked to one side, trembling.

"And there is another reason why you are stupid, Wei Jin-see. I helped you trick Carradine. I thought that your plan for tricking Carradine was very clever, and I was glad to help you. For your sake, I let Carradine call me 'old Ching' and 'old rascal' and 'swindler.' I thought that made a bond between you and me. But you didn't think so. My help meant nothing to you. You fooled me like all the rest. You made me lose face like all the rest, letting us think you were using one of us to trade your opium while all the time you were laughing at us—at me as well as at the rest."

Jin-see's sphincters had tightened in a painful spasm. It was worse than he had thought. For the first time it entered his mind that old Ching might really kill him, might really order his thugs to slit his throat. His gullet closed. It was hard to draw breath.

The vicious whisper went on.

"So why should I have feeling for you? I'll treat you as you deserve. Nobody knows you're back. If they'd known, your son or your daughter would have met the ship. Nobody was there, so they won't be looking for you. Not for some time yet. And then they'll be only a little uneasy. By the time they really start looking for you, whatever fish are left in the Whangpoo River will have eaten you down to your bones."

A great, icy tide rushed through Jin-see. Pounding curlicues of froth ate into his spirit as surf eats into sand. His life was ending. His *life*. Sweat popped out on his face and began to drip into the corners of his mouth. The old man saw it and grinned like a death's-head.

The door opened.

The old man turned, frowning, and the two thugs stepped forward alertly.

A servant stood in the doorway, a frightened man who had to lick his lips and swallow before he could speak.

"Sir, a messenger has arrived who says that there's been an explosion in your Yalu Road warehouse. It's on fire."

For the space of five seconds there was a pulsing, bubbling silence. Then another man pushed the servant aside. He was as large as the two thugs and, with his slit eyes and his tight, lipless mouth, as menacing. But his tone was polite:

"Sir, I have another message for you. If I am not seen outside your house *with Wei Jin-see* within two minutes, a man who is now at your gate will start running to your Kashing Road warehouse, where he'll arrive in under ten minutes. He's a very fast runner. There's no way you can stop him. When he arrives at your Kashing Road warehouse, it will explode and catch fire."

Ching si-sang's face was livid. His lips worked frantically around his toothless mouth. Frothy spittle dribbled from its corners. He heaved and panted and finally found breath to scream shrilly at his thugs:

"Do something! What am I paying you for? *Do something!*"

One of the thugs merely sneered and spat on the floor, but the other let out a stream of curses.

"Fornicator of goats! Violator of your mother! We can't make magic! If the life of this turd"—he jerked his thumb at Jin-see—"is worth all your opium, we'll slit his stinking throat and toss his stinking body into the river. But if you want to keep your opium, *let him go.* Either way you'll pay us, you cursed old son of a turtle!"

The messenger had come across the room and was pulling at Jin-see's arm, urging him toward the door. Jin-see's legs were trembling so strongly that he stumbled, and suddenly old Ching si-sang was in front of him, shuffling with astonishing speed to the door, glancing over his shoulder. He looked like a devil-god in a Taoist temple, his face almost black, his eyes white and bulging, the tip of his tongue showing red between his snarling lips. Then he was through the doorway and gone from sight.

"Quick!" the messenger said, and Jin-see's legs suddenly began to function again. They ran together out of the room, out the front door. At the top of the steps that led down into the courtyard, the messenger stopped to wave at someone outside the gate.

"Wei Jin-see!"

The whisper came from above. Jin-see looked up. The devil-god's face was grinning from a window six feet over his head. The devil-god made a flipping movement, and something splashed into Jin-see's face—something like liquid fire that burned with unbelievable pain. He flung up his hands to dash the fire away and the same pain seared his hands. Screaming, he began to run across the courtyard, trying helplessly to flee the savage pain.

He was in a carriage. The skin of his face steamed and bubbled like the surface of boiling water. His hands were on fire. Screams were issuing from his throat of their own volition. Someone was holding him, trying to keep his head still against the jolting of the carriage. Someone else was shouting urgently, trying to make himself heard over the screams: "We couldn't help it, Ah-fet! We couldn't help it!"

Ah-fet.

Alfred Pratt.

He tried to swallow a scream. His voice gurgled through it:

"Pratt?"

Someone bent over him. "Oh, God, Jin-see . . . "

"Macpherson," he gurgled. "English. Doctor."

"Yes," Pratt said immediately.

The pain was subdued, like a wild animal held in restraint. He knew that he was being cared for. He could move. He could hear voices and footsteps. But he couldn't see.

Someone said: "Can you hear me?"

He recognized the gruff voice that had said all those years ago: "She's deformed."

"Yes," he muttered.

The voice said: "Basically, you'll be all right. Able to function. You'll have full use of your hands, though they'll be a little scarred. Face will be scarred quite heavily. Vision of one eye will be reduced, but you'll be able to see out of it. Afraid the other eye is finished."

He said nothing, unable to believe it. He had left the valley in the fullness of manhood, with the ease of being free at last to take a concubine, loving Olan still, loving her more than ever, but able at last to lie with another woman. He had stepped off the ship, eager, vigorous, in command of his life.

It wasn't possible.

"Jin-see?" Pratt's voice. "Can you hear me? Macpherson's a wonderful doctor. He's saved one of your eyes. I can't say his bedside manner's any good, but he has saved your eye. It was vitriol. Ching threw vitriol on you, and then went up to the tower of his house and jumped out."

When Jin-see said nothing:

"Your family's fine. I've got a watch on your compound."

166

When Jin-see didn't answer, he sighed and fell silent.

One day Macpherson said: "Well, we'll see now," and propped him up on the pillows and began to unwind bandages from around his head. It got whiter as he unwound—whiter and lighter.

"Shut your right eye," Macpherson said.

He shut both his eyes and it grew dark again.

Macpherson said: "All right. Open very slowly."

He opened and found that only his right eye was opening.

He saw Pratt, smiling anxiously.

He saw Macpherson, the craggy face hardly changed, frowning anxiously.

He couldn't see both of them at once, though he knew they were standing close together. He had to turn his head from one to the other, and then he could them one at a time, as though each stood at the end of a tunnel.

Macpherson said: "Well, can you see?"

He closed the eye. "In a way."

Pratt said: "The doctor says you're to get out of bed and walk. He says there's nothing wrong with you except your— eye. You're to go home soon, so you're to get out of bed and walk about and get your strength back. Jin-see? Please, Jin-see."

Jin-see heard him only faintly from the distant place in which his spirit was dwelling, a cool place beyond emotion, a place in which it didn't matter that a man in full vigor had been cut down and was diminished.

And then, one day, in his distant place, Jin-see heard his daughter's voice.

"Father? Oh, Father, Father, Father!" No horror, no pity, only joy. "Oh, Father, you're *alive!*"

167

Julie, of the loving heart and the flashing mind.

In his distant place there was no daughter, so his spirit gathered itself for the long climb back to where Julie waited.

When Jin-see had grown a little accustomed to seeing everybody and everything one at a time at the end of a tunnel, Pratt said:

"D'you feel well enough to talk about what happened?"

"Ah-fet," Jin-see said, "if not for you I'd be at the bottom of the Whangpoo River. That's where Ching would have put me. He said the fish would eat me to my bones. I have to thank you for my life."

"Oh." Pratt coughed and mumbled. "Not at all. Let's not mention it. Let me tell you what happened here while you were in Shansi."

Tong Shao-yi had been exultant when Pratt told him that he'd been right about Jin-see and showed him the account opened on his behalf with the funds Jin-see's bank manager had made available. The impact on the activities of the anti-opium societies had immediately flared. The Guild merchants had found their worries escalating. At the same time they were inquiring among themselves and finding out that Jin-see had never traded opium.

"It was a mess!" Pratt was grinning. "They were buzzing like a hive of wasps. It's lucky, I suppose, that they've grown so rich and fat and lazy. They were all threatening this and that, but Ching was the only one who actually did anything. He bribed one of the waiters in a noodle shop Tog Shao-yi patronizes to put poison in his noodles. The man got cold feet at the last moment and didn't do it. When the . . . colleagues I'd hired to guard Tong Shao-yi told me about it, I reckoned that Ching might make a try for you too, maybe your family. I hired more colleagues to double the guard on Tong, to watch your house and family, and to watch the docks for your return. The day you docked in Yangtszepoo they saw you being kidnapped. We'd already made the plan about burning Ching's warehouses."

"It was clever," Jin-see murmured.

"Oh, it wasn't mine! The—er—colleagues planned it. In fact, after Ching threw the vitriol on you, they went ahead and burned his Kashing Road warehouse anyway. You understand, I don't *control* them. We're—well, I suppose colleagues is the best word for it."

He had made his connection with the colleagues during his days in the rice warehouse. He'd made a deal with them: set aside for them one sack of rice out of every hundred, even stored the sacks until it was convenient for them to collect. They could have got a lot more by raiding the warehouse, but Pratt's deal saved them trouble and danger, and they'd thought it sensible of Pratt.

"In those days they were small-scale crooks. Ex-rebels. The gangs were born in the old rebel societies. They got stronger and stronger. Today my colleagues can do almost anything, arrange almost anything. They advise that your return to Shanghai should be made known far and wide, and quickly. Ching took a crack at you because he thought nobody knew you'd come back. Once everybody knows it, nobody'll dare try for you because the police would look very hard for your murderer. A rich family like yours, they'd expect a big reward. If Tong Shao-yi's killed they won't bother much. We've got to take good care of him until we can get him to Peking."

Jin-see told Pratt about the arrangements he'd made in the Shansi valley. Pratt turned red.

"*I've* got a lot to thank *you* for! With what you're going to pay me for handling that crop I'll be able to get out of opium and into curios. Always been interested in those. How glad that's going to make my wife I can't tell you. She *hates* opium. She's pregnant. Our first child."

169

He smiled shyly. An insignificant little man with mousy hair and colorless eyes and a snub nose. A *nice* man.

Jin-see said: "Congratulations! But don't tell your wife about the opium from the valley. No one's to know. Can you imagine if news like that got out what the opium merchants would do to get ahold of that opium? No one's to know anything about it, not where it's grown, not where you store it, not that it exists even."

"Dead secret," Pratt said solemnly.

Jin-see went home one evening with Julie. He would stay in his room for a day or two, letting the news of his scarred face and eyepatch sink down into the household, and then he'd emerge and the life of the household would settle itself around him. Julie had told Great Dragon and Olan that he had been injured seriously. Great Dragon had nodded gravely. Olan had said almost casually: "He went to Shansi," as though that explained everything.

"She won't be shocked when she sees you," Julie said. "And, Father—you mustn't be shocked either. She's . . . stranger every day. She knows things now that she had no way of knowing."

He said nothing. Olan and himself, both of them . . . diminished, diminishing.

But on the evening he returned home, it felt natural to take Julie's hand so that she could help him out of the carriage. The gateman's voice as he greeted him was natural too, full of respect and tinged with pleasure. He could see nothing of the courtyard except the luminescence of the lanterns, but he could feel the faint warmth that the marble exuded, its smoothness underfoot. Marble was not hard like stone. It had a soft and living touch.

Julie said: "Father, Mother was tired tonight so I put her

170

to bed early. Don't disturb her till tomorrow. And don't go to bed yet. Stay with me for a while."

They went into the family room, and there he took her by the shoulders and adjusted his head until her face appeared in the tunnel of his vision—the awry face, flushed and smiling, happy.

Beloved.

She led him to the sofa, gave him tea, sat beside him, put her silky head on his shoulder.

"Now, Father, tell me! When Alfred Pratt and the doctor came to the *hong* to fetch me, the doctor said you'd lost an eye and he'd reported it, but the perpetrator did away with himself so there was nothing the police could do. And Pratt wouldn't tell me anything. Now, *you* tell me!"

He told her, choosing his words carefully, leaving out any mention of the opium from the valley, making it appear that the sole reason for Ching's attack was Tong Shao-yi.

"I'm convinced that Tong Shao-yi is the man to organize the Chinese National Anti-Opium Movement, and I'm going to finance him to the limit. We must get him to Peking as soon as possible. Until then he's still in danger, although Pratt has . . . colleagues who're guarding him."

She drew an audible breath and he knew, even though he couldn't see her, that she had whitened.

"And you, Father? Are you still in danger?"

"No. Anyway, Pratt's colleagues are also keeping an eye on our compound."

"Crooks," she said slowly. "Gang men."

He said: "Julie, you wanted a part of the life-duty. Well, this is it. Not just managing our money, but understanding this and not being afraid of it or disgusted by it."

"Yes," she said gravely.

There was a knock on the door, and she left his side. He

171

heard her cross the room and open the door. There was a moment of silence that suddenly, in his inability to see what was happening, deepened and took on meaning.

Julie said: "Come in, Great Dragon," but he heard no movement.

He raised his voice. "You had no need to knock, Great Dragon. You have the right to enter our family room whenever you wish."

"I didn't know who was here." Great Dragon's voice was cold. "I thought I heard your voice, but I thought it couldn't be—you wouldn't come home without sending for me at once."

He said: "I didn't mean—" and bit his lip. He'd been a fool! It wasn't explanation that was needed now. It was—love?

He rose and made his way to the door, stumbling only once. At the door he fumbled for his son's shoulders and focused on his face, which was stiff with hurt and a touching young dignity. He put his arm around his son.

"Come."

Within the circle of his father's arm, Great Dragon came, at first reluctantly, but after a few steps Jin-see felt his stiffness begin to relax, and in a moment he said, his tone full of concern:

"You can see, Father?"

"I can see as much as I need to," Jin-see said lightly.

They sat on the sofa, all three of them, and Jin-see recounted again what he had told Julie. But where Julie had been distressed, Jin-see sensed a growing excitement in Great Dragon. At last he broke off his narrative and said:

"What is it, son?"

Great Dragon thrust a piece of paper into his hand. He focused on it and saw that it bore rows of exquisitely brushed characters and great, square red chops, but in the dim light he could not read them.

"What is it?" he asked again.

"It's the letter from the Wai-wu Pu!" Great Dragon burst out. "My appointment's been confirmed! And better than I'd hoped! I'm to be Prince Kung's personal assistant! I can take Tong Shao-yi with me to Peking and introduce him directly to Prince Kung!"

When Great Dragon had gone happily away to write his letter of acceptance, Julie put her arm through her father's, and he closed his eye, which was feeling strained, and floated tiredly.

"Once long ago," she murmured dreamily, "I remember I called my brother 'prim.' "

He smiled over her head. "Once long ago I remember you hit your brother and sent him flying across the room."

She giggled. "But seriously, Father, I learned something about Great Dragon today. Did you?"

"I learned that I love my son, and he loves me."

"Yes. . . . I feel ashamed in a way. I hug you and kiss you and embrace you because I love you so much, but he loves you just as much without making any fuss about it. I suppose it's Li si-sang's teaching."

He laughed a little, caressing her cheek by lifting the shoulder on which it rested.

"Father," she said presently "While you were away a letter came from Donald. I opened it. His Committee got an anti-opium motion put before Parliament. It was voted down, 151 to 47, but he was very pleased that as many as 47 members voted for it. And . . . he got married."

Jin-see laughed with pleasure.

"That's fine! He needs a family!"

She said steadily: "He's forty-nine and his wife is twenty-nine. That's my age, Father. He wasn't really too old for me. It was just that when I first knew him, I was only five."

He caressed her hair, not knowing what to say. His heart ached for her, but was glad too. If she'd married Donald, she'd be far away from him now, in England.

After a while she snuggled closer and said gaily:

"Tell me what you did in Shansi."

The image of the girl swept into his mind—the broad-faced, broad-hipped girl who had risen out of the earth into the moonlight and commanded entry under his quilt, and had entered and taken her pleasure of him, and he of her. A common girl who had never heard the call of fairies. An unbreakable girl with whom a man could lie carelessly.

"Father?" Julie lifted her head from his shoulder.

He said: "In Shansi I took a girl to wife, as I have not taken your mother in all the years since your baby sister died. You understand, it's not the same thing. Your mother is the breath of my body and the beat of my heart. But a man needs a wife. In Shansi I thought that I would bring her here to live in our compound. But now—"

"You must bring her!" she said quickly, and then was silent. He felt a warm tear drop on his hand. In dismay, he bent his head to focus on her face. Her eyes were flooded, and tears streamed down her cheeks like tiny waterfalls. She flung her arms around his neck and hid her face from him.

"Father, I'm *not* crying because you found a wife. I'm *glad* of that! I'm crying because Mother already knows it! How can she know such things? But she does! On the morning after the last full moon of summer, she told me that you had lain with a girl under the night sky, in the light of the full moon. And she told me that that same night Great Dragon had finally pillowed Ching-mei. And it must be true, because now Ching-mei is pregnant, complaining all the time because she's sick every morning."

There was awe in her voice, and a kind of mystic fear. He said, "Shhh!" and laid her head back on his shoulder and rocked her in his arms as he had when she was a child.

After a long time she murmured sleepily:

"Did I say that my mother is glad too? Glad that you found a wife? She ordered a little house to be built for her on the other side of the compound, as far as possible from Ching-mei. Ching-mei, of course, is *furious*!"

Chapter XIII

1886

JIN-SEE PACED around Olan's reflecting pool. He preferred to be outdoors because his tunnel of vision was wider and brighter in natural light. Today was icy cold, but it was a perfect early January day, crisp and dry and brilliant with sunshine. He could see the blue of the sky reflected in Olan's pool, and the sunlight was a golden sheet draped around him.

Last night, Pratt's colleagues had conveyed Tong Shao-yi and his family aboard the seagoing junk that Jin-see had hired to take Great Dragon to Peking. The crew of the junk was composed of Pratt's colleagues, some of whom had once been pirates and, Pratt said, retained their sailing as well as their fighting skills.

Great Dragon would board the junk today, without Ching-mei. After long and acrimonious debate, Ching-mei and her father had had their way: she would remain in Shanghai for the birth of her child. All the commotion had obscured the very reason for the commotion itself: the fact of her pregnancy, the fact that she was carrying a child.

A male child? A grandson?

Jin-see paused to focus his gaze on the pristine blue of the water. Yin-kwa had said once that he and Charlie had sat together looking into the depths of Yin-kwa's reflecting pool while Charlie was making the decision to marry lovely Lingling, Jin-see's mother. Had Charlie seen in the water a foreshadow of her son, as Jin-see was seeing now deep in the sheet of blue a foreshadow of his grandson?

"Our son is coming," Olan called.

Stilling the beat of his heart, Jin-see turned toward the gate of the courtyard.

Great Dragon came into the field of his vision, dressed in his new mandarin robes. Long tunic of heavy gray satin, split up the front to reveal a pleated white silk underskirt. Sleeves long enough to hide his hands by several inches. Small white collar folded tightly around his neck. Round black satin hat. Black satin boots with white soles almost two inches thick, made of a hundred layers of white cotton sewn through with ten thousand stitches until they were hard as board.

But it was not the garments that made Great Dragon a mandarin. It was his demeanor. That touch of pomposity that had grated on Jin-see's nerves at his wedding—it suited him now to perfection. That deliberate walk, the long skirts of his robes rustling around his ankles. That judicious expression, calm and self-possessed.

Emotion ballooned in Jin-see's throat. His son was fully a man, highly trained, competent, honorable. And his son's son—please the gods it would be a son!—was growing in his wife's womb. The scene was changing. The life-duty was passing—already! so soon!—from his own hands to his son's. His son had come forth into the brilliant sunlight; he himself was receding into the dusk, his eyes blinded, his years numbered, his tomorrows yesterdays.

Swallowing the painful lump in his throat, Jin-see went to sit on the bench beside Olan to receive the farewell kowtow of their son.

The day the girl from Shansi arrived was cold and blustery, rain falling drearily, clouds pressing down as though they might never again allow the sun to peep. Driven indoors, Jin-see sat with Olan in her enclosed porch. They sat quietly, side by side, not speaking: speech was unnecessary to their communion. The warmth of Olan's presence was warmer to Jin-see than that of the big-bellied stove beside which they sat. Olan had never once commented on his eyepatch, on the scar tissue surrounding it that he could not see but could feel, hard and rough as the surface of a rasp. In her mind he had gone to Shansi and there he had done what he had to do, what was ordained in the primeval stars, and that was sufficient reason for whatever had happened. The thought gave him comfort, for it meant that what had happened was not a random convulsion of the great green turtle. Grandfather Wei had told him once of the great sea turtle that, when her time was come, labored up onto the beach and laid her eggs and, leaving them to whatever might befall, went back into the sea. In Ningpo, clinging to his grandfather, heart thudding, ears ringing with the sharp thunder of exploding shells, he had imagined a great green turtle in the sky, dropping from her womb little round eggs of good and evil to fall on whoever, lucky or unlucky, might happen to be below.

He heard Julie say: "Here is my father," and suddenly the girl from Shansi stood in the tunnel of his vision. She was dressed in new jacket and trousers of blue cotton, with black cotton slippers and an expanse of bright pink stocking between the slippers and the hem of her trousers. Her hair, which that night had cascaded about her, was pulled tightly back in a thick plait. Bright pink rouge had been spread around the eyes that, that night, had seemed to glow wide in the moonlight, but were now small and dull with awe or fear. She was staring at his eyepatch. When she saw that he was looking at her, she went awkwardly to her knees and kow-towed. Julie's hand raised her, and they moved out of his sight. He heard Julie say:

"And this is the Tai-tai, your mistress."

And Olan, in smiling tones: "Get up, my dear. I have known you since the last full moon of summer. I saw you in the moonlight. What is your name?"

And, when the girl didn't answer: "Never mind. To my-self I have called you Girl since the night I saw you, and that is what we'll call you. You're pregnant, are you not?"

Jin-see's heart gave a great leap that resounded so loudly in his ears, he missed any reply the girl might have made, but he heard Olan laugh delightedly.

"I knew it! It is a son! Jin-see, did you hear? We are going to have another son!"

In the evening, he went alone to the little house that Olan had ordered for Girl. Julie told him exactly where it was, and he found his way, following the map of his courtyards that was indelibly fixed in his mind.

The door was not locked, and he let himself in. The girl said nothing but he heard her breathing and adjusted the an-gle of his head until he saw her. She was still in her village finery, sitting on a bedroll on the floor, a large box tied with rope beside her.

He said: "You haven't unpacked."

She said sullenly: "Too much trouble to pack again when you send me away."

"What makes you think I will send you away?"

She shrugged. "They said you were rich, but I never dreamt *how* rich! This place is bigger than our three villages put together. And this house, for me alone—in the village fifteen people would be living in it. Your Tai-tai and your daughter—I didn't know ladies like that existed! And you—in the valley you seemed to be young, but now you're old. And that—" She pointed at the eyepatch, her hand trailing off into a hopeless gesture. "You don't want me anymore. You're going to send me back."

He said: "I will send you back only if the child you are carrying is not mine."

"It's yours, all right!" She grinned with sudden hope. "The village headmen will swear it. They and their fat wives watched me like hawks after you said you might send for me!"

He said nothing, for his throat had constricted. The girl rose and lifted her loose jacket. Her trousers were tied around her waist with pink cord, which bulged over the swell of her stomach.

"See? The harvest ended on the full moon of August. Now it's January. And this"—she patted the bulge—"is not more nor less than five months. Truly, it's yours."

He said: "You will stay here."

She sighed with satisfaction and rearranged her clothes, moving out of his sight.

"Thank you! The headmen said that your Tai-tai might have me beaten, but she was very kind, though strange. How could she have seen me that night in the valley, though it is true that the moon was full? I am afraid of her, but I'll try to serve her as well as I can."

"No one will beat you. And you need serve no one. There are many servants."

"What work shall I do?"

"Care well for yourself while you await the birth of your child. After it is born, you will care for the child. If it's a girl, my daughter will supervise her upbringing. If it's a son, I will see to him myself."

She said wonderingly: "But the child will belong to the Tai-tai! Won't she want to care for it herself?"

"No," he said.

Not Olan. Not Olan.

He rose to leave and heard her cross the room to stand beside him at the door.

"Thank you," she said again. "I know you won't come to share a pillow with me, but still I am glad to be here. I hate villages. And I hope the child is a son."

He put his hand on her body and felt the unmistakable swell of her womb.

A son?

And a grandson?

May it please the great green turtle!

On a fine night in May, another full moon high in a cloudless sky, within an hour of each other, the son and the grandson were born.

When the midwives had washed them and wrapped them in swaddling clothes, they brought them to where Julie waited with her father in the family room. Jin-see took them, one in each arm, and Julie led him to the ancestors' house, lit the taper, helped him lay the infants on the white cushion side by side, and left him.

He knelt on the polished wood beside the cushion and adjusted his gaze until he could see the altar. The soul tablets appeared as a whitish blur. He spoke aloud to them, his throat tight, his voice quivering.

"These are your descendants, my second son and my first grandson. I have named my second son Great Fish so that between him and his elder brother Great Dragon our family will be guarded over the land and the sea. My grandson has no name yet. . . ." He thought of all the names Ching-mei and her father had suggested, names of sages and poets, and said firmly: "His name will be chosen by his father. In the meantime, we will call him Didi, like all small boys. These two babies will grow and become men and in their turn they will make sons to carry our family into the future. They will bring honor and wealth to our name. And, if it is still necessary, they will inherit the life-duty and perform it faithfully. Watch over them, you who have passed to the other world, and guide their spirits."

When he had said these words, he remained with his face raised to the altar, his eye open, and suddenly he saw in his single eye's narrow strip of vision what he had never been able to see with both his eyes.

He saw his father. He saw beyond the twinkling of the sunbeam that had always hidden him from sight. He saw the boat distancing itself from the land and, on the deck, his father. He was red-haired. That was right! Yin-kwa had once said that his hair was bright red. They had called him Red Barbarian. He stood there on the deck, looking back, smiling, waving a hand. Not a wispy memory. Not the flat image of Yin-kwa's story. Not a shadow of Donald. Not a villain. Not a hero. A man. A man of love and honor and human frailty. A man—like himself.

One of the babies stirred and cried a thin cry. Smiling, Jin-see bent forward until he could see them. It was his son who was crying. He turned him over onto his stomach and gently patted his back to ease whatever troubled him.

GREAT DRAGON
JULIE

Yin-kwa = His Wife
1802 -
1872
Canton

Charlie * = Ling-ling
b. 1803
England
d. 1842
Chapoo

Olan _ _ _ _ m. _ _ _ _ Jin-see _ _ _ _ took "Girl"
b. 1835   b. 1832   Concubine
Canton   Macao
d. 1900   d. 1900
Tientsin   Tientsin

Julie   Great Dragon m. Ching-mei   A daughter
b. 1856   b. 1862   died at
d. 1906   d. 1906   birth
Shanghai   Shanghai   1872

Didi   Great Fish
b. 1886   b. 1886
Shanghai   Shanghai

* The Red Barbarian

Chapter XIV

1898

GREAT DRAGON ROSE from the crimson-cushioned seat and paced slowly to the windows of the sumptuous Reception Hall. This new Summer Palace was smaller and contained fewer buildings than the ancient one Lord Elgin had burned, but it was still large enough so that no other buildings could be seen from these windows. Through the gently stirring leaves of some silver birches, he looked out to a placid lake on which, propped up by some understructure that caused it to appear to float, was the Marble Boat. Paid for out of funds allotted to the Naval Board—after all, the Empress had said, it was a boat, was it not? A large, two-decked houseboat of veined white marble, its lower deck having eight arches on each side leading into the cabin, its upper deck actually a small roofed house. She used it for tea parties.

Donald had once recounted that on the day the English and French armies looted the ancient Summer Palace, he had fled the orgy and found a lake on which floated a complete miniature navy, drawn up in battle array, which he had thought must be the plaything of this same Empress, then only lately jumped up from her position as the concubine Yehonala. Did boats have some special fascination for her? Or was the Marble Boat merely a vent for her boredom?

Nine years ago, when the Emperor turned eighteen, she had been obliged to hand over to him the reins of government and retire to this new Summer Palace, built for her. Within a year it was well known that she hated the palace, detested retirement, and loathed the Emperor's zeal for what she considered to be crackpot schemes for reforming China. Visitors to the palace whispered that, these days, she was always in a towering temper. Certainly the Chief Eunuch had seemed a little reluctant to seek her out to announce that Great Dragon had arrived for his audience.

Great Dragon gazed out the window, his austere expression betraying none of his excitement. He had come to remind the Empress of a promise she had made years ago to him and to Tong Shao-yi. Would she remember? Would she hold to her word? Who could tell! The Empress was the Empress.

From behind him, the Chief Eunuch said in his soft, rotund voice:

"Tzu Hsi will see you."

The old name! It was almost forgotten now. Everybody called the Empress Lao Fo-yeh, the Old Buddha. Not derisively. With great respect. To the mass of the people she represented stability. Who cared that she had exercised imperial power for nearly forty years without the least right to it? She had governed well. She was clever and tough and durable. She had outlasted two Emperors—and perhaps would outlast a third, especially if he went on talking so earnestly with reformers. It would be fascinating to know the Chief Eu-

184

nuch's estimate of the young Emperor's chances!

"I will take you to her now," the Chief Eunuch murmured.

Great Dragon bowed. "Thank you."

They paced side by side along zigzag pathways that led through lawns and woods and massed plantations of flowering bushes. The Chief Eunuch was the taller of the two, a big man with a large, heavy face, the eyes so widely spaced that they approached deformity. He wore a brimmed hat and a flamboyant multicolored robe with sleeves so long that the cuffs almost brushed his ankles. By contrast, Great Dragon in his sober mandarin robes made an elegant figure. Conscious of it, he put his feet down precisely, taking small steps, forcing the Chief Eunuch to slow his pace. The notorious old scoundrel was the Empress's chief ally, and that made him one of the most powerful shadow-figures in the land, all the more powerful, perhaps, because their alliance was one of convenience. No affection was involved that might drag on either. He got a cut out of everything that took place at the Summer Palace, so he encouraged and facilitated her extravagances. How much had he made out of the Marble Boat? Out of the beautiful landscaping? Out of the Pearl Palace and the Jade Palace? And out of whatever was being built over there.

"What is that?"

Great Dragon pointed delicately with his folded fan at a high blank wall that workmen were erecting in the midst of a grove of trees.

"A wall of a small new palace."

The soft, bland voice went ill with the ugly, foxy face from which it issued.

"An outer wall?"

"Yes."

"Completely blank? No doors? No windows?"

"I believe there will be some doors and windows. Come this way, please. Tzu Hsi is in the Jade Palace."

They made a sharp turn to the left, leaving the half-built wall behind them. In front, through the trees, Great Dragon glimpsed the bright green tiles of the Jade Palace. A spurt of excitement caused him to draw a deep breath.

She was sitting in a splendid room on a carved blackwood armchair much too large for her small figure. She sat in a corner of it, leaning against one of the arms. From under her rich robe protruded gold-embroidered slippers mounted on tall gilded platforms that enabled her feet to touch the floor. Jewels dangled from her ears, flashed from her fingers, winked from her neck. Her face was thin and long, the eyes deepset, the mouth wide. There were lines and wrinkles—she was in her sixty-third year—but even in youth she could never have been a raving beauty. What was her secret? The secret that had brought her to the dragon throne and kept her on it for the better part of half a century?

Great Dragon prepared to lay himself down on the floor for the customary three prostrate kowtows, but she said sharply:

"No! I am no longer the ruler. And anyway it's all nonsense, all those grand fancies that made the kowtow so important. Do you know that a hundred years ago the English king sent us an ambassador to work out trade agreements, and the Chia Ching Emperor refused to see him because he wouldn't kowtow? How different everything would have been if he had seen him! The British wouldn't have made war on us. There would be no Unequal Treaties."

She glared at Great Dragon as though it were all his fault and gestured to a stool beside her armchair.

"Sit here. Yes, the age of kowtows is passing. Those silly young men think I don't know how to move with the times.

It's *they* who don't know! Trying to race *before* the times, trying to drag the times along like a mule who wants to remain where it is. Especially that young man the Emperor's so fond of—that heretical wild weasel who said, 'We cannot preserve the realm of the ancestors; what is the use of their institutions?' " She glowered at Great Dragon. "I will tell you something, Wei Ta-lung. You must never try to pull down an institution until you have something to put in its place."

She turned her scowling gaze to the window. When he followed her eyes, Great Dragon saw that she was staring at the strange wall being built in the middle of the grove of trees. It was in plain view from her window.

She went on:

"And while the Emperor flirts with young men such as that weasel, they ignore what the foreigners are doing who every day encroach more upon our country, enticing us with nothingnesses like loans and railways and mines. Oh yes, these things are very fine, but they are for *their* benefit, not ours. The foreigners! The Russians moving in a little here, a little there, at last getting their ice-free naval base in our port of Lushunkow. The British in Hong Kong and Kowloon and now in Weihaiwei, where they can watch the Russians. The French in Kwang-chowan. The Germans in Kiaochow. The Japanese, whom we used to call the Dwarf Pirates, worst of all, invading Manchuria, taking Korea and our best islands—the Ryukus, Formosa—forcing us to pay indemnities. All of them, the cursed foreigners, playing chess against each other, using pieces of China as their pawns."

She was still staring at the wall. Her voice had grown quiet, but it was all the more angry for that. Anger stood like an aura around her. Great Dragon sat on the stool beside the platforms of her slippers, feeling the power of her, the will of her.

187

The Chief Eunuch rose and poured tea for her from a silver teapot. She sipped at it and after a while turned to Great Dragon.

"And why did you request audience, Wei Ta-lung?"

He lifted his eyes to hers. The change in her was startling. She had completely dismissed her angry preoccupation. He had her entire attention. Was that her secret? This remarkable ability to regroup in full force almost instantaneously?

But not even the senior mandarin of the Wai-wu Pu dare stare for long into the face of Majesty. He lowered his eyes and drew a deep breath.

"Majesty, do you remember some years ago I told you that the British Parliament had passed a resolution that it is morally indefensible to raise revenue through opium?"

"I remember," she said promptly. "But what was the use of that? They went right on doing it."

"Not quite," he said softly. "Three years ago they sent a Royal Commission to India to investigate the situation of opium. That Commission has now returned to London. Its report is soon to be made public."

Her gaze became derisive.

"And you and Tong Shao-yi think the report will say, 'Oh, certainly, we must at once stop producing opium?' "

His throat tightened. He and Tong Shao-yi had indeed discussed the possibility that the report would find some way of backing out of that "morally indefensible" resolution.

He shrugged, and she cocked her head at him.

"You are more trusting than I!" Then: "Wei Ta-lung, aren't you the one with some English blood?"

He bowed. "One of my grandfathers was English."

"You don't show it. Do your sons?"

The image of Didi rose in his mind. Twelve years old and still called by the pet name because he and Ching-mei had never been able to agree on a formal one. But so heart-stirringly wonderful. Wide-eyed, solemn, shy, modest. And beautiful—all of Olan's beauty turned masculine and concentrated in him.

"I have but one son," he said, "and he is the image of his Chinese grandmother."

She nodded approval. "And you love him very much. But isn't there some other English mixed up in this?"

"Perhaps you are thinking of my father's old friend Donald Mathes. He lived in China for many years and is now back in England, Chairman of the Representative Board of the British Anti-Opium Societies. He and Tong Shao-yi have worked closely together from the beginning."

"I remember now. And he too is confident that this Commission's report will be satisfactory?"

"He is—very hopeful. The English societies have worked very hard for this. The first anti-opium resolution was put before Parliament twenty-eight years ago, and many after that, all voted down until the 'morally indefensible' resolution was at last passed. This Royal Commission is therefore a source of great satisfaction to the English societies, and to my father's friend."

"And to your father?"

"To him too, of course. He had an accident some years ago in which he was almost blinded. Since then he has not been able to do much, but he has financed studies to find ways of easing the sufferings of smokers who are trying to stop smoking."

"They have found ways?"

"Perhaps. The latest is something called the 'red pill.' A mixture of morphia and caffeine. It does stop a smoker's craving for his pipe, but then, my father writes, he becomes equally dependent on the pill. The cure may be worse than the disease, my father writes. It appears that morphia is the element of opium that causes the deadly addiction. Tong Shao-

189

yi believes that there can be no *cure* for opium smoking. There can only be an absolute *stop* of opium."

"Well," she said softly, her eyes seeking his. "I have not forgotten. The moment the British signify that they are prepared to abrogate the opium clauses in the Unequal Treaties, in that same moment I will issue an edict forbidding the smoking and traffic of opium throughout all of China."

He knelt and bowed. "Thank you, Majesty." The words came from his mouth in a little bubble of emotion, and she smiled sardonically:

"Wait for the Commission's report before you thank me. When you have the report, come back and tell me what it says."

It was only when he was walking away from the Jade Palace that the thought occurred to him. He had come to seek her confirmation that at the appropriate time she would see to it that the Emperor issued the edict. But she had said: "*I* will issue the edict."

He was once again passing the doorless, windowless wall.

A small new palace, the Chief Eunuch had said.

For whom?

Behind his impassive facade, Great Dragon smiled to himself. It was always the same. The first time an Englishman heard him speak in the accents Miss Crachett had so thoroughly inculcated, the Englishman goggled. This time it was the new Fourth Secretary of the British Legation, a very young man whose mouth dropped open.

"I say . . . I say . . . your accent's absolutely top drawer," he stammered, then recollected himself, his face reddening.

"You have something for me?" Great Dragon murmured.

"Yes, er, that report, you know." He lifted an attaché case and flusteredly let it thump down on Great Dragon's desk: it was remarkably heavy. "The Minister instructed that it be brought to you at once even though it hasn't been translated yet—but of course that won't trouble *you*."

He opened the case and with both hands lifted out a volume several inches thick that he plumped down before Great Dragon.

"As you see, it's extremely long. Two thousand five hundred pages. But there's a summary at the end."

Great Dragon stared down at it. The Royal Commission on Opium must have worked very hard to produce such an enormous report. It must contain a wealth of detail. Why was his heart turning cold?

He lifted a hand to the volume, then reached instead to ring the bell on his desk. He wanted no witness to his reading of the Royal Commission's summary. An office boy appeared, and Great Dragon bowed to the Fourth Secretary.

"He will show you out. Tell your Minister, please, that I will get in touch with him in due course."

When the Fourth Secretary had gone, Great Dragon sat motionless, staring down at the report, hands on either side of it, not touching it. His expression, as always, was impassive, but his heart thudded heavily as he stared at the series of pictures that interposed themselves between his eyes and the book. The Peking Years, they might be entitled. The twelve years since, heart sinking into his new black-and-white mandarin boots, he had stepped into this massive building and into the small, dark room on the ground floor assigned to Prince Kung's personal assistant. Was his post as lowly as his office indicated? Were all his years of study to be wasted on a fetch-and-carry job? A job in which he could do nothing for the life-duty, not even, perhaps, the primary task of introducing Tong Shao-yi to Prince Kung?

But those first days of trepidation had not lasted long. He had soon seen that his post was not lowly—it only seemed so because of the disorder into which Prince Kung had let the Wai-wu Pu fall. There were strings that he could pull, and he had pulled them, quickly beginning to inject system and efficiency into the Wai-wu Pu. Within three years he had moved from the small ground-floor office to this great corner room on the fourth floor, overlooking the roofs of the foreign legations to the south and, to the west, the walls of the Imperial City. From this office he now controlled the Wai-wu Pu, Prince Kung his boss in name only. His star had waxed fast in the Empress's firmament because she felt that somehow, by putting order into the Board of Foreign Affairs, and by knowing the foreigners' language so thoroughly, he was enabling her to control or manipulate the foreigners. Prince Kung's star had waned because, however cautiously and with whatever circumlocutions, he was one of those touting internal reform through imitation of the foreigners, whereas the Empress's idea of reform was simply to preserve the dynasty from further deterioration. Everybody talked of reform, and everybody's idea of reform was different. Everybody manipulated everybody else, or tried to, and was in turn manipulated. The Chinese government operated in chaos—nonsensical, crazy, stupid, venal, greedy, noble, idealistic, altogether preposterous.

In the midst of the chaos, Tong Shao-yi, with utter single-mindedness, had snatched and kept the initiative in anti-opium activities. Now there existed a national anti-opium organization spread throughout China, strong and ready to match the English societies in the final move against opium.

And here, before him on the desk, lay the report that might constitute the final thrust, the final blow that would force Parliament to abrogate the opium clauses of the Unequal Treaties.

But his heart was cold.

With a jerky movement he flipped the thick volume open,

192

riffled quickly through the pages, found those entitled "Summary of Findings," ran his eye down the list of items.

- The harmful effects of opium had been much exaggerated, they being no worse than those of alcohol taken in excess;
- The State monopoly on opium in India was tantamount to a strict limitation on production;
- India could not afford the loss of revenue which would result from the total prohibition of opium production;
- Indian opium was the best in the world; if it should be suppressed inferior Chinese opium would, of course, be resorted to.

Once again Great Dragon sat in a Peking cart, rumbling along the road that led to the Summer Palace. It was late September, the best season in Peking, the humid heat of summer gone, the sandy dust from the Gobi Desert no longer swirling, the air clear and chilly-warm in the sunlight. It was at a time like this, Great Dragon thought drearily, that the Summer Palace had been looted and burned, sending up such a pall of smoke that, as Donald had once recounted, it still obscured the sky on the day the Unequal Treaties were signed and opium was made legal. Thirty-eight years ago, in a sweet Peking autumn.

And legal still it was. Tong Shao-yi had taken the news of the Commission's findings at first in bitter silence, later with a grimace and a shrug. "Never mind. It will come eventually." But Great Dragon was still furiously angry, thinking of his father, sixty-six years old, almost entirely blind now, able to do little more than sit with Olan in her courtyard waiting for the moment when the life-duty would be accomplished.

As his cart approached the gates of the Summer Palace, Great Dragon sighed and straightened. He need not stay long.

He need only tell the Empress that the time for issuing the edict was not yet. He remembered her derisive glance. Would she jeer?

The gates of the palace were wide open and unguarded. The gatemen could be seen within the gatehouse, with a group of eunuchs, all talking excitedly.

There was no need to delay matters by trying to attract the gatemen's attention. Great Dragon walked quietly through the nearest gate and started down the pathway that led to the Reception Hall. There would be servants about whom he could send to find the Chief Eunuch.

But there was no one. The pathways were untrodden. The hills and dales and woods of silver birch were empty except for deer peacefully grazing and nuzzling each other.

The Reception Hall was locked.

It would be wiser to leave.

But that meant he would have to come again another day, all the way from the city, to report to the Empress, as she had commanded.

He would try once more to find the Chief Eunuch.

Turning, he took the zigzag path toward the Jade Palace.

As he approached the little grove in which the strange wall had been a-building during his last visit, he saw that the new palace had been completed. Whether it had doors and windows, or how many, could not be seen, only a sapphire-tiled roof above a high courtyard wall. The gate of the courtyard must be on the other side of the palace, where a few people stood among the trees. Not eunuchs. Soldiers? Startled, Great Dragon peered and caught glimpses of bright uniforms. Guards of the Imperial Palace in Peking!

He stood still. After a time, a pain beneath his ribs told him that he was holding his breath. As perhaps the soldiers were too—their figures seemed as tense and rigid as he himself felt. They were waiting. The riffle of breeze-blown leaves, the thud of a deer's hooves, the flaunt of its white-bobbed tail, seemed shockingly inappropriate. There should be silence and a cessation of movement. They were waiting, he and the soldiers.

It came, what they were waiting for: a woman's cry, despairing, heart-wrenching, very loud at first, quickly fading into a distant splash of water.

Abruptly, the figures of the guards relaxed. A moment later, they stepped back, giving way to another figure that came among them swiftly, walking away from the new palace—a tall figure, with what appeared to be grotesquely long arms, in a gown as brightly colored as their uniforms.

The Chief Eunuch.

Great Dragon composed himself, stiffened his knees, began walking slowly toward the Jade Palace. When he could hear the rustle of the Chief Eunuch's robe behind him, he turned, bowed, and waited. The Chief Eunuch came up to him and stopped. They faced each other in sunlight dappled by shifting leaves.

From the Chief Eunuch came a kind of emanation, an excitement.

Great Dragon said: "I have an audience with the Empress this morning, but I could find no one and the gates were open."

"The Empress is not here," the Chief Eunuch said. "She is in Peking, at the Imperial Palace."

A gleam that he could not extinguish shone suddenly from his wide-spaced eyes. Great Dragon felt the heavy thud of his heart. Again, the world seemed to stand still, waiting.

"And the Emperor is here in the Summer Palace," the Chief Eunuch said softly, on a long, panting breath. "In the new palace, over there. You remarked, you remember, about the doors and windows. There *are* windows, and a door. With locks and bars."

He turned, unable to stand still, and began to pace toward

the Jade Palace, extending an arm to draw Great Dragon with him.

"It is quite a nice little palace. Wtih a small courtyard, and a well. Quarters for concubines. Ten concubines. But—a pity!—no favorite. Emperors always have favorites. Most of their concubines they have two or three times a year. Some they never even see. But their favorites! You know, of course, that Tzu Hsi was a favorite. It used to be the custom, you know, for the concubines' names to be inscribed on little tablets that were placed on a table outside the Emperor's bedroom door. When he retired, he turned down the tablet of the one he wanted for the night. It was the Chief Eunuch's duty to fetch that concubine, carry her to the Emperor's room, and insert her under the quilt at the foot of the bed."

He stopped again and turned to face Great Dragon, glowing, twitching, inviting him to speak. Reluctantly, Great Dragon said:

"And this Emperor's favorite?"

The ugly eyes danced. The thick lips stretched in a fearful smile.

"Oh, Tzu Hsi ordered something else for her. She ordered me to offer her a choice. A rope—a silken one, of course, she was a royal concubine—or the well. She chose the well."

The eyes danced, staring into Great Dragon's. The lips smiled. Great Dragon turned away, his mouth dry.

"The Emperor had no objection?"

"I don't know," the panting voice said. "When I offered her the choice, the girl would not choose. We were in the courtyard. They had just taken the Emperor into the palace. The girl stared at the door with fierce eyes as though she could draw him back with her eyes alone. He did come back, not through a door but to a window. I saw her look up at the window. I did not follow her gaze, but whatever she saw, it must have been hopeless, for she cried out and jumped into the well."

"I see." It took the discipline of many years to make Great Dragon turn back pleasantly to the Chief Eunuch's face, flushed red with excitement. "Then I will tell my secretary to make a new appointment for audience with the Empress at the Imperial Palace. I wish you good morning."

He bowed and walked away. The voice called after him:

"It'll be all over Peking tomorrow! You're the first to hear the *rumor*."

He walked on, pretending not to hear.

The sapphire-blue roof gleamed in the distance. The leaves of the lovely trees stirred. The deer fed and nuzzled each other. The gates were still open and unguarded, the gatemen inside the gatehouse talking with the excited eunuchs. He slipped out, unseen.

"Back to the city?" asked the driver of the Peking cart.

"Back to the city," he said, his mouth still dry.

The driver clucked his pony into a lazy trot. The sun was lowering, and a chilly breeze was blowing up. The lovely day was coming to an end.

The lovely day on which a girl had died in the bottom of a well.

The Old Buddha was taking no chances. She, of all people, must know what a favorite concubine could do.

That was her secret, he thought. Not that she could regroup instantaneously, that she was willful, determined—all the things that were said about her. Not even that she was utterly ruthless—but that people couldn't believe she was. *Rumor*, the Chief Eunuch had said, and that was what the people would believe: it was all a rumor.

Chapter XV

1900

GREAT DRAGON PICKED UP a dumpling between his chopsticks and dropped it into his mouth. It was tasty. The new cook was good. Pray the gods he would last awhile! The average tenure of cooks in this household was three to four months before Ching-mei fired them or they stormed off, unable to stand her any longer.

At the thought of his wife, Great Dragon sighed, as always torn between exasperation and a kind of tired sympathy. Ching-mei had never been able to get rid of her father. After fifteen years of marriage, it seemed that Li si-sang still stood at her shoulder with his disapproving, thin-lipped look, pointing out that her husband, though a mandarin, could never overcome his lowly merchant origins. She must never be pleased by anything her husband provided, for that would be demeaning. She must disdain everything.

The only time she seemed able to escape her father was at

night, with the lamps blown out, the curtains drawn, deep darkness in the bedroom, when she would suddenly turn to her husband with a wild abandon that lasted sometimes for hours. The next day her air of disdain would be back in place, hard as concrete, and she never referred to those violent nights by the slightest word or look.

It had been thus all their married life: feast or famine, ever since that first night, weeks after their wedding. The wedding night itself had passed in exhausted sleep. Afterward, he'd been hesitant and uncertain. Jin-see's lecture had given him a clinical idea of what should be done, but in face of her disdain it had all seemed quite impossibly crude. Until the night of her first attack on him. He smiled, remembering. It really had been an attack. She'd known exactly how to go about it. Later he'd realized that she had learned from the gossip of the idle mandarin wives in whose company she'd been brought up. But at the time he'd been first astonished, then almost frightened by her ferocity, and finally delighted.

Now she entered the dining room and seated herself at the table, nervously clattering the bowls and cups.

"How does it taste?"

She dipped her chopsticks and nibbled.

"Not bad, but I'll have to tell him—"

Great Dragon interrupted

"*I* have to tell *you* something, so please postpone your argument with the cook."

She frowned pettishly. "What is it?"

"My father is coming to Peking."

"Your *father*! He hasn't visited us in fourteen years, why should he come now, of all times, with all this trouble about the Boxers!"

"He's coming with his old friend Donald Mathes."

"*What for?*"

"Donald wants to talk to Tong Shao-yi. They're still stuck

199

with that ridiculous Royal Commission report. My father is taking advantage of Donald's visit to come with him. My mother is coming too."

Ching-mei screeched.

"That madwoman! I thought your father said she'd never leave her courtyard again!"

"That was thirty years ago. He's bringing her because she begged so hard—the first time she ever asked to be let out of her courtyard. She wants to try and find her magician."

"You mean that wild man who was supposed to show her visions of the child she killed?"

Great Dragon compressed his lips.

"You know very well who she called her magician. She hasn't seen him for years, but she's kept on sending him money to an address here in Peking."

"That man's a Boxer! D'you mean your father's been giving your mother money to send to the *Boxers*? Your father's supporting the *Boxers*, on top of Tong Shao-yi and all those hospitals and the red pills and I don't know what else!"

"He supports us too," Great Dragon said coldly. "In fine style."

"When are they coming?"

"In a few weeks."

"I hope you don't expect them to stay with us! My nerves won't stand it! Not with that madwoman, your mother!"

She slammed out of the room before he could answer, and a moment later her voice was raised in the kitchen.

Didi slipped into the room and grinned at his father. Great Dragon silently grinned back.

"I'll get breakfast at school," Didi said, low-voiced, and went quickly into the hall. A moment later the front door closed softly behind him. By craning his neck, Great Dragon could see him hurrying down the garden path. Didi of the clear, grave look, the slow, sweet smile. Still shy and retiring, a little slow perhaps, but tenacious and persistent. The opposite, apparently, of his birthmate, Great Fish. Julie wrote that Fish was quick-witted, a "charmer." "I'm afraid I spoil him, but it's hard to resist him. Father spoils him too." Well, Jin-see would soon have a chance to spoil Didi, but Didi wouldn't spoil easily. Great Dragon's heart swelled with love, and with fear. It wasn't safe to have only one son, only one child. And he and Ching-mei, fierce as were their encounters, seemed incapable of another. He could, of course, take a concubine.

A servant came to say that the sedan chair-bearers were waiting, and Great Dragon went out to his chair, a large and sumptuous one with four bearers, a perquisite of his position in the Wai-wu Pu, which outwardly he took for granted, but inwardly was very thankful for. The narrow lanes of Peking, the *hutungs*, were choked with swirling dust in summer and, in winter, ankle-deep in churned-up mud in which pedestrians slipped and slithered. In the solidly built sedan chair, no matter the season or the weather, he was carried clean and unspotted between his home in the Chinese City and the Wai-wu Pu in the Tartar City, his bearers expertly avoiding the hurrying pedestrians, the heavily laden porters, the vendors crying their wares, the children playing their noisy games, the carts and wheelbarrows squeaking and lumbering. The hubbub was so familiar that he no longer heard it.

Ching-mei was right about one thing: it was not the time for visitors to come to Peking. The Righteous and Harmonious Boxers, as Donald had termed them, were becoming ever bolder, terrorizing the countryside, especially molesting foreign missionaries and killing their Chinese converts. The situation was made worse by the bands of wandering refugees that famine conditions in many districts were creating.

"At least don't bring Mother," he had written his father, but Jin-see hadn't even answered that. Donald had already sailed from Southampton. As soon as he arrived in Shanghai, he and Jin-see and Olan would travel to Tientsin on the new China Merchants Steamship line. From there they would come to Peking on the railway of the Kailan Mining Administration. Donald would stay at the British Legation, and Jin-see and Olan would of course stay in their son's home. Even Ching-mei would have to give in on that.

But none of that was Great Dragon's real worry. It was the life-duty. Didi did not even know of its existence. He had never mentioned it to Didi, thinking of the burden he himself had carried since he was six years old; it was fortunate he liked being a mandarin, for Jin-see had left him no choice. Let Didi enjoy his childhood, he had thought. Let him have a choice of career. Perhaps, when he grew up, the life-duty would be accomplished. If not, there was plenty of time to tell him about it later. But would Jin-see agree? Didi was fourteen now. Would Jin-see insist that he be formally told of the life-duty when he reached fifteen?

At the great door of the Wai-wu Pu, Great Dragon absently stepped out of the sedan chair and into the square, thick-walled building with its deep-embrasured windows. People stood aside, bowing respectfully, as he passed along the corridors and up the broad flights of stairs. In his large fourth-floor corner office, his secretary was waiting, the elderly mandarin whom he called "Uncle" when they were alone. It was Uncle who, during those first anxious days, had chuckled encouragingly, had nodded and twinkled and shown him what strings to pull and how to pull them. It was Uncle who was now Personal Assistant to the Personal Assistant, and would be forever, as far as Great Dragon was concerned, until he went to his ancestors or chose to retire, and the latter was unlikely, for he thoroughly enjoyed the doings at the Wai-wu Pu, poked fun at the pompous solemnities, made little jokes and plays on words at which he laughed silently, shoulders shaking. He would be young forever, Great Dragon thought, no matter how old he got.

Now, as Great Dragon entered his office, Uncle waved a yellow banner wrapped around an ivory stick.

"The Old Buddha has issued an instruction to the provincial officers, of which you are to inform the foreign legations."

Great Dragon smiled. When he smiled, something of his mother and something of Jin-see sparkled into being, but he smiled only rarely, usually only when he was alone with Didi or Uncle.

"Let me guess. It's about the Boxers."

Uncle laughed and spread the yellow banner on the desk.

In the past few months, the eleven foreign ministers resident in Peking had presented numerous notes to the Wai-wu Pu demanding that the strange, wild sect of militants who were persecuting foreign missionaries be suppressed. The Empress had issued one set of instructions, with which the foreigners had not been at all satisfied. The instructions had declared that there were good and bad elements among the Boxers; provincial officers, while suppressing the bad elements, must carefully discriminate in order not to harm the good. In the face of such equivocation, no provincial officer had taken any action at all against any Boxer.

Now, Great Dragon scanned the new instructions. More of the same: provincial officers should exercise perception in dealing with the Boxers, for they had worthy ends of keeping mutual watch and giving mutual help.

Great Dragon barked a short laugh.

"What d'you think that means, Uncle?"

"I think that for a document that's supposed to discourage the Boxers, it's remarkably encouraging!"

"Would you say it sounds as though the Old Buddha is

inclined to believe that nonsense about the Boxers being impervious to foreign bullets?"

"I'd say that she's at least prepared to take a chance on it. Just think! After forty years of enforcing foreign privileges under the treaties, the Boxers might really get rid of the foreigners for her!"

Great Dragon laughed.

But that night he had his chair-bearers carry him through the Legation Quarter on the way home.

The Legation Quarter covered three-quarters of a square mile in the southwest corner of the Tartar City, abutting the Gate of Heavenly Peace, which gave access to the Imperial City and the Imperial Palace. The eleven foreign legations were grouped loosely, the largest, the British, nearest to the Gate. South of it was the Russian, and south of that, across Legation Street, was the American. A few hundred yards to the west, the Japanese and French. The other, smaller legations were scattered farther away.

Four hundred and seventy-five diplomats and their dependents lived in the Quarter, plus several dozen foreign soldiers, symbolic guards of the ministers. The chief duty of the diplomats was to see to it that their treaty rights were exacted in full. Since the Unequal Treaties and their numerous protocols and amendments and conventions covered practically every aspect of relations between China and the foreign countries, the relationships were ruled by treaty, not by international law. The diplomats and their counterparts in the Wai-wu Pu were experts, not in international law, but in every word and phrase and nuance of the treaties.

When not engaged in enforcing the treaties, the foreigners led a gracious life. They dined in state at each other's legations, served by white-gloved "boys," with flowers floating in the finger bowls. They played out their intrigues and had their clandestine love affairs. They provided employment for hundreds of servants, for the suppliers of their mountains of food, the tailors who made their extensive wardrobes, the shoemakers, the haberdashers, the caterers, the wine merchants, the bakers and pastry-makers, the endless string of people whose service was found essential to the elegance of the Quarter.

Now, as the lights of the legations twinkled in the gathering darkness, Great Dragon peered out through a slit in the curtains of his sedan chair. Would the Old Buddha really go so far as to allow the Boxers to attack the foreigners? The legation guards were show figures, in magnificent uniforms, standing at attention outside the legations with shouldered arms, or marching back and forth with firmly stamping boots. They'd be of little use against those wild men, the Boxers. The ministers would certainly expect the Wai-wu Pu to provide imperial troops to protect the legations. Would the Wai-wu Pu be able to do so? Who, in the final analysis, commanded the imperial troops?

The Old Buddha.

The day after the foreigners were informed of the Empress's new instruction regarding the Boxers, Great Dragon entered his office to find the anteroom crowded with chit-book coolies. The chit-book was a notebook in which the sender of a letter entered the addressee's name and the date. The chit-book coolie delivered the letter and obtained the signature of the addressee in the chit-book as proof that the letter had been delivered and received.

Normally, Uncle signed chit-books on Great Dragon's behalf, but today it appeared that all the chit-book coolies had been instructed to get Great Dragon's personal signature in their chit-books. The room was buzzing with their chatter, and as Great Dragon entered, they crowded forward expectantly.

Great Dragon looked around coldly and turned to Uncle.

"They can leave the letters with you as usual, or they can take them back. They're not going to make me into another kind of chit-book coolie, signing chit-books."

When Uncle later entered the office, he was chuckling.

"Every foreign minister demands that you personally arrange to have his person, his family, his dependents, his legation, his residence, his property, and all his nationals resident in China, and all their homes and properties and dependents, protected against the Boxers."

Great Dragon laughed.

But all the same he went to the Palace to sniff the air. It didn't smell good. The Chief Eunuch received him.

"The Empress is in seclusion."

"I am sorry to hear it. Her health is poor?"

"Not at all. It is her spirit that is in decline."

"I should have thought that it was her spirit that was never poor."

"I am afraid it is your fault."

"*My* fault?"

"A few days ago you sent over for her consideration a request for audience from Italian emissaries who also want a piece of China."

"They want to lease—"

"They want a piece of China. That's what she said. The English and French, the Russians, Germans, Japanese, are all gobbling up pieces of China, she said, and now the Italians want to nibble too. She was so angry that lightning was flashing from her as from the sky during a summer storm."

They stared at each other. The Chief Eunuch said in his cushiony voice:

"It is not the time to speak to her about troops to guard the foreign legations."

Great Dragon left the Palace with his usual deliberate stride, his heart thumping, his head humming. The dam was bursting.

Back in his office, the young Fourth Secretary of the British Legation was waiting. Great Dragon might refuse to sign chit-books, but he could not refuse to see a Fourth Secretary to receive directly from his hands a letter from his minister. The Fourth Secretary handed it over:

"It's about the security of the Legation Quarter, sir. The ministers had a meeting this morning. It doesn't seem sure that you'll be able to provide troops . . . er, what I mean is it'll probably take you too long—"

"I'd better read the letter," Great Dragon murmured, and the young man stopped his stammering, looking both grateful and admiring. Great Dragon's command of English still clearly impressed him.

The letter bore the day's date: 2nd June 1900. It stated that since the Boxer threat was increasingly serious and the Wai-wu Pu seemed unable to provide guarantees of protection, the foreign diplomats had arranged to bring seventeen naval vessels to Tientsin that would provide a force of twenty-five hundred sailors and soldiers to protect the legations, should the Boxers attack. Within the next two or three days the force would march from Tientsin to Peking along the roadbed of the Kailan Mining Administration's railway. Could the Wai-wu Pu assure free passage of the force along the designated route?

Great Dragon looked up gravely.

"The roadbed is guarded by imperial troops. According to the treaties, they will not oppose the foreign force since its destination is the Legation Quarter."

"Thank you."

The Fourth Secretary bowed and left, looking relieved. Great Dragon wished that he could feel as relieved as the Fourth

Secretary looked. The general commanding the imperial troops along the roadbed woud be instructed to let the foreign force pass unmolested. But if the Boxers attacked it, would the general in turn attack the Boxers, militant rebels with no sanction under any law or treaty? It would be his duty. And if he did, what would the Empress think of it?

Great Dragon looked up to find Uncle's eyes on him, gleaming sympathetically out of the network of laugh wrinkles.

"It's beginning to pinch, eh? Well, this is one of those periods when histroy spurts out of a convulsion of society as lava spurts from a volcano. It's rare and interesting. Watch it and enjoy it, for there's nothing you can do about it."

He seemed to like the idea of being able to do nothing, for he left the room chuckling.

The Chien-men, one of the five gates that pierced the wall between the Tartar and Chinese cities, was one of the places where news posters were put up every morning. There was always a crowd within the walls of the gate, for those who could read would read the posters aloud for the benefit of those who could not. It was usually necessary for chair-bearers to push and shout in order to get through the crowd, but on a morning some days after the Fourth Secretary delivered his minister's letter, Great Dragon's chair-bearers could not get through the gate at all because of the size of the crowd and the surging excitement that caused them not to hear the loudest calls for right of way. The excitement was felt rather than seen or heard. The crowd was hushed, tense, straining to hear what a reader was reading aloud. Great Dragon, immobilized behind the curtains of his chair, strained to hear too.

"Foreign forces have invaded our land."

Great Dragon sat up sharply.

" . . . Imperial troops guarding the railway naïvely let them pass. . . . The fearless Boxers, rushing to the defense of the nation, attacked the invaders. . . . The general commanding the imperial troops compounded his misbehavior by firing on the Boxers, for which the Empress has suitably reprimanded him. . . . The Empress has ordered the Boxers to oppose all invaders. . . . "

Great Dragon sighed heavily as the crowd began to break up in a loud babble of voices, even some cheering. The story that the Boxers were impervious to foreign bullets was just the kind of thing they loved to believe. Few of them were old enough to remember that the last lot of invaders had taken only two hours to caputre the great forts at Taku; had raped and sacked whole towns on their way to the desecration of the Summer Palace, the looting and burning of its buildings, its priceless treasures; and the siege of Peking itself.

In the Wai-wu Pu there was a strange silence. The corridors, without the usual bustle of people, seemed to echo. Upstairs, the corner office was empty. There was a small pile of papers on the desk. Absently, still thinking of the scene at the Chien-men, Great Dragon glanced through them. On the top was a telegram.

He was still staring at the telegram when Uncle came bustling in.

"I've been going around telling everybody to leave, buy as much food as they can, and barricade themselves in their homes. It's too late for anything but to sit this out as safely as possible. Why don't you go home now?"

"I can't," Great Dragon murmured, still staring at the telegram. "I must go to Tientsin."

"*Tientsin?* That's where the Boxers are rushing to! The foreigners are going to send more troops from Tientsin and the

Boxers are rushing there. You can't go to Tientsin!"

Great Dragon looked up from his contemplation of the telegram.

"I must. This is a telegram from the China Merchants Steamship Company. Yesterday they delivered my father and mother and my father's old English friend to the Tien-an-men Hotel in Tientsin. They accept no further responsibility for their safety."

"Oh!" For a moment Uncle stared in consternation. Then, shrugging: "Well, tonight's train to Tientsin will probably run, though it'll probably be the last for a long time. I'll send one of the clerks to the station immediately to buy a ticket, get a seat on the train, and sit in it until you get there this evening." Then, the smile, the chuckles, entirely missing: "Take care."

"What about *me*?" Ching-mei cried furiously. "You go rushing off to Tientsin and leave me with only Didi to defend me against these madmen?"

"There're a dozen servants in the house to defend you, and in any case the Boxers are going to attack the foreigners, not you."

"How are you going?"

"By the train this evening."

"When will you be back?"

"I don't know. If the train stops running, I'll have to bring them back by cart, by the old road."

"You won't bring them here to our house! I told you, my nerves won't stand it!"

"Of course I'll bring them here," he snapped, swinging on his heel and hurrying to the door. She followed him angrily, but when he opened the door and she saw the excited crowd eddying in the *hutung* outside, heard the rumbling roar that crowds make, she let out a small gasp: "Oh . . ."

The sedan chair-bearers had brought the chair into the garden and he went to it quickly. As he was about to step in he heard her call: "Great Dragon—take care." Surprised, he turned to look at her and saw that her face was pale and strained. For the first time since he had known her, she had forgotten to look disdainful—at least in daylight. At night, it was too dark in their bedroom to tell. Smiling at his fancy, he raised his hand to her, and she gave him back a little wave.

Sitting in the chair, the hubbub around him unheard, the anxiety forgotten for the moment, he thought of his wife. Perhaps at last she was rid of her father. Perhaps at last she could become her own person. His person. Their son's person.

The thirty-five-mile train ride from Peking to Tientsin usually took an hour, but tonight, with innumerable stoppages and mysterious waits and pauses, it took almost five hours. When the jam-packed train jerked to a stop in Tientsin station it was after midnight, but it might have been noon, judging from the crowds that lined the platform. Passengers erupted from the train as soon as it stopped, pushing and shoving into the people already on the platform, creating a huge, straining bulge that, it seemed, would crack the walls of the station. But somehow the people bumped and wriggled their way past each other and eventually the platform began to clear. Great Dragon waited another five minutes before leaving the train, and even then was badly jostled.

It took nearly an hour to negotiate the ten-minute walk to the Tien-an-men Hotel. He threaded his way through the crowds, waiting while interminable lines of laden carts inched by, while terrified ponies bucked and reared between the shafts, while people rushed about getting in each other's way, tripping over each other, parents searching for lost children, lost children shrieking their woe, all in a turmoil of anxiety and fear, everybody straining to get himself and his family and his belongings to some safer place, the west running to the east, the east running to the west.

At last Great Dragon stepped into the lobby of the hotel, which was almost as chaotic as the street. With relief, he recognized a man who had worked for the Wai-wu Pu, who saw him and began at once to push his way over.

"Excellency! How can I help you? I am the manager of this hotel."

Great Dragon blew out a big breath.

"Thank heaven! I have come to fetch my parents. I was informed that they are here with an English friend."

"Yes, yes! Wei Jin-see and his wife. The Englishman is no longer here. This morning the British Consul sent someone to fetch him aboard one of the English ships. But your parents are upstairs. Do you wish to stay here too, Excellency? I could—"

"No, no. I wish to take my parents back to Peking as soon as possible. At dawn tomorrow. The train service has stopped. Can you hire me a cart to go back by the old road?"

"Yes, I will send someone immediately. But—excuse me, Excellency—I think you and your parents will have to walk to the cart depot. It would be impossible to bring the cart here. Do you know where the depot is, on Li-hu Street?"

"Thank you. I know."

"Excellency, take care. Your parents are old, and your father's sight . . . You know that the foreigners are preparing an army of soldiers from their warships to march up to Peking? And the Boxers are on their way here, if not already here. Take care. . . ."

Fourteen years had made a very great difference! When he had left Shanghai, he and his father had been of a height. Now his father was a good deal shorter. His thick black hair had turned iron gray. His skin was more yellow than it had been, and was stretched tightly across his cheekbones. The black patch over his eye was concave, as though the eye socket beneath had sunk in. The other eye was no longer round and foreign-shaped and dark. The eyelid drooped, and what could be seen of the eyeball was filmy gray.

His father had turned at the sound of his entrance, a big smile stretching his lips. He was walking forward, hands outstretched, at a tangent. In a moment he would crash into a table. Great Dragon sprang forward.

"Father!"

They met in the middle of the room and embraced, Great Dragon not speaking, for the lump in his throat was choking, but Jin-see chuckling, saying over and over in a husky old man's voice that caused Great Dragon's heart to overflow, "My son! Great Dragon of the Land! My eldest son!"

He clutched his father tightly around the shoulders. He had forgotten! So many things he had remembered: his father's singlemindedness about making him a mandarin; his father's strictness; the brooding look of disappointment he had sometimes caught in his father's eyes; the efforts his father had made to conceal the fact that he loved Julie more. All these things he had remembered, not resentfully, but simply, as facts. But he had forgotten the day his father, newly blinded, came to the door of the family room and put an arm around him and said, "Come." He had forgotten walking into the family room in the circle of his father's arm. He had forgotten—and now, holding his father, he remembered, with an exquisite rush of love.

Then his mother was there, clinging to him, his beautiful child-mother. Ching-mei called her mad, and perhaps she was, if a beautiful child who played with fairies could be called so harsh a name.

When they had all embraced again, his father drew back, peering hard, struggling to see his son's face.

"You haven't changed, Great Dragon!"

"Of course he has," Olan cried gaily. "He's a big mandarin now, and he looks it!"

"And how is our grandson?"

"Fine! He looks like Mother—and a bit like you too, Father."

It was true! Didi was like his grandfather. He had the same fundamental simplicity, the same refusal to parlay his values.

"Great Dragon," Olan trilled, "did your father write you that I want to look for my magician? I have an address for him. In the Tartar City of Peking."

"We'll look for him as soon as we get to Peking."

"You must come with me to see him when we find him. He will show us pictures of your little sister—you know, the one who was born crippled? She's got both her legs now, in the other world. She's beautiful and happy!"

His heart hurt sharply.

Jin-see said: "How are we going to Peking?"

"By cart, by the old road. We'll have to walk from here to the cart depot. We'll start out at first light."

"Should we take our things?"

"The fewest possible. Nothing heavy. We can leave the rest here with the manager."

His father began to fumble with luggage, and Great Dragon went to help him

"You know," Jin-see said, "they came this morning to take Donald to a British ship. They were very angry with him, said he had made a nuisance of himself coming to Tientsin at this time. When he started to scold them about opium, you should have seen their faces!"

He grinned, and Great Dragon remembered how sharklike his father could look. But then the grin turned nostalgic.

"It was good to see Donald! I didn't realize how much I missed him. I wonder if I shall ever see him again!"

"Why not?" Great Dragon said in his severest mandarin tone, but his heart trembled.

When they left the hotel, the predawn was laying a pale silver brush against the sky. Great Dragon walked between his parents, a hand gripping the arm of each. The streets were less jammed than they had been, but still there were many people, a butterfly crowd, flitting about, going nowhere, waiting for something to happen. The main object of their curiosity was the foreign soldiers who seemed to be everywhere now, briskly marching to some central meeting point. They wore different national uniforms, but all had the same expression, proud and disdainful. They ignored the Chinese mobs who ran along beside them, chattering and gesturing, nervously ready to flee at the slightest hostile movement but unable to resist the spectacular excitements of the night.

Great Dragon walked slowly and carefully, steering his almost-blind father on one side and his carefree, oblivious mother on the other. She stopped often to stare round-eyed at the foreign soldiers, and then Jin-see too would stumble to a stop asking anxiously: "What is it? Is your mother all right?"

"Look, Jin-see," she called happily. "Try to see these men. They've got on red jackets and blue pants with white stripes, and fur hats—are those fur hats, Great Dragon?"

"Mother, we must hurry. We're going to Peking, remember? To find your magician?"

She beamed at him. "Oh, yes!"

"Is she all right?" Jin-see said again.

"She's all right," he reassured his father.

He felt as though drops of blood were oozing from his heart. He remembered what he had seen so often in his youth and not comprehended. He remembered his father's eyes, when they were whole, seeking Olan, following Olan, deep and tender with love. He remembered his father's love for his mother.

She stopped again, staring into an alley. Turning toward

215

her to urge her on, he saw that her face was shining, her eyes sparkling. She raised a hand to point into the alley.

He was turning his head to follow her pointing finger, and Jin-see was saying, "Why have we stopped?" and "Where's Olan?" when, around a corner, a column of foreign soldiers came swinging, plumed helmets shining in the first rays of the sun, knee-high black leather boots thumping, sabers slapping rhythmically against the boots. All around them, and running after them, the usual crowd of chattering spectators. And then, in a great gust that seemed to sweep him and his parents aside, a mob of wild, screaming men erupted from the alley, brandishing knives, clubs, broken bottles. With a screeching roar, they flung themselves upon the foreign soldiers. Immediately, a huge struggle began, men heaving and flailing violently against each other, yelling, panting, grunting, weapons flashing, screaming spectators squirming, trying to flee, becoming engulfed inextricably in the tangle, blood spurting everywhere, shockingly red and liquid. Out of the tumult of sound and fury words spouted—English words:

"Mucking swine!"

"Bloody muckers!"

"God-blasted murdering Boxers!"

And Chinese words, more ominous: "Kill, kill, kill!"

And a happy cry from his mother: "Look! My magician!"

She was pointing at a man in the center of the strife, clearly visible because of his great height. A skeletally thin man with long, tousled hair, slashing right and left with a broken bottle, blood dripping from the bottle, from his hands.

She wrenched her arm from Great Dragon's grasp and darted out into the street, making a beeline for her magician.

He pushed his father against the wall, ignoring his cries. "Stay here, Father. Don't move. I'll be back in a moment." And rushed after his mother. He almost caught her, but his fingers slipped on the smooth silk of her gown. "Mother!"

he shouted frantically, and she turned for the fraction of an instant to give him a joyous smile before burrowing into the surging mass of men. He flung himself after her, clawing, butting, but his father was before him. His father hadn't needed a guiding hand; he'd been guided by his son's desperate cry of "Mother!" and now he ducked under his son's arm and plunged into the fight, crying out with ineffable love and fear, "Olan! Olan!"

Everything became dreamlike. A club raised high above his father's head began to descend slowly, slowly. He tugged at his father's arm, his sweated hands slipping, his arms weak against his father's frenzied determination. The club cracked down onto his father's head and his father's blood and brains splashed hot over him. Something exploded in his own head, and fierce pain spread through him in quicksilver ripples. The blood-soaked cobbles of the street came floating up and slapped him in the face as consciousness flicked out.

Chapter XVI

1901

O N THE SEVENTH DAY of September 1901—the four-teenth day of the eighth moon of the twenty-sixth year of Kuang Hsu—at four o'clock in the afternoon, Great Dragon entered the Hall of the Board of Ceremonies. Behind him came Uncle, carrying a pile of documents: twenty-four copies, twelve in Chinese and twelve in English, of the Boxer Protocol.

At their entrance, the signatories of the Protocol, who had been standing about chatting stiffly, hastened to the green baize-covered table. There was a flurry of chair legs scraping and morning-coat tails flipping as the plenipotentiaries of the eleven foreign powers whose legations had been besieged by the Boxers seated themselves in a row on one side of the table. On the other side there were only Prince Ching, who would sign for the Chinese government, and the Empress's representative, seventy-seven-year-old Li Hung-chang.

Watching the old man shuffle precariously to his seat, Great Dragon felt a surge of frustrated anger against the Empress. She had brought about catastrophe by throwing the Boxers at the foreigners, and when it became clear that the foreigners were about to annihilate the Boxers, she had taken the Emperor from his hiding place and fled the capital with him and called once again on her old stalwart Li Hung-chang to come to her aid.

He had come—perhaps for the last time, for the shadow of death seemed to lie on him—but he had not been able to finesse her out of paying for her willfulness. The terms of the Protocol were disastrous. Twenty-five Chinese forts to be destroyed to assure the foreigners access to Peking from the sea. The Legation Quarter, on the imperial doorstep, to be fortified and permanently garrisoned by foreign troops. Ten high officials who had helped the Boxers to be beheaded and a hundred others punished. Examinations to be suspended in forty-five cities to humiliate Boxer-sympathizing gentry by preventing their sons from competing for the mandarinate. And, of course, China to pay an indemnity: the staggering sum of 333 million dollars, in gold, over forty years, at interest rates that would double the amount, the funds to come from customs and salt revenues vital to China's scarecrow treasury.

The distinguished gathering today was to sign these awful terms into treaty law. Uncle began to pass out the documents. From hand to hand they went around the table, each man signing each copy as it came to him. A hundred and forty-four signatures. No one spoke. There was no need. Everyone knew exactly what was in the Protocol; it had taken many months to negotiate.

Great Dragon watched the signing, his head throbbing with the pain that had nagged him ever since the day a year ago when he'd awakened in that Tientsin hospital surrounded by white-clad figures who asked him over and over who he was. He had kept his mouth shut and his eyes fixed on the ceiling. If they didn't know who he was, how should he? This ill-smelling place was theirs, they must have brought him here. . . . Until the day he suddenly knew who he was and jumped up to rush dizzily along the rows of chipped iron bedsteads, heart and head pounding, searching for the loved faces, knowing he wouldn't find them.

By that time he'd been in the hospital nearly three months. They told him that rescue workers had brought him in with hundreds of others, wounded and dead. The wounded, all except himself, had recovered and left or been taken away by relatives. The dead—most of the bodies had been identified and claimed. The rest had long since been buried in a common grave.

The papers rustled as the signers pushed them to each other over the green baize. Great Dragon's head pounded as though a devil were in it clanging cymbals. But now, at least, with the Protocol completed, he could do what he should have done a year ago: go to Shanghai to talk to Julie. They had exchanged telegrams and letters, but the discussion they had to have could not be entrusted to paper.

The signing took a long time, and after it there was a reception at which Prince Ching stoically offered champagne to the foreigners. When Great Dragon reached home, Ching-mei called out snappishly:

"You're late. Didi's late too—something at school. I was obliged to dine alone."

Ordinarily he wouldn't have answered her, but tonight bitter words came to his lips.

"I've been watching some more of our country's lifeblood signed away to the foreigners."

"You mean the Protocol? What does it cover?"

"What we deserve for our stupidities."

He sat down to his dinner, grateful that she said no more. When he had finished he rose and went to stand by the mantel, where he could look down upon her.

"I'm going to Shanghai the day after tomorrow."

"Why?"

"To see my sister about our inheritance."

She looked up eagerly. "You mean we'll have our own money? Your sister will no longer be in control?"

He looked at her coldly. "Have you ever lacked for anything?"

"I want to go with you," she said sharply. "After all, I'm part of the family. I should have a part in the decisions."

The devil in his head thumped and rumbled. He said: "I'm going alone. There can only be one decision about the inheritance. Why d'you think I forbade you to talk of my father's death? Because *we have no proof of it*. If we go to Court with no proof of his death and try to have his assets transferred into our names, it would be like walking into a den of tigers. Everybody from the doorman to the chief judge would be on us for squeeze. The case would never come to judgment. They'd delay it until they were sure they couldn't squeeze anything more out of us—and then there'd be no case, would there?"

She was staring at him apprehensively.

He said: "We have no alternative but to continue using the power of attorney Father gave Julie when his sight began to worsen. So we don't want to attract any attention to Father's absence. Besides, I have other business in Shanghai. I'm going alone."

He left the room quickly before she could say any more. Ching-mei's company in Shanghai was the last thing he wanted. He longed to be alone with Julie in the old compound where the ghosts so violently thrust into the other world must still be lingering. And there was the young half-

brother he had never seen. And the meeting Tong Shao-yi
wanted with the Opium Merchants Guild. Certainly, he must
go alone.

As the steamer was warped to the dingy Shanghai waterfront, Great Dragon saw Julie in the crowd waiting on the
wharf. She stood a little apart, her face both grave and smiling, eyes raised to scan the people on the deck. The look of
her was instantly familiar to him, though the planes of her
face were sharper and there were lines. She was forty-five
years old now, and the years showed.

When the gangway was lowered he hurried down and
pushed his way toward her. Her face lit up when she saw
him, but she said nothing, just his name, as she hugged him
hard. He heard the little gulp she made to control tears, and
when he held her away from him her eyes were smiling but
misty.

"Is that all your luggage?" she said quickly, pointing to the
bag at his feet. "Good! Then we can get a carriage and go
home at once."

As they drove out of the dockyard onto a road marked
Broadway, he stared about him, amazed at the changes of the
last fifteen years. Since he had last seen the old waterfront
district of Yangtszepoo, the International Settlement had been
expanded to include it. Now the tumbledown shacks, the
smelly flocks of quacking ducks, the slimy green ponds had
all disappeared. Broadway was a broad way, lined with shops:
ship chandlers, hardware merchants, sellers of small ma-
chines, oil, kerosene, dozens of items, including, of course,
opium. Nothing fancy. No divans. Just small hole-in-the-wall
shops selling opium in little packets, mainly to dock workers
who carried their pipes in their waistbands and smoked their
opium on the spot. He watched a bone-thin coolie puff a pipe
quickly, then turn back, thews popping, to shifting bales larger

than himself. What would take the place of opium for men like these who smoked it, not for pleasure, but to gain the short-time strength they desperately needed?

Julie touched his arm.

"Don't look, Great Dragon. Don't be serious. For now, let's just be glad you've come. Look there instead—across the river, all those factories. They all belong to Jinsey Mathes. It's twice as big as when Father and Donald left it. Father used to say, 'Thank the great green turtle Donald and I had the sense to leave when we did!' "

He smiled at her. The smile came more easily than it did in Peking.

"We still have shares?"

"Oh, yes! They bring in lots of dividends! But we'll talk of those things later. Look there, Great Dragon. It's the new Astor House Hotel. . . ."

The carriage rumbled on, over the Garden Bridge, past the new British Consulate in its sea of green lawns, past great commercial buildings new to Great Dragon, taller and bulkier than any he remembered, past the new Customs House with its clock tower, past the Hongkong & Shanghai Banking Corporation, a broad sweep of steps leading up to its bronze front doors, bronze lions on guard. Everything clean and orderly. Uniformed police directing traffic.

Julie said: "What you can't see is even more wonderful than what you can. *Underground sewers.* See how the road slopes down on both sides? And those gutters, with gratings every few yards? Those carry rainwater and dirt into sewers that run under the roads. In the Settlement and French Town only, of course. The Chinese City and Nantao and Chapei are the same as ever, dirty and broken down. But here in the foreign areas they're even starting to have machine chamberpots: you pull a chain and water comes rushing down from a tank and cleans out the pot and everything goes down into the sewers. Did you ever hear of such a thing? But what's most wonderful of all, I think, is that it all *works!*"

He thought of the reckless, willful Empress, of dying old Li Hung-chang laboring on her behalf, losing, being forced to agree to the Protocol. Everything always worked where foreigners were in control: the Customs Service, the Postal Service, the Salt Monopoly. The foreigners installed efficiency—in exchange for more encroachment. The foreigners created new sources of revenue for China to pay them more indemnities.

She closed her fingers around his wrist.

"And you should see the new shops, Great Dragon. Department stores, they're called. Everything under one roof. They let Chinese in if we look as though we have money to spend and won't spit on the floor. I've been in several times. I bought some lovely things. Beds with spring mattresses! Just wait till you sleep in yours!"

They came to where the old Yang King Pang Creek had been, with its horrible little opium dens and its predatory gangs of abandoned children. The creek existed no longer. In its place was a broad thoroughfare called Avenue Edward the Seventh.

In a short time, the carriage rumbled off macadam and began to shake and bump on a pot-holed road: they had left French Town and were in the Chinese City. Their driver, who had been half asleep behind his steadily clopping horse, suddenly woke up and began to flourish his long whip, shouting at the other drivers and rickshaw-pullers and cart-pushers and pedestrians, all shouting too, who made their way about untidily without benefit of traffic policemen. No one moved a jot faster, no one gave an inch.

Julie began to laugh and a moment later Great Dragon joined her. Laughing, they arrived at the old, familiar gate, which opened in the old, familiar way. The gateman, stooped and gray now, stepped forward, beaming, to kowtow. Great Dragon embraced him and stepped into the lovely old courtyard, the marble underfoot rubbed to a silky sheen by myriad footfalls, the moon door of the ancestors' house glowing. A great entanglement of emotions flooded his spirit. The years of his youth rushed in upon him, the years of study and endeavor, dominated by Jin-see's will, by Li si-sang's exigencies, and always, always, by the life-duty. He turned to Julie, unsayable words trembling on his lips. Gravely, she said, "Come," and led him toward the ancestors' house, slowing her pace so that the gateman could shuffle past them to slide open the golden door.

As soon as they entered, Great Dragon saw the new soul tablet, of dark green jade, carved and inlaid with gold. WEI JIN-SEE. It stood in a row with the other two. The candles in the pewter holders were burning. Incense sticks were alight in the vase. Julie must have given orders that these things be prepared for his return, for he, the eldest son, was now the guardian of the ancestors. Silently, he stepped forward, prostrated himself, performed the ritual kowtows.

When he rose, he saw that Julie had tears in her eyes.

"I didn't wait for you, Great Dragon. I went ahead and had the tablet made because—It was so lonely. I miss Father so much. Mother, too, of course, but Father . . . I didn't realize till he was gone that he filled the whole place for me. I loved him so much."

He swallowed his own emotion.

"He loved you too, Julie. More than me. In a way more even than Mother, for he loved you with his mind as well as his heart, and perhaps there's nothing more enticing."

She smiled mistily.

"Great Dragon, let's sit here for a while."

They sat side by side on the big white cushion. It was peaceful. He imagined layers falling from him like the layers of an onion. The Empress. The Protocol. Sick old Li Hung-chang. The plenipotentiaries, so pleasant to each other in public, so bitterly quarrelsome in private. His situation with Ching-mei, still ambiguous: her father was back, standing stubbornly behind her shoulder. When all the layers had fallen away, he would be pure again, young again.

Julie said softly:

"I had a letter from Donald, blaming himself for their deaths: if he hadn't given in to his anger about the Royal Commission, none of them would have been in Tientsin at that fatal time. I tried to make him see that although we are sorrowful, they are happy. Father and Mother are happy. It was time for them to die. Mother was already more than halfway in the other world—had been for ages. In another year, Father would have been completely blind. As it was, he managed to see Donald—I mean, he had enough sight left really to see him. And anyway, he couldn't have lived without Mother."

He said nothing, for he felt that there was more that she wanted to say. After a while she said it.

"Donald has a baby daughter. He called it a miracle, for he's sixty-five and his wife's forty-five. Like me. They've called her Noelle, for she was born at Christmas." She was silent another moment. Then: "If I'd had Donald's daughter, I would have called her Precious Dawn."

"You should have married!" he burst out, his heart aching for her. "With Father's money and position, you could have married anyone you chose!"

"No, I couldn't." She gave her head a decisive shake. "The only person I could have married would have been Donald. Great Dragon, d'you think it's our English blood that makes you and me so un-Chinese about marriage? Look at me. And you. You're not happy with Ching-mei, I'm sure, yet you haven't taken a concubine, though you could afford two or

226

three. I think . . ." She raised her head toward the altar and shut her eyes, as though to absorb emanations from the soul tablets. "I think Father took it for granted that you'd take a concubine. He wanted you to marry Ching-mei only because of the prestige she'd bring you."

He felt very close to her. She'd always been older, wiser, quicker-witted. He'd always felt some awe of her, looked to her for cues. But today she had needed him, and that made him very happy in spite of sorrow. He wanted to tell her things, to share with her.

"I've thought of taking a concubine, of course. One of the reasons I haven't is that I don't think my son would be indifferent to it. I think it would diminish me in his eyes. He's that kind of person. And there's another reason. I did get prestige from Ching-mei at first, but later I built up a lot more for myself. I'm known as a man of judgment. Ching-mei says it isn't judgment, I'm just stuffy and slow to make up my mind. In a way she's right. I find it impossible to make snap decisions. I have to look at all sides of a matter and consider. And I consider that a concubine is more trouble than it's worth. If the wife has given permission, the concubine is sulky because that makes her inferior. If the wife has not given permission, then it's the wife who sulks and nags. Either way, you're in trouble."

Julie laughed aloud. "I once told Father that you were prim, and I was right—you *are* prim! 'Looking at all sides of the matter'! 'Considering'! About taking a concubine!"

Her laughter was teasing and he hugged her, loving her, glad that he had lightened her mood. They sat awhile in companionable silence, the setting sun glowing mysteriously through the frosted glass of the windows. Slowly, he felt her mood turn somber again.

"Great Dragon, does Didi know about the life-duty?"

"No. I didn't want to—burden his youth. I wanted to let

him choose his own career. Maybe there'll never be a need to tell him. If there is, there's time. Do you agree?"

"Yes," she said slowly. "At this time you're the inheritor of the life-duty, and you're right in Peking where whatever happens will happen."

"Does Fish know?"

"What d'you think? Living with Father? He knows all about it. He knows all the ins and outs of the opium trade."

She rose and went to the altar, took up the lovely jade tablet.

"Father was like this tablet—made all in one piece." She traced the carving with her finger. "Wei Jin-see. Just his name. I've been thinking that the foreign style is better. A big tombstone on which a lot of words can be carved. 'Beloved Father.' 'Rest in peace.' Lovely words like that."

She sighed and put down the tablet.

"Come, Great Dragon. Fish will be home from school by now. We'll have dinner, and then we can talk about what we have to talk about, and then you can go to sleep on your lovely spring mattress."

In the courtyard, three women passed them walking briskly the other way. Great Dragon looked questioningly at Julie. She laughed a little.

"Girl's mah-jongg partners. Girl is the living *dis*proof of your theories about concubines. Of course, as it turned out, she wasn't really a concubine, but she's never been any trouble. She loves to eat and she loves to play mah-jongg, and as long as she can do those two things, she's happy."

"Does Fish live with her?"

"No. He's lived with us since he was weaned. Father sent him every day to see his mother, and he still does that, but otherwise he was entirely Father's son. And now, in a way, he's mine. Not a daughter called Precious Dawn, but a son called Great Fish." She smiled a little sadly. "Well, I'm not complaining. He's been a wonderful comfort to me since our parents died."

As they passed the passage leading to Olan's courtyard, Julie caught Great Dragon's arm.

"There's one more thing I want to show you."

They entered the courtyard, no longer locked. The day's light was almost gone, and the colored lanterns were not lit. Nothing was reflected in the still pool of water but dark shadows that seemed to stir sluggishly. A prickle crept along Great Dragon's spine. In this courtyard he had made his farewell kowtows to his father and mother, and had never seen them again till the day of their deaths.

They walked around the pool to the little pink marble house that enclosed the grave of the crippled little sister. Over the miniature archway characters had been carved into the soft marble. Peering, Great Dragon made them out.

"Olan has joined her daughter."

Julie had thought of everything.

In the family room, a tall boy rose from the table, advanced to the middle of the room, and kowtowed respectfully to Great Dragon.

"Elder Brother."

The young half-brother. Strangely, for his mother was a Chinese peasant, there was something vaguely foreign about him. His hair was very fine and not quite black—dark foreign hair rather than Chinese hair—and his eyes were something like Jin-see's in their roundness. At the moment, they were bright and sparkling. From the boy's gravely correct greeting, Great Dragon would not have expected the smiling, inviting glance. A charmer, Julie had written. Certainly, he was very attractive.

Great Dragon caught Julie's quizzical gaze on him.

"Looking at all sides of the matter? Considering?"

He laughed.

The meal passed pleasantly. The atmosphere at the table was warm and loving. The ache in Great Dragon's head seemed to lessen. If only Didi could be here to see what family life could be like! Didi didn't know how to banter as Julie and Fish were doing so easily and fondly.

Julie put down her bowl, but before she put down her chopsticks she leaned over to pick both wings out of a dish of chicken and lay them in Fish's bowl.

"You won't mind, Great Dragon. I remember you never liked the wings." She sat back. "Well, if you've had enough we might as well talk about the inheritance while Fish finishes dinner, and get it over with. I suppose you've come to the same conclusion I have—that we dare not lay claim to our inheritance?"

"Not if we want to keep the money!"

"Then there's not much to be said. We have no alternative but to continue as we are, with me operating under the power of attorney Father gave me. Later—well, I suppose Didi will follow you in the mandarinate or something like that—anyway, I don't suppose he'll go into business. Fish is taking economics and business courses, as Father planned. When the time comes, he'll be well qualified to take over the *hong*, and I can give him a power of attorney. D'you agree, Great Dragon?"

"Yes," he said. "I don't see what else we can do for the time being, at least." He had a vision of the Chief Eunuch. Shanghai officialdom would be as rapacious. "But later, I hope we can come to some firmer arrangement."

Fish turned quickly, and Great Dragon realized that he had been listening intently.

"I'm studying hard, Elder Brother. I'll do the very best I can for our family."

He spoke with such pleasing diffidence that Great Dragon found himself smiling kindly.

230

"I'm sure you will, and I'm sure you'll do fine. Well, that settles that, for the next several years at least. The only thing now is to remember not to speak of Father's death. If court officials should come to hear of it, they might start wondering why we don't claim our inheritance, and that might lay us open to squeeze as badly as the other way around. Will you remember, Fish?"

"Of course," he said. "Long ago I told the teachers and the other boys at school that Father had gone completely blind and that he never goes out anymore, so nobody's wondering why he hasn't been seen."

Julie regarded him with surprise: "You never told me you'd told them that."

But Fish had lost interest. "Didn't I?" he murmured absently, picking up a chicken wing and giving it his full attention. Julie watched him indulgently, then smiled over his head at Great Dragon.

"All sides of the matter looked at? All things considered?"

"Yes!" he said wholeheartedly. Julie was right—Fish was a charmer, and a fine, bright boy.

The meeting with the Opium Merchants Guild took place in the same old offices in which Jin-sec had presided. Tong Shao-yi had seen to it that invitations on Court stationery were sent to every merchant, and none had dared to stay away, but what surprised Great Dragon was that many of the British importers were also present. In the early days, the Guild had controlled the importers by being their only customer. Now, the Guild and the importers were like partners with a common interest. As Great Dragon began the speech he and Tong Shao-yi had prepared, he could almost hear his words thudding dully against their joint hostility.

He told them that the Royal Commission's report, which had so pleased them, was now discredited, it having become

231

known that the members of the Commission and the witnesses they interviewed in India had largely been hand-picked and rehearsed by the British India Office, whose interest in maintaining opium was self-evident. Donald's Board had reported that new moves in Parliament were to be expected. On the Chinese side, the Empress would issue an edict forbidding opium the moment the British signified their willingness to abrogate the opium clauses. The Guild merchants should not, therefore, be surprised if they found themselves being phased out of business within the next few years.

Moreover, opium was no longer simply a matter of treaties between China and Britain. It was assuming worldwide implications. A Dr. Marshall Mead Chipman of the American National Bureau of Medicine had recently read a paper to Congress. Great Dragon read them excerpts:

"The licensed opium traffic in India and the enforced traffic upon China is the greatest national sin and the most far-reaching in its consequences perpetrated by any nation of the century. . . . These are hard things to say of a nation whose head citizen is designated Her Most Christian Majesty and Defender of the Faith, but the facts are there. . . . As this matter is obviously of an international character, a convention should be called to consider it."

An American bishop in the Philippines, who was in frequent correspondence with Tong Shao-yi, was writing the President of the United States urging him to convene such an international conference to consider not only opium but also morphia and the recently discovered heroin.

When he stopped speaking, the merchants and the importers turned to each other, ignoring him, tacitly discounting his speech by their rudeness. They shrugged their shoulders and spread their hands. Until the treaty clauses guaranteeing opium were actually abrogated, opium would continue to be sold. If the smoking of opium declined because morphia and heroin were easier to use and were odorless, then the manufacture of morphia and heroin would rise, and in either event opium would be needed.

Great Dragon sat impassively listening until an old man rose, pulling himself up by clinging to the back of the chair in front of him.

"Excellency." The old voice was squeaky. "I know your father, Wei Jin-see. I haven't seen him for a long time. I heard that he is blind. I am very sorry. He is seventy years old, isn't he? I'm a few years older. I'm not blind, but my legs . . ."

He broke off and stared around confusedly, then began again:

"Your father invented the plan for ruining Carradine. You did not know Carradine. You and all these others are too young. What I want to say, Excellency—I've seen it all, from the rough days of the smuggling to these days when my grandsons sit in comfortable offices in long gowns of silk and brocade to trade opium. And I know that you and Tong Shao-yi are right, Excellency. Opium is a very evil thing and should be stopped."

He stood there, nodding his trembling head and blinking his rheumy eyes, until a young man came and led him from the room. It was a signal for all the others to leave too, and they hurried out, avoiding Great Dragon's gaze.

When he was alone, another old man came up to him.

"Excellency, I was your father's secretary. I think of him often. It was a terrible thing, that accident. Apart from his eyes, he is well?"

Great Dragon inclined his head. "Thank you."

"Excellency, no one uses your father's old office now. You could sit in it for a while to rest. I could bring you tea."

He looked hopeful. Great Dragon said: "I would like that," and the old man hurried to open the door of a room that looked out on the alley in front of the building. Great Dragon entered the room, and it seemed that ghosts accompanied him. His father. A foreign ghost named Carradine. His father had ruined Carradine in—he calculated—1868, thirty-three years ago. Half a lifetime. In that year he himself had been six years old, starting his studies. . . . He sat down behind the bare desk and spread his palms on it. Wood, like marble, was warm. Had life. Something of his father might come to him through his hands on this old, worn wood.

The meeting hadn't been bad. In some ways it had been quite good. There'd been no outcry against the issuance of the Edict. It seemed that, rather than resist the Edict, the merchants and the importers would concentrate on how much time they had left, and how much money they could make in that time. Of course, merchants and importers alike would nitpick, scrutinize every detail of whatever arrangements were made, claim every jot and tittle of advantage they could, delay matters as much as possible, drag everything out. The importers would hold forth about their "treaty rights" and scream "treaty violation" on every possible occasion. The merchants, now so cosily in bed with them, would probably try to cover themselves with the same blanket.

There was a knock on the door and Great Dragon called, "Enter," expecting the old secretary with the tea he had promised. But the man who entered was a foreigner—a short and tubby middle-aged Englishman with a snub nose and thinning hair, who advanced diffidently toward the desk, saying in English in accents Great Dragon at once recognized as not "top drawer":

"I'm sorry to disturb you." And then: "You don't look like your father!"

Taken by surprise, Great Dragon, for once, spoke quickly:

"You knew—know—my father?"

"Yes. Is he dead?"

A cold wave of alarm held Great Dragon motionless for a

moment. Then he gestured toward the chair at the opposite side of the desk.

"Who are you? And why do you ask such a strange question?"

The man sat down apologetically.

"I'm sorry, I should have introduced myself. My name is Alfred Pratt?" He made the statement a question, looking inquiringly at Great Dragon. "You've not heard of me? Well, of course, it wasn't you I met, it was your sister. At the time of your father's—er—accident."

Was this the Englishman who'd rescued Jin-see and taken him to a doctor? Great Dragon kept his face expressionless.

"Then perhaps, whatever your business is, you should go and see my sister?"

"Well, I've been racking my brains what to do. I didn't think it right to go to your home because of your young half-brother. Didn't think your father'd want him to know. When I heard you'd be here today, I came rushing. Please believe me—it's important for me to know if anything's happened to your father. You see, if your father was all right, he'd surely have come to see me in May or June, as he's done for the last fifteen years. He didn't come, so I think something must have happened to him, but in that case I can't understand why you or your sister haven't got in touch with me. He *told* me he'd written the letter."

"What letter?"

"The letter about—" Pratt broke off, looking agonized. "I promised your father I'd tell nobody. If he's alive . . ."

Great Dragon made up his mind. Surely this couldn't be a trick.

"Very well. Assume that he is—incapacitated."

Alfred Pratt sighed.

"All right. Don't see what else I can do but tell you. The letter about the opium. The opium from the valley. I'm in

235

possession of nearly seven thousand pounds of it, belonging to your father."

"*What?*" Great Dragon felt completely blank.

Pratt nodded vigorously.

"That's right. D'you remember your father left Shanghai for several months in 1885? He went to Shansi then, to buy the valley. In fact, I told him about it. I met him on the ship going upriver, when I told him about Tong Shao-yi. Then he said he was looking for land that would grow seeds of the Patna poppy, and I told him about the valley in Shansi. It was when he returned from buying the valley that he was attacked and blinded."

Great Dragon rose abruptly and went to the window. It was evening. The people in the narrow, crowded alley below the window were hurrying to get home, hungry for their dinners, their rest, their wives and concubines, their opium. The opium shop next door was doing a roaring business. By all the gods and devils, what was this about a valley?

He turned to face Pratt.

"You must excuse me. I am . . . astonished. I know absolutely nothing about this. Nor does my sister, or she would have told me."

"But she must know! You father *told* me he'd written the letter and left it among his papers for her to find in case something happened to him, so she would know."

"There was no such letter, nothing at all like that. I'm sure she would have told me if there had been."

Pratt looked bewildered.

"I asked him to write it, and he told me he had. I said I couldn't be responsible for all that opium in case something happened to him. You see, the arrangement was for the farmers from whom he bought the valley to keep on working it, growing opium from the seeds of the Patna poppy that your father gave them. He wanted opium of that quality to

236

use against the British importers if necessary—if, in the end, the British won't stop shipping Indian opium to China. Your father planned, in that case, to flood the market with his own Patna-quality opium at the price of ordinary domestic. That would have ruined the British import trade in a minute!"

Great Dragon felt the high beat of his heart. His father! Almost blind. Sitting all these years with Olan in the shell-pink courtyard, keeping this secret.

Pratt went on. "I acted as his agent. The crop is harvested in summer every year. He came to see me every year at the end of May and gave me the money to buy the crop. I went up to the valley, paid the farmers, took delivery of the opium, arranged to get it across the Yellow River and into a warehouse in Chengchow. Nobody knows it's there but me and your father. The seven thousand pounds that are there is fifteen years' production from the valley. The best opium ever grown in China. Any day as good as Patna. This year, when your father didn't come, I used my own money to buy the crop. But of course, if he's dead, you and I must decide what to do."

"Yes, of course," Great Dragon said faintly. He had to consider this matter from all sides! He was still too astonished, too perturbed, to reach any kind of decision.

Pratt said: "He didn't want anyone to know. You can imagine what a row the Guild would have kicked up if they'd known about that opium, how hard they'd try to get hold of it. And he didn't want you to know because you're a mandarin and it would have complicated your life to know. He didn't want your sister to know because, he said, she was already doing a man's job running your *hong*, and he was getting blinder and blinder and she was having to do more and more, and he didn't want to lay any more burdens on her. And your half-brother was so young. He wasn't even born yet when your father bought the valley. It was in the

237

valley that he—er—found the woman who is your half-brother's mother."

There was a timid knock on the door, and the secretary entered with a pot of tea on a tray.

"Excuse me, Excellency. I didn't know if you would want to be disturbed."

Great Dragon rose.

"Thank you." He smiled at the kind old man. "I will tell my father that I met you, that you're looking well, that you think of him. He will be happy."

The old man turned red with pleasure. It wasn't a lie, Great Dragon thought gently. He would tell the spirit of his father.

He turned to Alfred Pratt.

"Let us go home and talk to my sister. It's a good time now because our young brother is having a series of examinations and he won't be home till late."

Pratt said, as though he dreaded his own words: "Then your father is dead?"

Great Dragon said: "Yes."

The pain in his head started up again with a soundless roar.

Julie stared wide-eyed.

"There was nothing like that in Father's papers! I went through everything very carefully, and there was certainly no letter like that."

Great Dragon felt drained. That last meeting with his father—that last, loving meeting in the Tientsin hotel—was more to be appreciated than ever. Without that to remember, he'd be empty. How little he had known of his father! Julie had recognized Pratt at once, had greeted him with pleasure, and he himself had never even heard Pratt's name before tonight. And Pratt had known so much about their father that even Julie hadn't known. Pratt said that the valley was beautiful, high up in the Chungtiao Mountains of Shansi. And Girl

238

had come from that valley. Somehow, that irrelevant detail made it all doubly unnerving.

Julie said slowly:

"I suppose it's conceivable that Father destroyed the letter after writing it. Sometimes he got very despondent. The day he found out that patients in the hospital who he thought were cured of opium smoking by the red pill weren't cured at all—in fact, they weren't even taking their pills, they were going into the washrooms to *smoke* them. They crushed them into powder and mixed the powder with the tobacco in their cigarettes. They got away with it because there was no opium smell. On the day Father found that out, my heart ached for him. . . . But, no. I can't believe that Father would have destroyed the letter once he said he'd written it."

"No," said Great Dragon.

"No," said Pratt.

"Well," Julie shrugged, "it's a mystery. Perhaps one day we'll find out what happened to the letter, but there's no use wasting more time on it now. We'd better go on to decide what to do about the opium from that valley. Great Dragon?"

Great Dragon found himself answering promptly.

"We'll have to go on buying it up. If we didn't, the farmers would sell it to the Guild, of course. We'll have to go on buying it every year until they can be stopped from growing poppies. I mean, until we reach an agreement with the British, and the Empress issues the Edict forbidding opium."

"You're right," Julie said. "Mr. Pratt, do you mind continuing as our agent? I'll see to it that you get the money every year, as Father did, and of course we'll reimburse you for what you spent this year."

"I don't mind," Pratt said. "Your father was very good to me. I was very fond of him. But, as I told him, I don't want to be the only one responsible for all that opium in the warehouse. What I'd like—I think we should get a safe deposit box in a bank and keep the storage receipts in there. Two of us, or all three of us, can be 'either/or' signatories, so that any one of us can have access to the box."

"Good," said Julie. "You and Great Dragon, Mr. Pratt. I don't even want to know what bank you choose. I'm too close to Father's affairs. There shouldn't be any mention at all, at home or at the *hong*, of that safe deposit box, and I don't want to know anything about it."

Great Dragon smiled at her. In Peking he was the mandarin, in command of the Wai-wu Pu, having access to the Empress herself. In Shanghai, Julie commanded. He loved her very much.

"And we won't tell Fish anything about it," she said. "I think Mr. Pratt's right that Father wouldn't have wanted him to know. He's too young."

In the morning, Great Dragon went to the address Pratt had given him, Pratt's home on Bubbling Well Road. A tall brick wall enclosed it, on the top of which were cemented thick shards of broken glass bottles. The gate, like the wall, was protected by a sheet of metal that covered it completely on the inside. Shanghai-style precautions. He pulled the bell-pull and was peered at through a peephole before the gate was opened.

He entered a pretty garden and walked up a sandy path toward the front steps of a large, solidly built brick house. A Chinese woman stood on the steps, a short, stocky woman with a broad face, hair in pigtails. He took her for a servant until she said, in the flattest of Shanghainese accents:

"You are welcome. My husband is waiting for you."

He bowed, to hide any astonishment that might show on his face.

"I'm sorry we have all these precautions," she said pleasantly. She was smiling and her eyes were bright. "But my husband is afraid of robbers and kidnappers. We have a lot of crime in Shanghai. Not like Peking."

"We have crime in Peking too, but perhaps a different kind."

She laughed delightedly. "Come in, please."

She led the way into a spacious hall and shouted up the stairway: "Ah-fet! Ah-fet! Your visitor is here!" Her lungs were powerful.

Alfred Pratt came hurrying down the stairs.

"Good morning! You've met my wife, I see. And here is our daughter." He smiled at a girl of about twelve years who had come in from the garden. "Her name is Belle. And now, please come into my study. Mei-mei, we don't want to be disturbed."

He patted his wife's cheek and led the way into a large and well-proportioned room to the right of the hall. Great Dragon looked around admiringly. Three curios of excellent quality—museum pieces—stood on pedestals.

Pratt smiled. "All due to your father's kindness. The commission he paid me for acting as his agent enabled me to get out of opium—I was a small dealer when I met him—and into antiques. I'd always been interested in curios. I've done quite well. Now . . ."

He bustled to the desk, an ordinary little man, balding, acquiring a paunch—and happy. A happy man, Great Dragon thought. He opened a drawer and produced a map, which he spread out on the desk.

"Here, let me show you where that valley is." He traced a cross with a pencil. "Just about here. I can't pinpoint it exactly, it's a hidden kind of place, four hours up on pony-back. I could take you to see it, if you like."

Great Dragon shook his head. "Not this time—I'm due back in Peking. Perhaps one day."

He handed over the parcel of money Julie had given him.

241

"Here's the reimbursement for what you paid for the opium this year." Pratt locked it away in a drawer.

"About the bank. I thought the Hongkong & Shanghai Bank. The one with the lions, you know? It's the safest for our purpose, I think. One of the biggest, and British. They'd never let anyone get to the safe deposit box without proper authorization."

"You know best," Great Dragon said.

As they left the house, the wife came hurrying out to the steps, calling after them in her loud shout:

"Don't be late, Ah-fet! Don't go into a curio shop and forget the time!"

He turned and waved, laughing.

A happy marriage, Great Dragon thought with a twinge of what might have been envy. His own marriage a turbulent affair of secret orgies and verbal daggers. His father's a gentle idyll of madness. Julie, unmarried, dreaming of Donald and a daughter called Precious Dawn. And this oddly assorted couple, a lower-drawer Englishman with excellent taste in curios, and a Chinese woman of the servant class, probably illiterate, with a flourishing, loving, happy marriage. "Mei-mei" he had called her, the common term for any Chinese girl—"little sister." Had she no name of her own? But it didn't matter, did it? They were happy.

On the day he was leaving to return to Peking, Great Dragon said to Julie:

"Don't come with me to the ship. It won't sail till the tide is right, and that won't be till after midnight. I've already said good-bye to Fish."

She looked at him sadly.

"Fifteen years since last I saw you. How many years till the next time?"

"You could visit us in Peking."

"I can't leave the *hong*. And there's Fish to supervise. He's too lively to leave alone. Anyway"—she smiled a little—"I don't think Ching-mei would be happy to see me. I don't think she's ever forgiven me for drinking that glass of brandy for her at your wedding."

They stood together, smiling, remembering. Ghosts of Jin-see and Olan and Donald flitted through the lovely, empty courtyards and faded into darkness. The fairy lights were never lit now. Olan's house was closed. So was the house in which he had studied with Li si-sang for so many years, in which he and Ching-mei had begun their married life by not sharing a pillow for weeks. Only the family house was occupied now, and Girl's house. The clack of mah-jongg cards coming from there was often the only sound in the compound.

And of course the ancestors' house was occupied.

"What about the soul tablets?" Julie said softly. "Will you take them with you? You're the one who should be performing the rituals."

"Let them stay here," he said. "They belong here. One day I'll come back."

She nodded. "I'll be glad to have the tablets here. I love taking care of the ancestors' house. Before you leave, Great Dragon, will you go and say good-bye?"

She walked with him across the courtyard and watched silently while he made his farewell kowtows.

Chapter XVII

1906

GREAT DRAGON HAD NOT SEEN the Empress since she had seized the Emperor and moved back from the Summer Palace to the Imperial Palace. Watching her now, he thought that the years had hardly touched her. The lines and wrinkles were no deeper, the coal black eyes were as alarmingly sharp. Power suited her, nourished her. She sat much more easily on the high throne of the imperial audience chamber than she had in the parlor of the Summer Palace. The ruthless, crafty Old Buddha! Two months after the Boxer Protocol was signed, her devoted Li Hung-chang had died, but she had stayed away from the capital for two more years to give the foreigners time to begin forgetting the Boxers. On her return, almost her first act had been to have herself photographed as the Goddess of Mercy standing benignly amid lotus flowers and waterfalls. Then she had received in audience the wives of the foreign diplomats and had had another photograph taken, herself seated, the wives grouped around her, standing, towering over her. It must have cost her a lot to tolerate that, but in the photograph her expression was gracious and she was holding the hand of the American minister's wife, who had lived through the Boxers' siege of the legations but now declared herself deeply impressed by the Empress's "womanly tenderness."

"Madame," Great Dragon fancied himself saying to her, "you are speaking of the woman who is suspected of responsibility in the deaths of two Emperors, her husband and her son, and who is certainly responsible for the incarceration of a third Emperor, her nephew, and the drowning of his favorite concubine."

But even as he fantasized, he knew that such a speech to the American minister's wife would awaken little comprehension. Of all the foreigners now crowding China, only the English really understood the Chinese. Great Dragon and the Englishmen with whom he dealt had a kind of fellow-feeling, a mutual respect for each other, a mutual contempt for those other, more recent, enemies. Chinese who hardly knew each other patted each other's backs and called each other "old friend" by way of compliment. Great Dragon sometimes had the impulse to pat an Englishman's back and call him "oldest enemy."

And some Englishmen felt the same. Yesterday, the First Secretary of the British Legation—he who, as Fourth Secretary, had so admired Great Dragon's accent—had sat across the desk from Great Dragon, leaning forward, saying, low-voiced, as a Chinese might:

"If you can persuade her to take the first step, it's safe to say that the India Office will simply have to follow. They'll have nothing more to hide behind. And I'm sure you'll be able to persuade her. She knows her nuts and bolts, she does, that old . . . Buddha."

After several years of close association, the First Secretary and Great Dragon sometimes did each other the honor of using lower-drawer English in their more intimate conversations.

Great Dragon had only said mildly, "I will try to persuade her," but he had known, and Tong Shao-yi had known too, when Great Dragon told him, that at last, at last, the moment had come.

The Empress was dismissing her visitor, sitting impassively while he kowtowed: her disapproval of the kowtow had apparently vanished with her resumption of power. But when she saw that Great Dragon was her next visitor, she signed to the Chief Eunuch. Four eunuchs immediately came forward with a palanquin. One of them reverently held up to her a padded handrest. Holding on to it, she stepped from her throne to the palanquin and was borne away to a side room. The Chief Eunuch signed to Great Dragon to follow.

In the side room, the Empress was seated in an armchair on a dais. Beside her was a stool, to which she beckoned Great Dragon.

"It's a long time since you've been to see me. Have you and Tong Shao-yi been failing in your job?"

He smiled. He felt very calm. Success brought with it, not excitement and a wildly beating heart, but a kind of tranquility.

"Majesty, as we've said before, the English are stiff-necked, and in their land anyone has the right to speak. To pass matters through their Parliament takes a great deal longer than, for example, through your Government Council."

She smiled grimly.

"You are bold, Wei Ta-lung. You must have some very good news for me."

He bowed. "I hope you will think so. There are, in fact, two pieces of news." He would tell her the second first, to

246

soften her, and also for the sake of the timing. He wanted to end with the gesture he had planned. He glanced up at her. "The first is that President Theodore Roosevelt has given orders for an international conference to be convened to consider the problems of opium. Shanghai has been suggested as the site of the conference, to acknowledge that China's problems with opium are greater than any other nation's."

She nodded and said "Good!" emphatically.

"The second piece of news . . ." He leaned forward, as the First Secretary had done, spoke softly, slowly. "You will recall, Majesty, that the Americans became an independent nation by defeating the British, who had tried to force them to pay tribute. The British are therefore especially sensitive to pressure from the Americans, and of course this American call for an international conference puts pressure on the British."

He cleared his throat. That sounded well and suited his purpose, and if it was not entirely true, she wouldn't know the difference.

"Pressure has also been put on the British Parliament from other sources. You will recall the infamous report of the Royal Commission on Opium? It has been proved largely a fraud, and there has been a public outcry in England about that. The English anti-opium societies have continued and increased their activities. Finally, in May this year, Parliament was persuaded to pass another resolution confirming the one it passed fifteen years ago that to raise revenue through opium is morally indefensible, and demanding that the government bring the opium trade to a speedy close."

Again she nodded. Her shiny eyes were fixed on him. He went on:

"The branch of the British government concerned with the government of India is called the India Office. For it, of course, the closure of the opium trade means the loss of many millions every year in revenue. It is struggling against Parliament's order. It is insisting that if China wants to stop opium, China must take the first step."

She said sharply: "What! *We* take the first step, when all the world knows that they forced opium upon us! And what step can we take? There is still the guarantee in the treaties!"

He answered her very softly. "Majesty, what the India Office is saying, in essence, is that we want to get rid of Indian opium in order to promote our own. The Royal Commission's report said that in so many words: that if Indian opium were to be stopped, Chinese opium would take its place. The India Office has enjoyed the revenue from opium for so long that they have come to think of it as their right, and they cynically attribute to us their own base motives."

He stopped and drew a long breath, waited a moment, then looked up into her eyes.

"Majesty, we must prove our good faith before the world. The Edict forbidding all opium, foreign and domestic, throughout our empire, must be issued immediately. We must ourselves, unilaterally, abrogate the opium guarantee."

Her eyes flashed fire.

"And what about war? Twice before the British have sent armadas against us because of opium. If we unilaterally abrogate the opium guarantee, how do I know that they will not do so again?"

"They will not do so," he said, his eyes steadfast. "The challenge of the India Office is its last stand, and it will collapse like a balloon the instant it is pricked. You asked if Tong Shao-yi and I have been failing in our job. We have not, Majesty. We have been having intense discussions with the English societies about plans for ending opium shipments from India. The best plan, the one most likely to be accepted by the India Office, is to reduce shipments of Indian opium by ten percent a year, to end in ten years, provided that we can reduce domestic production at the same rate. And we can do better than that, Majesty. Tong Shao-yi thinks that with the organization we already have for suppressing opium, we can do it in *five* years."

Her gaze was still fierce and dubious. He said:

"Majesty, if you will issue the Edict *now* forbidding opium throughout our empire, the India Office will have no alternative but to accept that plan."

He slid from his stool and knelt before her, raised his folded hands to touch his forehead, and bowed until his hands touched the floor. The nape of his neck was exposed at her feet, at her mercy.

"Majesty, here is my neck on it."

After a moment she said, "Rise."

He slipped back onto the stool. She was smiling, sardonic, lips compressed. She knew very well that he had rehearsed the gesture, and she was pleased, as he had known she would be, for thus he had honored her.

"Very well," she said. "But remember—your neck is on it."

The Edict, written in vermilion characters on a yellow silk banner, read:

> It is hereby commanded that within a period of ten years the evils arising from foreign and native opium be equally and completely eradicated. Let the Government Council frame such measures as may be suitable and necessary for strictly forbidding the consumption of the drug and the cultivation of the poppy. Do not oppose.

Great Dragon read and reread it. So simple. So short. As though it had not been forty-six years in the making, since the day the Unequal Treaties were ratified in the pall of smoke from the burning Summer Palace. As though it had not cost millions of lives. As though it would not take colossal effort to put into effect. For the first time in the millennium of Chi-

249

na's existence, the entire country, from the frozen north to the lush south, from the western heights of Tibet to the sea-washed eastern shores, would be engaged in a single undertaking: the eradication of opium.

All the way home in his sedan chair, he felt his heart thudding in time to the quick rhythm of the chair-bearers' footsteps. Replicas of the yellow banner were on display in all the places where news posters were regularly put up. Crowds of excited people eddied around them. More crowds flowed toward them. The news was momentous. Two generations of Chinese had grown up with opium as common and available as cabbages. Two generations of mothers had sent children out with the errand: "There's no more opium—go buy some before your father gets home." Two generations had grown it, sold it, traded it, smoked it, died of it, without the slightest ban. And now, suddenly, the Old Buddha had forbidden it. It was inconceivable! How could opium be got rid of? It was ingrained in every nook and cranny of life!

Great Dragon walked up his garden path, the scattered flakes of an early snowfall disintegrating beneath his feet. As soon as he entered the house, he knew that Ching-mei was not there; there was a peaceful quiet that did not exist when she was around. He felt glad. He could spend some time alone with Didi. He could tell him about the Edict—and of course he could now tell him about the life-duty! The eradication of opium would be accomplished in his own lifetime! There'd be no more life-duty to pass on to Didi! There was no reason now to delay telling him about it.

He pushed open the door of his son's bedroom. Didi sat at his desk surrounded by books and papers. At twenty he was a larger version of himself at five and at ten, both in appearance and spirit. As handsome, and as sensitive. Great Dragon watched him a moment, his throat contracting. Life was going to hurt this young man, so beloved of his heart. At least he would be free of the life-duty.

"Son," he said quietly.

Didi looked up, the rare wide-open smile illuminating his face.

"Hello, Father. Mother's gone to the bank."

"Do you have time for a talk? An edict was issued today— an edict forbidding opium. I want to tell you about it, and about a piece of family history in which your great-grandfather, your grandfather, and I have been very closely involved. . . ."

Later, when they heard Ching-mei come in, they fell silent, listening for the signs of her mood. Then they both sat back and turned to the door, unconsciously making the same gesture. She was stamping down the hall. She was in a temper.

The door banged open. She stood in the doorway for a moment, glaring, then flung something at her husband's feet. A roll of silver dollars, wrapped as they came from the bank. The roll broke and the dollars scattered around the floor, tinkling.

"That's it," she cried. "All that remains in the bank. Nothing left in our account."

"What?" He stared at her uncomprehendingly.

"That's right!" she snapped. "You heard me. Your precious sister whom you admire so much. She hasn't sent any money for the last two months."

He began to pick up the dollars, Didi helping him. It couldn't be! The money had always been deposited in his account on the first of the month, ample for the month. There must be some stupid mistake. The bank had credited someone else's account. But that could hardly be, either.

He piled the dollars on the hall table and went into his study, opened the drawer in which he kept Julie's letters. She didn't write often, no more often than he wrote her, and he hadn't written for months. Not since May, when the new resolution in Parliament had been passed, and he and Tong Shao-yi had suddenly become so busy with the torrent of letters from Donald.

He opened her last letter. It was dated May, six months ago. It was short. The characters were shaky. He remembered it now. She had written: "Sorry if this isn't readable. I am sitting up in bed. Not feeling well. Perhaps just getting old! Fifty this year—half a century! Fish is looking after me well."

She must be seriously ill now, if she hadn't sent the money for two months. But why hadn't Fish written or telegraphed? What in the name of all the devils was happening?

Cursing his own neglect, he went to find Ching-mei.

"I'm going to Shanghai on the first available ship."

"How are you going to pay? And what about me?"

"The bank manager will give me a loan, of course. I'll leave money in the account for you and Didi."

"See that you do," she snapped.

It was almost dark, the sky heavy with fat black clouds, when the ship docked in Shanghai at the end of a late November day. He had sent a telegram announcing his arrival, but no one was there to meet him. He stood on deck, peering in vain at the shadowy crowd on the wharf, telling himself that his sense of abandonment, of foreboding, was unreasonable.

Rain was pattering as he descended the gangplank, carrying his small suitcase. Disembarking passengers and those who had come to meet them were hurrying in droves to the line of carriages. By the time he got there, there were no vehicles left but two or three rickshaws. It would take a long time to get to the Chinese City in a rickshaw, but there was no alternative. He hailed one. The coolie kept him standing in the rain while he belligerently bargained for the price of the ride, obviously taking advantage of the lack of other transport. When Great Dragon agreed to an exorbitant price, the coolie let him step into the rickshaw, picked up the shafts, and started off at a slow, pounding run.

The hood of the rickshaw, raised because of the rain, was of cheap and smelly oilcloth, leaking in many places. An oilcloth sheet stretching from the base of the shafts to hooks just inside the hood was supposed to prevent the rain from beating into the rickshaw, but that too was leaking. The coolie's steps grew more effortful every minute. The animosity he had displayed bespoke his hopelessness and misery. Yet the life of the foreign city flowed by, rich and prosperous and flourishing. A bluish glow came from the gas streetlamps, yellow light flooded from the buildings and the lanterns that flickered on every vehicle on the road and every craft on the river. The reflection of the lights made a shifting web of dazzling streaks upon the wet macadam. The night, the lights, the chilly damp of the rickshaw, the coolie's suffering . . . Reality and unreality disputed Great Dragon's spirit. The pounding in his head became more painful. The sense of foreboding grew.

When at last they reached home and Great Dragon paid the coolie, he raised his hands in supplication and, panting heavily, begged for more. He was bone-thin and so ragged that patches of skin showed through rents in his sodden clothing. He was shivering spasmodically.

"You're going to buy opium?" Great Dragon asked.

"Yes, if you'll give me a little more money. It's raining. There'll be customers. I need the strength to run."

"And when the opium wears off, it'll be harder than ever."

The coolie's humility turned into vicious anger.

253

"Son of a turtle! Mother violator! Don't put your fat tongue to what your fat brain can't imagine! D'you know what it's like to eat bitterness?"

Silently, Great Dragon gave him another coin and he shuffled off, still muttering angrily. For a moment Great Dragon stood in the rain, looking after him. The Edict would not affect him. He'd be dead long before it filtered down to his level. He was dying now, on his stumbling feet, between the shafts of his leaking rickshaw.

Great Dragon turned to the gate and was astonished that it was a new one. No more the old varnished wooden one, but iron bars backed by sheet metal. And the wall had glass shards cemented into the top of it. Julie had said nothing about these changes. Why not? Why not? Cold fingers touched his spine.

The gate was solidly shut. The old gateman had delighted in watching through the little window in the old gate to be able to open it to members of the family before they were obliged to ring.

Perhaps the old gateman was dead.

Great Dragon pulled the bell-pull beside the gate.

He heard the click as a peephole was opened, and felt the eye that inspected him through it. A voice growled:

"Who are you?"

Suddenly furious, he shouted: "I'm the oldest son of this house!" and heard the loss of control in his voice.

One leaf of the gate was slitted open just wide enough to admit him. He squeezed in. The gate was quickly shut and locked again. The gateman turned. Even in the darkness, Great Dragon knew that he was a stranger.

"Didn't my telegram arrive?" he snapped.

"Yes," the growly voice said, "but I don't know you. I have to be careful. Sorry."

He took up a lantern and began to lead Great Dragon across the courtyard.

"I know my way!" Great Dragon said curtly, but the man walked on stolidly in front of him to the door of the family house and banged on it. It was opened immediately, by another stranger. The level of Great Dragon's anger rose. He brushed past the man into the hallway and was at once struck by a stale, musty odor. Alarm joined the anger, swirling up gray and ominous. He began to hurry through the lamplit passages, making for the family room. The man who had opened the front door followed him: he could hear his quick, slithering footsteps. As they neared the family room, a woman stepped out of it—another stranger, tall and heavy. She shut the door behind her and stood with her back to it, looking uncertain.

"Where is my sister?" Great Dragon said, his voice harsh and too loud.

The man behind him said to the woman in a worried tone: "She's not in there, is she?" The woman's glance flickered to him over Great Dragon's shoulder. She nodded briefly, wetting her lips. For an instant graven in time they stood thus, the two servants looking at each other, Great Dragon between them, rigid, alarm now choking in his throat.

Then the door of the family room opened slowly and Julie stood in the doorway, clinging to the lintel. The lamplight was too dim for Great Dragon to see her clearly, but the set of her head was unmistakable, and relief swept through him. He pushed past the woman and hurried toward her—and, two feet away, stopped short, horror drowning every other feeling.

She looked like the ghost of Julie returned from a visit to hell. Her face was all trembling lips and huge, dull eyes. She was all gray: iron-gray hair cropped raggedly short, fog gray skin stretched so tightly that her cheekbones seemed about to crack through.

"Julie," he whispered. "Julie."

Her eyes focused, passing slowly through stages from blank incomprehension to a kind of incredulous hope.

"Great Dragon?"

Her voice was a croak. She took a wavering step toward him. Her hand slipped from the lintel and she staggered. He caught her—she was feather-light—and carried her into the family room.

The woman hurried after him.

"She needs her medicine!"

"Get out!" he said fiercely, and laid Julie on the couch. Her face was even grayer now, if that were possible. She began to tremble, and then to shake spasmodically, her body rattling, arching itself rigidly, then collapsing and beginning again to rattle. Sweat was pouring from her, darkening the pillow behind her head, darkening her garments. Beneath her half-closed lids there was only a flicker of white—her eyeballs had turned up into her head. Her lips were fixed in a rictus of agony. Her distress was appalling.

The woman pushed at his shoulder.

"She needs her pipe! Can't you see how she's suffering? Get out of the way and let me give her her pipe!"

He turned stiffly in the direction of the woman's pointing finger. On the side table, access to which he was blocking, lay the paraphernalia of opium smoking. A tin of opium. A long needle. A lamp. Matches. A pipe.

His blood turned to ice. Like an automaton, he rose and went to the window, stood looking out into the dark courtyard. Behind him he heard the woman preparing the pipe. There was a sudden gush of the strong, sweetish odor of opium. That was what he had smelled when he entered the house, subconsciously recognizing it yet refusing to give it credibility—the stale smell of opium dross. He heard the hiss of Julie's breath as she inhaled. A pause. Then a long sigh as she exhaled the vapor. There were little sounds as the woman tidied up, then the click of the door as she left the room.

He waited. His head was throbbing. His whole body hurt, the broken pieces of his heart and spirit rubbing painfully against each other as the icy flow of his blood displaced them.

After a while he heard her whisper his name. He went to her. It was amazing what the pipe had wrought. Her body was quiet, limp. Her face had a little flush of color. Her eyes were open, and intelligence had returned to them.

She did not smile. She did not greet him. She stared at him with almost frightening intensity and began at once to whisper.

"There's not much time. Before long I'll need another pipe, and he may come back at any minute. Listen, Great Dragon . . ."

He knelt beside her and she took his hand, her touch light as a butterfly's yet vibrating with urgency.

"Fish did this. A long time ago—I can't remember how long—I got sick. I know now that it was Fish who made me sick with something in the food. He got me a doctor, and the doctor made me worse. For weeks I was in a kind of dream, sleeping while I thought I was awake, and sometimes I would be really awake, and then everything was strange. All the servants were strange. That woman who makes my pipes—she's kind, but she's terribly afraid of Fish and the one-eyed man. There's a one-eyed man. . . ."

She swallowed dryly and he hurried to get water, helped her to drink, trailed water over her forehead and her temples. She blinked and frowned and passed the tip of her tongue around her mouth. It seemed bright red against her flaky gray lips.

"One day when I first was sick, Fish came with the doctor.

257

He said I wasn't to worry, he'd quit the university for the time being and was taking care of the *hong*. But he needed a power of attorney. He gave me a paper to sign. I signed it. Then one day, a long time later—it's so hard to remember—I felt better. I got up. I thought I'd go to the *hong*. But the one-eyed man stopped me. Fish came and said I mustn't go to the *hong* anymore. He said if I stayed home quietly and made no fuss, he'd take care of me and see I had as much opium as I needed."

Her whisper had been weakening and now it trailed off and she fell suddenly into an exhausted sleep, her eyes half closed, her mouth half open. He watched her for a moment, then rose quietly and began to pace the room, heart and head thumping.

It was fantastic! What was Fish trying to do? Annex the whole of the family fortune for himself? But how did he think he could make Julie's power of attorney stick? An indirect power of attorney, father to daughter to the youngest son. The eldest son, Great Dragon, a mandarin of note, could demolish Fish's claims in a single court appearance!

She stirred and he went back quickly. Her eyes were dulling but she swallowed and, with effort, spoke again.

"He's used the power of attorney to transfer everything into his mother's name. When he was born, Father registered him at the municipality as the son of himself and Girl. It's all legal. We never claimed our inheritance, so it's all still Father's according to the law, and Mother's dead, and lots of men when they get old transfer assets into the names of younger concubines. Fish says the court accepted the transfer without question and accepted him as his mother's representative because she's not well enough to appear herself. I think he's giving her opium too."

Her voice trailed off again, and her eyes drifted shut. Stunned, his mind stumbling, he leaned forward to wipe the sweat from her face with his handkerchief. Suddenly her eyes opened wide. She was staring at him from a distance of six inches. Her voice came loud and clear.

"Great Dragon, just believe me. Don't look at all sides of it and consider. *Just believe me!*"

The effort drained her. The color fled her face and left it ashen. Her eyeballs turned up again into her head, and sweat began to pour from her brow.

Then Fish spoke. Startled out of his skin, Great Dragon jumped up and found Fish standing beside him, looking down at Julie, his face blanketed with worry. The woman was there too. Fish was speaking to her.

"You know she's too weak to walk about! You could kill her by letting her! Take her back to bed at once!"

Without a word the woman picked Julie up in her arms and turned toward the door.

"Wait!"

Great Dragon leaped forward to bar the way. Fish turned to him with a beseeching look.

"Elder Brother, I'll tell you all about it—I'm so glad you've come!—but please let the woman take Elder Sister back to bed first. You can see how ill she is!"

He smiled, the attractive smile Great Dragon remembered, strained and diminished by worry and a deep fatigue, but still charming. Slowly, Great Dragon stepped back. Of course, there was no need to keep Julie from her bed while he thrashed out the matter with Fish. The woman quickly left the room, Julie's head sagging against her shoulder.

Fish sighed deeply. "Poor Elder Sister!"

Great Dragon searched his face, searching for signs of the lies, the treachery, but there was only anxiety and a small, sad glimmering of the smile.

"What's the matter with Julie?"

Fish sank down at the table, leaned an elbow on it, put his

head into his hand in a hopeless gesture of abandonment and sorrow. His voice was so low and muffled that it hardly reached Great Dragon's ears.

"She's gone mad. Like your mother. She must have inherited that streak." He looked up, his eyes tight with pain. "For a long time I didn't know it. I was working hard at the university. The old servants had died—the old gateman, Father's valet, your mother's Old Woman. Most of the servants were new. I didn't know anything was wrong until they all came to me one day, all together, and told me they were resigning because they couldn't stand it any longer. Elder Sister was giving orders, forgetting them, scolding the servants for doing what she'd ordered. She had cut down on the food money— they were having to spend their own money to keep from starving. She hadn't paid their salaries that month, insisting that she'd already paid them. I didn't know what to do. I asked them to stay on a few days, I'd talk to Elder Sister. But the next day the same thing happened with the staff from the *hong*. The older ones from Father's time had died or been pensioned off, and many were new. They came to me with the same complaints about Elder Sister."

He sighed and stretched his shoulders in a weary gesture.

"You can't imagine what it's been like! I could have replaced the servants if necessary, but I couldn't let the staff of the *hong* go! I had to take everything over within a week. She began to deteriorate very quickly. Luckily I was able to get her to sign a power of attorney to me before everything went to pieces. I got doctors for her, of course, but they could do nothing. There's nothing physically wrong with her—I mean, she has no illness, except of course for the terrible effects of the opium. But we had to give her opium. When she began actually raving—shouting, screaming, throwing things—it was the only thing to keep her calm, to give her rest."

A little soothing balm was creeping into Great Dragon's

spirit. Fish's story didn't make anything better, but at least it did clear up some of the confusion—the new servants, the power of attorney, even perhaps the new precautions, the barred gate, the glass shards on top of the wall. They might be necessary to protect Julie.

"Why didn't you tell me all this?"

"Well, you know how it is, I hesitated. I kept thinking it was temporary, that she'd recover. And I was so busy, and any letter I wrote you would have had to be very long, of course. I got your telegram saying you were arriving today, but I couldn't take the time to go and meet you—though I did manage to get home early. Ten, eleven, midnight—that's been the norm for the last couple of months! I can't tell you how glad I am you've come."

"You could have telegraphed me to come."

"Well, again, you know, I hesitated, hoping she'd recover. And I knew how busy you'd be after that new resolution about opium was passed in Parliament." His lips twitched wryly. "I know all about opium, you know—Father saw to it—and I followed the news about it. The Edict's been issued, I saw in the newspaper?"

"Yes." Great Dragon walked to the window. He needed time to think about all this! Obviously, Julie's condition needed immediate attention, whether or not she was out of her mind. Was that old English doctor who'd taken care of their father still practicing? What was his name? Macpherson? Well, he'd be very old now. . . . . If only he'd known about this earlier! He turned back to Fish.

"You should at least have let me know that something was wrong! As it was, I had no idea until the remittances stopped coming."

Fish's mouth fell open. He clamped a hand to his head, jerked upright, then slumped back in his chair.

"The remittances! I forgot! I am so *sorry*! I simply forgot!"

Great Dragon found himself giving a short laugh. It was such a youthful reaction. Fish was only twenty after all, like Didi.

With a clatter, a servant entered with a large tray full of dishes. Fish brightened at once.

"Dinner! Let's eat before we talk more. You must be hungry, and I'm famished. Food'll do us both good."

Great Dragon smiled. Tragedy there might be, but it didn't affect youth's appetite!

They sat silently while the servant laid the table. A simple family dinner—a pork dish, a chicken dish, greens, and a soup. Great Dragon realized that he was, after all, quite hungry; the relief of what Fish had said had given him back some appetite, and the food was good. Julie's madness might be treatable. Macpherson, if he was still alive, might recommend a good English doctor. Or it might abate of itself. Their mother, after all, had been very gentle and amenable.

Fish was leaning across the table, a bowl of soup stretched out in his hand.

"It's Peking-style hot and sour. It's too spicy for me, but the new cook makes it awfully well. Try it."

Great Dragon took the bowl and spooned a little of the soup into his mouth. It tasted fine—peppery, vinegary, with just the right amount of chihli. It had cooled a little while the bowl stood on the table, and was just the right temperature. He put the spoon down and raised the whole bowl to his mouth.

"Great Dragon," Julie's voice said clearly in his ear. *"Just believe me!"*

He hesitated, the bowl at his lips. Of course, he wasn't taking Fish's word over hers! He'd look into the whole matter thoroughly.

"Drink it," Fish said. "It's really good."

He drank the whole bowlful without pause.

At once, the pain in his head, which had quieted a little,

slammed back again, fiercer than ever, so fierce that he clutched at his head in desperation, digging his fingers into his temples. But the pain spread like wildfire, down his gullet, to his stomach. Hot needles pierced him—tz-tz-tz—hotter and hotter, faster and faster, leaping and dancing to all parts of his body. He tried to rise and got halfway to his feet, leaning over the table. He tried to cry "Help me!" to Fish, but his throat convulsed and no words came. In despair, he raised his eyes pleadingly and saw Fish's eyes, bright and black, fixed expectantly on his face.

Those eyes were the last thing he saw as he crashed face forward to the table, smashing the dishes and splashing the remains of the soup all over the floor.

Chapter XVIII
November 25-26, 1906

THE GRAY MIST SWIRLED slowly, and for a while Julie was content to swirl with it. She was in that heaven-sent time of well-being between pipes, when the last one was still bathing her in its afterglow and the need of the next one had not yet started.

The gray mist was lighter than usual. Not a thick fog—an eddying cloud, like the remnant of fog. There was a lamp burning somewhere that made a bright, round spot of light on the ceiling that was clear and white, no swirly gray. It was very tranquil.

Beyond the light was darkness. Night. That was strange. It was a long time since she'd been awake in the night.

Other strange things had happened.

The woman had come as usual with her food, but the one-eyed man who always came and watched while the woman fed her hadn't come.

And the woman hadn't fed her the food. She had scurried over to the chamberpot in the corner and emptied the food into it.

And then she had hurried back to the bedside with a pork bun that she produced from under her garment. The bun was one of those that the old man made, the old man who, as far back as she could remember, had set up his traveling kitchen outside the front gate every morning. This was surely one of his, the steamed dough fluffy and soft and delicious. She'd eaten all of it.

Her usual food lay in the chamberpot.

After a while she'd felt stronger than in a long time. Had she really got up and walked alone to the family room? Yes, indeed, she had done that! How wonderful! And she'd stayed there a long time, until she began to feel the need of the next pipe, and the woman had come to fetch her.

Fish had told the woman to take her back to bed.

Fish had been in the family room.

And someone else.

Great Dragon.

A little surge sprang up in her body. It disturbed her tranquility and she tried to ignore it, but it became a swift tide that jerked her upright.

Great Dragon was in the family room!

She raised herself on an elbow and then on her hands until she was sitting on the edge of the bed. She felt for her slippers, slid her feet into them, stood up slowly, took a step. It didn't make her dizzy, for the swirling mist was all gone now. She went into the corridor, shuffled along, her soft-slippered feet silent on the polished wood floor. She met no one. The door of the family room was open. She slipped in.

The room was a shambles. The dining table overturned, broken dishes scattered among sticky pools of spilt food. What had happened? Where was Great Dragon? And Fish? And the one-eyed man? She stared at the litter and grew cold and began to shiver.

Footsteps came down the corridor. Fish's voice said on a note of triumph: "They'll never identify him!"

Then Fish and the one-eyed man were in the room, staring at her. The one-eyed man cursed and began to shout for the woman, but Fish stopped him. Fish was smiling, that wide, engaging smile that used to enchant her. He said:

"One-eye, I want to talk to my sister."

One-eye grunted and left the room.

Fish drew her to the sofa and sat beside her, still smiling, his bright black eyes fixed on hers.

"You are *wonderful*, Elder Sister! All these months, all that opium and the pills and the powders, and still you're walking about with wits enough to tell stories to our brother! It's really a pity! You'd make a marvelous partner if you'd join me! But you won't, will you?"

"Won't what?" she whispered.

"Join me in our new enterprise. The *hong* is going into the opium trade. I've been planning it for a long time. Now that the Edict is out, the price of opium is going to shoot sky-high. There'll no longer be thousands of chests of it piled high in the warehouses, common as dirt. It'll be scarcer and scarcer, until it's worth its weight in gold. I'm going to make as much money handling ten chests as the dealers are making now handling a hundred."

She kept her eyes on his eyes. Their brightness stimulated her, made her angry, and that was good. She needed anger.

"Where's Great Dragon?"

"Behind some crates on the dock where he landed this afternoon, with a dagger in his back. They'll think some waterfront villain got him as he came off the ship. It's in the International Settlement. D'you think the British police will bother much with the body of an unidentifiable Chinese?"

A great and painful load had descended on her as he spoke, but she kept her eyes expressionless. He grinned at her, eyes shining.

"But I'm not totally blackhearted. I knew he was going to die, so I had this made for him in advance."

He went to a drawer and showed her something that he took from it. A soul tablet, the exact match of the one she'd had made for their father, this one carved with Great Dragon's name.

"We'll put it on the ancestral altar with the others, and you can sit and mourn him. I'll have a couch moved into the ancestors' house, and one of those low opium tables, and you can lie and smoke your pipes and gaze at the soul tablets of our ancestors."

The cruelty of his words was at direct variance with his charming smile. Anger flared in her, and again she was glad. More than ever she needed anger to keep the tears back, to keep her wits working.

"You enticed him here to kill him," she whispered. "Why? He was far away. He never interfered with the affairs of the *hong.*"

He shook his head in mock sorrow. "You disappoint me, sister! He'd have been jumping on me in a minute when he found that the *hong* was in the opium trade, and he would have found out as soon as I started to recover that opium you know, Father's opium that's stored in Ah-fet's name?"

He glanced at her sideways. For a moment she was confused. Then, with a great thump of her heart, she remembered. Ah-fet was Alfred Pratt! How did Fish know about him? As she and Great Dragon had agreed, she had never said a word to Fish about the opium from the Shansi valley, stored in Chengchow, the storage receipts accumulating in a safe deposit box to which only Pratt now had access, since Great Dragon was dead.

267

She drew her robe around her to hide the trembling of her hands and leaned back, closed her eyes, as though exhausted.

He touched her arm. "Who's Ah-fet?

"I don't know," she said languidly.

"You do know. I've read the letter Father wrote you about him."

"I don't know," she murmured. "I never had a letter from Father about someone called Ah-fet."

"I took the letter after Father died." He laughed lightly. "I used to go through your and Father's papers whenever I liked. You were very careless—trusting, I suppose you'd call it. But now I have to know who Ah-fet is and where the storage receipts are."

His voice had grown threatening. She kept her eyes closed, gathering her forces, formulating her answer. Careful! She must convince him that she didn't know. It was the last thing she could do for her father, for the life-duty that he and Great Dragon were no longer here to carry.

She said slowly: "You should have asked Elder Brother before you killed him."

"*What!*" She felt him leap off the sofa. "You mean that— that *mandarin* dealt with Ah-fet?"

"I don't know," she shrugged. "But he must have because I didn't."

"Father wrote *you* the letter!"

"And you stole it," she whispered, her voice beginning to crack. "If I'd received it I'd have made inquiries and found out. But you stole it."

He began to curse violently.

She no longer had to pretend to be exhausted. The trembling had started in her stomach, the first symptom of withdrawal. Soon she would be shaking all over, sweat pouring, the craving rampant, tearing at her as though her body were turned inside out, being dragged back and forth over a giant rasp, and her whole being, her whole mind and thought, the whole of the future, life itself, would be contained in that single holy, unholy object, the pipe.

She heard One-eye hurry into the room and ask, "What's wrong?"

"She doesn't know who Ah-fet is!" Fish screamed. "She doesn't know where the storage receipts are! It was that devil-cursed mandarin who dealt with Ah-fet!"

One-eye growled something, and Fish began again to scream.

"I've asked my mother where the valley is, and she doesn't remember! She's sunk in that devil-cursed opium trance, she can't remember yesterday, let alone twenty years ago! And even if she could remember, the letter says the crop from the valley is only four hundred pounds a year! Ah-fet's got *twenty-one years'* worth stored away somewhere, and I don't know who he is!"

One-eyed said suddenly: "Why is your sister here? I put the powder in her food! She should be asleep!"

"Maybe she's getting used to it!" Fish's fury vibrated in his voice. "Put in double next time. Put in *triple!* She's no use to me if she doesn't know who Ah-fet is and where the receipts are! Call the woman to take her away! I can't stand the sight of her any longer!"

It was morning. The woman was there again, and again without One-eye. Again, she scuttled across the room and emptied the breakfast into the chamberpot. Again she produced a bun from under her garment that she thrust into Julie's hand. She watched while Julie ate it, muttering:

"I can't. I won't. If they want to kill you, let them do it themselves. Not through me."

When Julie had finished, she wiped her face and hands with

a wet cloth and combed her hair. Then, whispering:

"Listen. Your brother and that son of a turtle One-eye have gone out. There's someone outside asking for you. An Englishman who speaks Chinese very well. He says he's an old friend of your father."

Donald? *Donald?*

"The watchman won't let him in, but he won't go away. He says he'll wait at the gate until he sees you. Do you want to see him?"

"Yes," Julie breathed.

"You'll have to walk out to the courtyard. Can you manage it? I'll help you inside the house, but once outside, you're on your own."

"I can do it," Julie said.

They walked together through the corridors, Julie leaning on the woman's arm. When they came to the front door, the woman opened it and waited until Julie had grasped the lintel before removing her arm. One more little step, and Julie was outdoors for the first time in months, in the beautiful courtyard glittering with cold sunshine.

"Julie!"

An old man came hurrying toward her across the courtyard. An old man. White-haired, wrinkled, cheeks concave, thin jowls shaking. He reached her and folded her in his arms.

She burst into tears.

He spoke in English. "For God's sake, Julie, what's wrong? I'm on my way to see Tong Shao-yi about the Edict and the Agreement with India, and of course I stopped to see you. *What's wrong*, Julie? There's a scoundrel at the gate who wouldn't let me in! And you look so ill!"

She rubbed her head against the sleeve of his coat. Donald! Really Donald! And what was the use? He was so old! If she involved him it would put him in grave danger from Fish and One-eye. He was too old to cope with them.

270

He was murmuring anxiously, patting her, pressing his handkerchief into her hand. She took it and dried her eyes and looked up at him, smiling shakily.

"It's nothing. Seeing you made me think of my father."

"Oh!" His faded blue eyes misted. "Of course. Your father." He smiled at her encouragingly. "But you, Julie? You're in trouble. What can I do?"

She looked at him helplessly. What could he do?

But there *was* something he could do!

She freed herself from his embrace and took his arm. The watchman had followed him across the courtyard and was standing a few yards away, regarding them with intense suspicion. Drawing Donald with her, she took a step. The watchman took a step. She took another, this time clearly in the direction of the ancestors' house. The watchman looked undecided. She took three more steps, Donald with her. The watchman stood still. He wouldn't dare follow her into the ancestors' house.

Clinging to Donald's arm, she drew him across the courtyard to the golden moon door. Excitement buoyed her. She felt no fatigue. Donald unfastened the door and they entered and he closed it behind them. She glanced quickly at the altar and sighed with relief. It was there, the tablet that Fish had had made for Great Dragon. It stood on the altar with the tablets of his ancestors.

Donald had seen it too. He looked at her, his face crumpled with distress.

"How did he die?"

She spoke quickly, softly:

"Donald, I won't tell you what's been happening to this family since my father died. It's too long and too complicated and you can do nothing to make it better. But there is one thing you can do that would make me happy. Take the four soul tablets with you to Peking and give them to Didi, Great

Dragon's son. The Wai-wu Pu will tell you where to find him."

"I will," he said without hesitation and went to the altar and stored the tablets away in the capacious pockets of his coat.

"And now you must go," she said. "Quickly, before they come back and stop you."

"And what about you?"

"It doesn't matter! The only important thing now is for those tablets to get to Didi. My father would want it."

He regarded her doubtfully. She took his arm again and led him back to the courtyard. The watchman, looking relieved, took a step toward them. She waved a dismissive hand, and he stepped back. She was glad. Donald would think she still had command of the household.

They walked slowly back to the house.

"I can't leave you like this!" he said. "You should be in a hospital. You need a doctor."

"I have a doctor," she murmured. It wasn't a lie. Fish's doctor came every now and then. "Donald, please don't worry about me. Please go quickly."

She smiled up at him. She knew that her desperate sense of urgency was flushing her cheeks and making her eyes shine. She knew that she looked well for the moment, and at that moment the woman, who was standing just inside the open front door, had the courage to step into the courtyard and take her arm.

"You see!" she said gaily. "I'm well looked after!"

Still dubious, he held on to her hand.

She withdrew it gently.

"Good-bye, Donald."

He said, with a catch in his old man's voice: "I always loved you, little Julie. God and your father forgive me if I'm wrong to do as you say."

He went away quickly.

The woman helped her back to bed, and now she was exhausted, panting, feeling as though her strength were water running out through a drain. The woman made a pipe for her, and then sat and gently massaged her feet.

She thought of the golden sovereigns Donald had given her, one each Chinese New Year from the time she was five until he went away. She murmured to the woman, who went to the cupboard and brought her the little box in which they were kept.

"Take them," she said to the woman, "and go away. One-eye will harm you when he finds out that you helped me."

The woman shook her head, though her eyes were frightened. Julie said again:

"Take the gold and go back to your village. You and your family can live on it for generations. You have helped me and I am grateful, but you can't help me anymore. You know that."

The woman nodded. She went down on her knees and kowtowed. Then, tears streaming from her eyes, she took the little box and went away.

When it grew dark, One-eye came. He was angry, but he was not explosive, like Fish. He kept his anger within him, and it was all the more dangerous for that.

He had a bowl of soft rice and chicken. He propped her on pillows and began to feed her. Strength came to her from somewhere and she took the bowl from his hand and fed herself while he watched. She ate the whole bowlful. It was good. The poison was tasteless.

When he had gone, she lay watching the darkness come. When it was too dark to see anything at all, she closed her eyes. Who would prepare her next pipe, when the agony of withdrawal started? Perhaps it didn't matter. Perhaps she wouldn't need another pipe. Her body, her legs, her arms, her hands, felt very heavy. She lay very still. It was very quiet.

273

After a while she knew that someone was standing beside her bed. Not the woman, for she had gone. Not One-eye, for there was no feeling of malevolence. Not Fish, for he couldn't stand still for so long.

At last she lifted her heavy lids to see who it was.

It was her father.

Not old and blind as she had last seen him, but young and vital as on the day he presented her to the ancestors. He was smiling. He didn't speak, but she knew what he was telling her.

"Darling Julie, you did well to send our soul tablets to Didi. The life-duty is his now. You can lay down your share of it. You performed it well. . . . Come with me. We will go to your mother."

He stretched a hand to her. Filled with joy, she lifted her own hand, which was no longer heavy, and laid it in his.